THE YOUNG EAGLES

THE YOUNG EAGLES

a novel by

Ian Cameron

W. H. ALLEN · London
A Howard & Wyndham Company
1979

Κάρτιστοι μὲν ἔσαν καὶ καρτιστοις ἐμάχοντο

Iliad Book 1, line 267

(The mightiest were these, and
        with the mightiest they fought.)

Photoset, printed and bound in Great Britain
by Redwood Burn Limited, Trowbridge & Esher
for the publishers W.H. Allen & Co. Ltd.,
44 Hill Street, London W1X 8LB.

ISBN 0 491 02338 3

1

The sky was blue. The sun was warm. The fields were bright with flowers. The four of us hadn't a care in the world that morning as we cantered over the meadow and up to the hedge.

But the hedge – think of it if you like as symbolic – had wire in it.

My horse must have seen it a second before I did, for she stopped dead, and I was catapulted ignominiously over her head. It was a strange sensation: as though time had been suspended and I was falling in slow motion, until with the most almighty crash I fetched up in the hedge; a branch struck me across the side of the head and I passed out.

From what the others told me I must have been unconscious for only a few seconds, but for those seconds I lay motionless, my head at the most peculiar angle, and Otto for one felt certain I was dead. As I came-to his face was the first thing I saw and his voice the first thing I heard. He was bending over me, his eyes enormous: '*Mein Gott! Mein Gott! Mein Gott!*' he was repeating over and over again. Then, as I blinked and tried to push aside the branches digging into me, his eyes lit up. It was a funny thing; it wasn't only his expression that changed; it was as though his whole body had been transfigured with relief. 'Jack! You're all right! Lie still. In case anything is broke.'

It was sound advice. But seventeen is a resilient age, and I levered myself to my feet and said I was fine. By the time Jessica and her brother Gavin had reined in their horses and come back to see what had happened, I was walking up and down, feeling more shaken than I cared to admit but insisting I was all right to ride on.

Otto had more sense. 'It is time', he said firmly, 'for lunch.'

Jessica took one look at me and dismounted: 'I'm starving!'

So we tethered our horses at the side of the field and settled down to a picnic.

The picnic was fun. And at odd moments during the meal I found myself looking at Otto and thinking of the way his expression had changed – had sort of lit up – when he realised I wasn't seriously hurt. I knew I would have reacted in exactly the same way if I'd found *him* in a ditch and had thought him dead and then suddenly he had opened his eyes. And I told myself that a friendship such as ours was a friendship for life.

And so I am convinced it would have been, if all over Europe people that summer hadn't been basking in the last of the sun and savouring the last of the wine. For the year was 1914. . . .

'How's the head?' The others, it seemed, were still anxious about me. It was too good an opportunity to miss. I feigned dizziness, and Jessica cradled me in her arms – until she realised I was having her on, and then instead of the hoped-for kiss I got a resounding slap, and we rolled over and over in the grass until I ended up a second time in the hedge. Then we got on our horses and rode off towards the Helford River.

It was the sort of day it's good to be alive in. The wheat was young; the sun was warm; the world was our playground. The Helford peninsula is one of the most sparsely-populated corners of southern England, and in two hours' riding the only living creatures we set eyes on were rabbits and birds. Then unexpectedly, just as we were thinking of heading back for the Pendowers' farm, we realised we had company.

It was Gavin who spotted it: 'Look!'

We reined in our horses. Aircraft in the spring of 1914 were still enough of a novelty to be stared at.

It was an odd-looking contraption: rather like a flying bedstead, all flat surfaces and festoons of wire. And even to our untutored eyes there was something ominous about the way it was behaving. One moment the pilot seemed to have it under control, the next its engine faltered, its nose dropped and it came drifting earthwards like a falling leaf until the engine burst again into spasmodic life. Otto's voice was anxious. 'I'm

2

afraid it has the engine failure.'

'You mean it's going to crash!'

We stared at the airplane with fearful anticipation. The horses, sensing something was wrong, moved restlessly.

The plane was coming almost straight towards us, losing height and weaving from side to side – if I'd known that afternoon one-hundredth of what I knew six months later I'd have realised the pilot was searching frantically for somewhere to land. The engine was silent now. Indeed the whole world seemed suddenly to have become silent, as though the very trees and hedgerows were holding their breath. It looked for a moment as if the plane was going to hit a cluster of elms about a hundred yards from where we were standing; but at the last second it did a kind of sideslip and landed with a fearful thud in a meadow. It ploughed across the grass, gradually losing speed; then it must have hit a depression, because it lurched onto its nose and lay still.

For a moment none of us moved. Then Gavin flung his cap high in the air: 'Tally ho!'

His horse, startled, reared up, very nearly unseating him.

'Come on,' I cried. 'Let's see if we can help.'

We galloped across to the plane.

By the time we got to it the pilot was trying to struggle out of the nacelle. He seemed more dazed than hurt – from what he told us afterwards he'd cracked his head on the windshield as the machine nosed over. When he saw us he started jumping up and down and flailing his arms like a windmill: 'Keep back! Fire!'

Fire was a hazard I hadn't thought of. We came to an uncertain halt.

The pilot was blundering about in the network of struts and wires, holding his head in his hands, unable apparently to extricate himself. Otto and I had the same thought at the same moment. We jumped off our horses and made a dash for the plane.

Now I'm sure the pilot wasn't so dazed that he couldn't in time have freed himself. But he was mighty glad of our help. We

3

half-dragged, half-carried him clear and collapsed in a heap at what we hoped was a safe distance. 'You all right?' I panted.

He nodded: 'Thanks! Jolly plucky of you both.'

Otto was staring at the plane: 'Where's the fire?'

Fire, the pilot explained, was always a risk after a crash landing. 'Happened to a friend of mine last week,' he added cheerfully. 'Poor chap was *carboneezayed*!'

We stared at him uncomprehending.

'You know. Carbonised. Turned to charcoal. . . . Hello there!'

This last was addressed to Jessica. Her cascade of auburn hair was tucked demurely under her riding hat, but the pilot nevertheless seemed to think her well worth staring at. 'This', I said, 'is Miss Jessica Pendower. And her twin brother Gavin. It's their father's field you've landed in.'

The pilot told us his name was Douglas Reid – 'Captain Reid of the Flying Corps.' He was a dapper figure, with neat moustache, flamboyant 'kerchief and what he obviously thought was a way with the girls. We gathered that he'd done over a hundred hours solo, that he'd actually flown across the Channel, and that this was his third forced landing. We gathered also that he was anxious to get in touch as soon as possible with his airfield, 'So they can send some mechanic fellows, you know. To fix the plane.'

Contacting the airfield, however, was easier said than done; for the Helford is sparsely populated and there wasn't a telephone for miles. We decided eventually to make for the Pendower's farm. This would involve a ride of nearly an hour; but once we got there the pilot would be assured of telephone, transport and whatever he needed in the way of first aid.

It was at this point that things began to get out of hand.

The pilot drew me aside. I couldn't think what was embarrassing him. 'I say, old chap,' his voice was apologetic. 'Someone ought to stay with the plane.'

This was a complication I hadn't thought of.

'It's a military plane, you see. I'd stay myself. But I ought to talk to our chaps at the airfield.'

4

I didn't like the turn the conversation was taking. There was a dance that night at the Pendower's farm; I was taking Jessica, and I'd no intention of sitting up half the night with a wretched airplane!

The pilot was speaking again. He seemed more embarrassed than ever. 'That friend of yours. Seems a decent enough chap. . . .'

'He's jolly decent. Why?'

'Is he English?'

I shook my head.

'He's not a Hun, is he?'

'What if he is?'

The pilot held up his hands in mock alarm: 'Whoa there! Steady, boy! Steady!'

I was angry. When Otto had first come to Charterhouse a couple of years ago no one had thought it the least bit odd that I should have a German friend; but recently, with the growing possibility of war, there'd been an increasing number of snide remarks and innuendos. 'It's jolly unfair,' I said hotly. 'Didn't he risk his neck for you? To get you out of your plane?'

The pilot had the grace to look sheepish. 'I *said* he seems a decent chap. But we could be at war with them any moment. We can't leave him in charge of a plane!'

'Why not? He isn't going to pinch it!'

The pilot sighed: 'Listen, lad. If there *is* a war, a machine like this'll be worth its weight in gold. I'm not leaving it with a Hun. No matter', he added quickly, 'how decent a chap he is.'

Well, there it was. I thought of riding off and leaving the pilot to sort things out as best he could – but this seemed hardly playing the game; I thought of suggesting Gavin stayed with the plane – but he was too young and accident-prone (if there was a way of damaging the plane he'd find it!); I thought of suggesting the pilot stayed himself – but I wasn't sure how bad his head was, and besides he wanted to talk to his airfield. In the end I decided ruefully there was only one thing for it: 'How long', I muttered, 'would I have to stay?'

The pilot clapped me on the back: 'Jolly sporting of you!

We'll be as quick as we can. Our chaps ought to be here in a couple of hours. Three at the most.'

Now I thought at the time, and I still think now, that I made the only possible decision, that there was nothing else I could decently have done. Be that as it may, I soon discovered I'd touched off a powder keg: explosion followed explosion: and by the time the reverberations had died away, life for none of us was ever quite the same.

When I told the others I was staying with the plane I couldn't make out if Jessica was angry or hurt, because she turned away and started adjusting her stirrups.

Gavin looked at me in surprise: 'What about the dance?'

'Let's hope,' I said shortly, 'I get back in time. Sorry, Jess.'

'It's all right,' she said. But I could tell that it wasn't.

Otto laid a hand on my shoulder: '*I'm* not going to the dance,' he said with a smile. 'Let *me* stay.'

It was the one thing I had wanted to avoid. I couldn't think where to look or what to do.

The pilot let out an assinine bray of a laugh. 'If you youngsters get a move on, we can *all* go to the dance!'

Otto looked at him very straight. 'Why', he said quietly, 'am I not permitted to stay with your airplane?'

There was a silence that went on and on.

'So!'

Otto had gone red as a beetroot. It was a beastly situation for him. I felt utterly rotten about it, and I had a sudden and not very logical wish to prove to him that I at least still trusted him – and with something a great deal more important than an airplane. 'Otto,' I said. 'Do us a favour. If I don't get back in time, take Jess to the dance.'

He hesitated; but he was too much of a gentleman to refuse. He clicked his heels. 'If she will accompany me,' he said very formally, 'I shall be honoured.'

Looking back, I am amazed at what a torrent of events was to stem from this seemingly innocuous incident!

When the four of them had disappeared, I took a look at the plane.

It was, I'd gathered from the pilot, a Farman Longhorn, fitted with dual controls for training. It was easy to see how it had got its nickname, for a pair of the most enormous skids curved up in front of its body like the horns of a cow. It was a fair size: about thirty feet long and fifty wide. Its construction struck me as primitive in the extreme: panels of fabric which seemed to be held together with a forest of struts and a complexity of wire. There was wire everywhere; I reckon you could just about have caged a canary in it! Taking care not to put my weight on anything fragile, I clambered into the nacelle. The cockpit was painted blue, and contained pedals, a stick and what looked like a pair of home-made handlebars. It seemed incredible that such a Heath Robinson contraption could actually fly!

My inspection over, I settled down under one of the wings. It was a pleasant evening: warm and tranquil, with a curious aroma which I couldn't at first identify but which I eventually decided was the Longhorn. (I didn't realise then that planes, like people, each have their own individual fragrance, that of the Longhorn being a compound of burnt oil, varnish and dope.) It wasn't long before the warmth, the stillness and the smell of the Longhorn combined to make me feel pleasantly drowsy. I lay back and shut my eyes and wondered how far the others had got on their way to the farm. A bee droned lazily through the clover. After a while it settled on my arm. But I didn't feel it. . . .

When I woke, the sun had vanished and it was several degrees colder. I looked at my watch and cursed. Seven o'clock. The dance would be starting in less than an hour. I hadn't a hope of getting back in time. I wondered what had woken me. Then I heard the drum-drum-drum of a horse's hooves coming nearer.

It was about the last person in the world I expected who came galloping over the meadow: Jessica. She swung off her horse and shook loose her hair. 'You don't', she said, 'look very pleased to see me!'

'I'm jolly pleased! But what's going on?'

'I'm afraid', she said, 'I'm the bearer of bad tidings. You'll have to spend the night here. With the plane.'

'Oh, I say!'

She unstrapped a bundle from her saddle: 'Don't look so glum! I've brought blankets, coffee and lots to eat. Almost enough', she added enigmatically, 'for both of us.'

I didn't know what to make of *that*. Surely Jessica couldn't be thinking of spending the night with me? Alone? I looked at her with a mixture of eagerness and apprehension. 'What', I said, 'about Otto? And the dance?'

'I am not a parcel', she said quietly, 'to be handed round. *I'll* decide who I'm spending the evening with.'

Jessica, I knew, had a rebellious streak in her and some funny ideas – Gavin reckoned she might even be a suffragette! I decided to stick to practicalities. 'What about the mechanics? Aren't they coming?'

The ride back, she told me, had been a disaster. The pilot had felt dizzy; twice he'd fallen from his horse, and every few hundred yards they had had to stop and rest. By the time they got to the farm and the pilot's head had been seen to and he'd contacted his airfield, it was too late for there to be any chance of repairing the Longhorn that evening. Reid apparently had told his airfield that he'd be happy to spend the night with the plane; but the Pendower family, afraid that he might have concussion, had dissuaded him. 'So' – Jessica's eyes dropped and she seemed suddenly loth to look at me – 'you and I have volunteered!' She helped me to lay out the blankets under the wing of the Longhorn.

I wonder what would have happened that evening if I'd been a few months older, a little more sure of myself, a little less callow. Maybe nothing at all. Maybe my whole life would have been different. I'll never know. . . .

Jessica sat down and drew the blanket over her knees: 'I love the twilight, don't you?'

'Yes.' I sat beside her. 'It's so quiet.'

'It's so quiet', she said, 'that I can hear the beat of your heart.'

'And I yours.'

Our eyes met. Her hair brushed my cheek.

I wanted to kiss her. But I wanted also to be fair to Otto. 'What about the dance? Isn't Otto expecting you?'

'I've talked to him. He understands.'

'He's having a wretched time, Jess. It can't be much fun nowadays, being a German. I thought that pilot was beastly to him.'

She didn't say anything. She just looked at me.

'Jess!'

'I'm here. In case you hadn't noticed.'

'Didn't you think that pilot chap was beastly to him?'

For a long time she sat very still. I'd no idea what she was thinking. Then she seemed suddenly to come to a decision. 'Oh, jolly beastly! Perhaps I ought to go back and console him.'

I didn't know what to say to that, so I said nothing. There was a long silence. It wasn't a comfortable silence; it went on and on until it became like an almost physical barrier between us. And eventually Jessica stood up and put on her riding hat.

I wished more than ever now that I'd kissed her; but the opportunity had all too obviously escaped me. The twilight seemed suddenly to have lost its magic; all that was left was the chill.

Jessica was looking at me in a way that I wasn't sure how to interpret: part-exasperated, part-regretful. ' 'Bye Jack,' she swung herself onto her horse. 'Sweet dreams!'

As she disappeared into the woods at the far side of the meadow I felt – as many wiser men than I have felt before me – that you never know what you want till it's gone.

You're a fool, Jack Cunningham, I told myself, but it's no good sitting on your backside lamenting; you'd better make yourself comfortable for the night. . . . I collected an armful of bracken from the edge of the wood and stuffed it under a blanket – the great thing when sleeping out, I seemed to remember, was to have plenty *beneath* you. I checked the lashings that the

9

pilot had put on the Longhorn; I checked that the gates leading into the meadow were closed – I'd no wish for my *vache méchanique* to be visited in the night by a herd of its sisters! – then I sat down to sample the coffee and sandwiches which if I'd had any sense I might have been sharing with Jessica.

By now the great gold disc of the moon was rising over the hills. It was the perfect evening for a dance. The music, I told myself, would be in full swing now, with some couples doing the waltz and the new-fangled hesitation in the big panelled hall, and others, I didn't doubt, drifting hand-in-hand across the terraces and onto the beach. I wondered what Otto and Jessica were up to? I hoped they'd confine their activities to the dance floor. But if they don't, a voice whispered, you've only yourself to blame. I closed my eyes and tried to will myself to sleep.

Sleep, however, was elusive. The ground was hard, the night was full of unfamiliar sounds, and my thoughts like pigeons to cote kept homing to the dance. It must have been midnight before I dozed off. And in my sleep I dreamed.

Three bizarre monstrosities were disporting themselves in the night sky. They were half-airplane half-animal, parodies of the Longhorn. I was 'riding' one, Jessica another and Otto the third, and we were waltzing in and out of the stars in a sort of *danse macabre*. At first it was rather exhilarating. But as the music grew faster and more discordant, the Longhorns began to creak and groan in protest. Suddenly they started to fight, charging at one another like celestial hippopotami. Exhilaration gave way to fear; and fear to horror; it was as though I had some premonition of how the fight was going to end. It ended with my nightmare-creature colliding with Otto's. There was the most terrible explosion, a cloud of smoke and twin balls of flame plunging comet-like to earth. In my dream I could hear myself screaming in terror: again and again and again.

It was the screaming that woke me. Shriek after hideous shriek as the owl flew low over the moonlit meadow.

I woke next morning stiff and tired, as though I'd had no more than a cat-nap. By the time I'd splashed about in the Helford, however, and drunk the last of my coffee, I was feeling if not on top of the world at least able to cope with it.

The meadow was still glistening with dew when Reid and a veritable retinue of mechanics drove up in a Crossley transport. From what I'd seen of him the day before I hadn't greatly cared for the pilot; but I have to admit he now went out of his way to be pleasant. Which, he asked me, would I prefer: to be driven straight home, or to help with reparing the Longhorn? I opted to help with the Longhorn.

The repairs didn't take long. As soon as a fractured fuel-pipe had been replaced, the engine started first time, and was soon ticking over like a pair of well-oiled but ill-synchronised alarm clocks. The skid, which had buckled on landing, proved more recalcitrant; but at the end of a couple of hours it had been spliced and splinted – rather like an injured limb – and after a trial taxi round the meadow, Reid pronounced the plane ready for take-off. He looked at me quizically: 'Care for a flip, young fellar?'

I wasn't sure if he was serious. Or – if he was – if I wanted to risk being *carboneezayed.*

He must have read my thoughts, because he seemed suddenly to lose interest in me 'Forget it. If you're scared.'

That needled me: 'Of course,' I said mendaciously, 'I'm not scared.'

He tossed me a helmet: 'In you hop then.'

Now I know that in popular flying stories the hero is invariably an *aficianado,* ever reading books on aerodynamics and longing to leap into the great unknown. It wasn't that way with me: at least not to start with. As I climbed that morning into the cockpit of the Longhorn I felt like Daniel being fed to the lions, and nothing would have pleased me better than if the engine had failed to start. However, no sooner had I strapped myself in than the wretched thing exploded into life, unpleasantly close to the back of my neck. (The Longhorn was a 'pusher': that is to say its engine was at the rear of the fuselage with its propeller facing backwards.) One of the mechanics checked that my harness was taut; and before I quite realised what was happening the plane was lurching ponderously across the meadow like a cow being driven to pasture.

Once I'd got used to it, I found taxying not unpleasant. Looking back, I could see the grass being flattened out by our slipstream; looking sideways, I could see the hedgerows flashing past the tip of our wings – a smart canter I reckoned we were moving at. I put my hands on the dual-control-bars, and soon got the hang of what the pilot was doing. We trundled up to the cluster of elms at the top of the meadow, and swung into wind. Reid signalled me to let go of the controls. The engine began to tick louder and louder, faster and faster, and suddenly we were careering through the long grass like a charging hippopotamus to an accompaniment of the most alarming clatters and bangs. For five, ten, fifteen seconds both noise and plane gathered momentum. Then there was a sudden lurch, and the only sound was the tick-tick-tick of the engine. I was wondering what on earth had gone wrong, when I realised we were airborne.

It was a curious sensation: a moment of trembling uncertainty, like a salamander venturing for the first time into flame; then, as the airflow built up around us, a feeling of growing stability. There was no need, I told myself, to be afraid.

I looked out. Already we were beyond the meadow, climbing steadily as we crossed the blue ribbon of the Helford. And suddenly, as we lifted clear of the hills, there unfolded in every direction the most magnificent panorama: a breath-taking vista of woods and fields, cliffs and sea, clouds and sky, all seen not in the usual two dimensions, but as a bird sees them in three. I was conscious at that moment, as I had never been conscious before, of the beauty and complexity of the world we live in.

We turned, and I can't say I cared for *that*: the earth tilting one way and my stomach the other. I clung to the side of the cockpit, fighting instinctively to get back to an even keel. Reid must have realised how I felt, because he gave me a grin and shouted 'Relax!' – I could sense the word rather than hear it –

then he went into another and gentler turn. And this time I began to get the hang of it; it was like riding a bicycle; one had to think of one's body as being part of the machine, to go with it not against it.

We were flying parallel to the coast now, heading into the wind and moving so slowly that we seemed almost to be hovering. I rested my hands on the controls. It would be rather fun, I thought, to be able to fly: to be free to go where fancy took one: to explore beyond the sunset, above the clouds . . . . I followed Reid's movements, noting how he kept our airspeed steady at fifty-five, and the horizon level at the confluence of bracing wires and skid. Flying didn't seem to be difficult.

We must have been airborne for about ten minutes – though it seemed longer – when I saw to my disappointment that we were coming back towards the meadow. Reid pointed down. It was obvious he intended to land.

Now I can only think that the rarefied air must have made me a bit intoxicated; because I shook my head, pointed upwards and indicated that *I* wanted to have a go! I could see he was amused. He climbed to three thousand feet and handed over.

Some people, though in my experience very few, take to the air as a newborn babe to water; I had a pupil once who the first time I took him up did a near-perfect loop in a Tiger Moth. I wasn't so lucky. It was a long time that morning before I was able to keep the Longhorn straight and level, and even longer before I was able to turn without very nearly shuddering into a stall or toppling into a dive. But Reid was patient; the Longhorn was docile; and once I'd got the hang of a thing I didn't forget it. And suddenly, as I eased out of one of my smoother turns, it came to me that I was the Longhorn's master. It was the most wonderful feeling: to know that the airplane, like a horse beneath me, was obedient to the touch of my hands and feet; to know I could take it wherever I chose – should I explore the Lizard, or look for the Pendowers' farm, or play with those cottonwool clouds above the Helford? I was filled with exhilaration. This, I told myself, was the life!

But too soon Reid was directing me back to the meadow. Too

soon he was taking over the controls and preparing to land. Before we dropped below the crest of the hills I took a long look at the magnificent vista of sky and cloud, woodland and meadow, and hoped this wouldn't be the last time I'd see the world as eagles see it.

When we had landed, taxied up to the Crossley and clambered out of our cockpits, I didn't quite know what to say. 'Thanks a lot, sir,' I blurted out. 'That was super!'

He looked at me quizzically: 'I thought you were sold on it.'

I thought of telling him that I *wasn't* sold on it: that I'd been uncomfortable, uncertain and at times afraid. Yet I knew that if he'd said 'Come up again', I'd have gone like a shot. Thinking to change the subject I pointed to a metal boss in the cockpit – the miserable thing had been digging into my back for most of the flight: 'What's that?'

'That', he said, 'is a gun-mounting. For a Lewis machine-gun.'

Now this was something that hadn't occurred to me: that aircraft could be weapons of war. It seemed all wrong. Here was man, venturing for the first time into an unknown and most wonderful element – the air – and already, before he had even explored it, he was using it to fight in. It struck me as evil: a sort of prostitution. I remembered my dream, and the Longhorns fighting, colliding and plunging comet-like to destruction. And though the sun was shining and there wasn't a cloud in the sky, I shivered.

A couple of weeks later Otto and I were back at Charterhouse, struggling with the *Iliad*. And a couple of weeks after that the Archduke Francis Ferdinand was murdered on the borders of Bosnia and Hercegovina.

The names didn't mean a thing to me. 'Where on earth', I said to Otto, 'are Bosnia and Hercegovina? And a place called Sarajevo?'

14

2

The summer of 1914 will always be an enigma to me. Were its skies *really* so cloudless, its wines so mellow, its girls so desirable? Or do my generation look back through rose-coloured spectacles at an age which in fact was flawed beyond redemption by the canker of inequality? I can't judge. I only know that for me at any rate that summer evokes a cornucopia of memories, all of them golden – like that penultimate Saturday in July, Old Carthusian Day, the day my generation drank the last of the wine. . . . There were teas and marquees, top hats and cucumber sandwiches, champagne and epigrams from Aeschylus; there was the thud of leather on willow, the martial strains of the band, and Jessica still young enough to blush at my friends' admiring glances: '*Now* we know why Jack and Otto are always dashing off to the Helford!'

I felt myself blushing too. 'What rot! I just happen to live there.'

'Some people have all the luck!'

Applause rippled politely round the cricket ground. The Old Carthusians had a demon bowler, and he had just uprooted our opening batsman's stumps. 'I'm next for the slaughter,' I said. 'I'd better get my pads on.'

Jessica wished me luck. I had rather hoped she'd stay and watch when it was my turn to bat; but Otto offered to take her down to the river, and away the two of them went, hand in hand, the sunlight bright in her hair – they had, I thought to myself, been seeing a lot of one another lately. . . .

Now you could, I suppose, see the events of that afternoon as symbolic. For there was I, facing up to the demon bowler, playing a schoolboy's game; and there were Otto and Jessica, by the side of the river, playing an older and far more meaningful game – a game they had started playing, though I didn't realise this at the time, on the night of the Pendowers' dance. That was the night it all started. . . . From what I learned later it seems that Otto had been very formal and undemonstrative on the dance floor, and Jessica had teased him about this. 'But Miss Pendower,' he had said, 'how can it be otherwise? When you are Jack's girl? And Jack is my friend?' This hadn't pleased her. She had said she *wasn't* my girl – 'For all the notice he takes of me,' she had said, 'I might be a piece of farm equipment!' And there was truth in this. For Jessica to me had always been the kid next door, a trusted but younger and somehow quite asexual friend. Until suddenly that summer, as a butterfly springs from its chrysalis, she had made the leap from girl to woman. While backward me was still preoccupied with keeping a straight bat to the demon bowler! Given time, my mood would have matured to match hers. But time for all of us that summer was running out. Before I realised what was happening Jessica and Otto were on the threshold of love, love given an added poignancy by the knowledge that their countries might soon be at war. She was sixteen, he seventeen – the same age as Romeo and Juliet. It was inevitable that their hearts should rule their heads. Inevitable too that there should come a time – Old Carthusian Day – when they had to say goodbye. 'One day soon, my little Jessie,' he said as they sat by the slow-moving river, 'I must to steal away, like the thief in the night. You know why.'

'Do you *have* to, Otto?'

'If your brother was in Germany,' he said, 'and there was a war, wouldn't you wish him to come home? To fight for his country?'

'I suppose so.'

'In the same way, I wish to go home and fight for *my* country.'

She was silent.

'Surely, Jessie, you understand?'

She wouldn't look at him. She had in her hand a stick of cow parsley and she kept breaking pieces off and tossing them into the river. Her voice was so low that he had to lean forward to

16

hear what she was saying. 'God said "thou shalt not kill".'

'But men have *always* fought and killed – for what they believe to be right. Would you wish us to have no courage? No loyalty? No honour?'

Her eyes were full of tears. 'What use are courage, loyalty and honour if you're dead?'

'What use is it to be alive,' he said, 'without them?'

She tossed her last piece of cow parsley into the river. 'I expect,' she said, 'it's because I'm a girl. And in love. I can't see things as you do.'

He took her chin, very gently, between his forefinger and thumb. 'The war won't last for ever. And when it is over I shall come back for you. That on the Bible I give you my oath.'

They kissed. Faintly from the playing fields above the river came a ripple of applause – the demon bowler had knocked my middle stump clean out of the ground. They didn't hear the applause. They didn't see the gold and sapphire dragonflies hovering over the reeds. They clung to one another with the despair of those who fly in the face of the gods: in their hearts the same fear, that their lips would never meet again.

Later they sat side by side, not wanting to speak, not daring to touch. Then he said quietly: 'Would it be fair to ask you to wait for me?'

'All's fair,' she said, 'in love and war.'

'So you will?'

She hesitated. She hesitated not because she was uncertain, but because she wanted very deliberately to make herself assemble, face up to and then dismiss as unimportant all the heartaches which she knew a promise would lead to. 'I'll wait for you,' she said. 'I give you my word.'

That's how they left it.

There were no histrionics, no declarations of undying passion, no railing against the gods; just a very ordinary boy and a very ordinary girl who loved one another and made a simple promise. Simple, but to the pure of heart, binding.

By the time they got back to the school the sun was setting, the cricket was over, and the band were marching away

17

through lengthening shadows to the tune of *Semper Fidelis.*

I was rather pleased with my innings against the Old Carthusians – thirty-one runs and nearly as many bruises. And when I had showered and changed I found waiting for me in my study something which pleased me even more: an official-looking envelope embossed with the frank of the War Office. I opened it eagerly:

> *Dear Sir,*
>   *I am in receipt of your communication of the 2nd instant.*
>   *I am instructed to inform you that commissions in the Royal Flying Corps are available only to those who already hold a Certified Pilot's Licence.* [Damn and blast it! How on earth do I get one of those?]
>   *However, a limited number of cadetships for those wishing to learn to fly will shortly be available at the civilian Flying Schools of Brooklands and Shoreham.* [Now *that's* more like it!] *Should you wish to be considered for such a cadetship you are instructed to attend for interview at Room 613A, the War Office, London, on the morning of August 7th.*
>   *I have the honour to be, sir, your obedient servant. . . .*

Only one person at Charterhouse knew I'd been trying to join the Flying Corps. I burst into Otto's study, where he was entertaining Jessica. 'Look! Look!' I thrust the letter at him. 'I'm going to be a pilot!' That I might fail the interview or fail to make the grade at Flying School simply didn't occur to me!

Otto was almost as pleased as I was. Much to my embarrassment he embraced me: 'Well done, Jack! You lucky blighter!. . . . I say, this calls for a celebration.'

'Rather!. . . . Jess – remember those crates of champers? Behind the tea tent?'

We pooled our resources and found we had eight shillings and four pence: just about enough, we reckoned, for a bottle. Jess's eyes were sparkling. 'I'll say it's for my parents. But how do we get it up here? Without being seen?'

For a moment we were nonplussed. Then Otto handed her her parasol.

Half an hour later, thinking ourselves no end of devils, we were pouring the champagne into tooth mugs and drinking to my wings. Glasses were drained and filled and drained again. It was the perfect finale to a perfect day. Only at the very end, when I least expected it, did I catch a glimpse of the pit towards which we were sliding.

Otto's cheeks were flushed, his eyes were bright. 'I too', he announced, 'will join a *Fliegerabteilungen.*'

'What on earth's that?'

'You know. A section of aircraft. How do you call it. . . . A squadron!'

'You mean you want to be a pilot too?'

He nodded.

'Oh, how ripping! Perhaps we'll meet!'

Our delight was spontaneous, our joy ingenuous. We pranced round the study in an elephantine *pas de deux*, knocking a line of books off a shelf, slopping champagne all over his beautiful orange carpet, and provoking a violent hammering from the room next door. Otto leapt onto a table. He raised his glass: 'To knights of the air!'

The glasses were drained. It sounded all so romantic, all such fun: like a medieval joust with all the trappings of pageantry and chivalry . . . until quite out of the blue, I remembered the machine-gun-mounting in the cockpit of the Longhorn. It made me think. I looked at Otto and all of a sudden realised it would be a great deal better if we *didn't* meet. And having started thinking along these lines I found I couldn't stop. It was silly, I know. But the champagne seemed suddenly to have lost its sparkle, the evening its magic.

I didn't tell the others what was bothering me. I said I'd a headache, 'too much champers, I expect', and left them to it and went for a walk through the twilit playing fields. It was as though I knew in my heart that it was a night for saying goodbye.

19

A fortnight later Otto vanished. In the evening he climbed as usual into his bed in the monitors' dormitory. Next morning he was gone.

The date was August 3rd, and one of our politicians was making yet another speech. 'The lamps are going out all over Europe,' he told us. 'We shall not see them lit again in our lifetime.'

We listened. But we didn't yet understand.

3

On the morning of August 7th I was up with the proverbial lark. If there was going to be a queue for the cadetships at Brooklands and Shoreham I'd every intention of being at the head of it.

It was still misty as I left the friend's house where I had spent the night, and the occasional hansom as it trundled past was invisible until it was almost on top of me. By the time I got to the War Office, however, the sun was breaking through, and my first glimpse of the building was spectacular: a pyramid of sloping roofs and classical façades rising like some mysterious fairy palace out of a backdrop of plane trees and mist. The inside of the War Office was mysterious too; there were buff-coloured forms to be filled in in triplicate, spiral staircases to be climbed, and blue-coated messengers to be followed down a seemingly endless labyrinth of corridors, until I came at last to the Mecca of my dreams: Room 613A.

But alas for my hope of being first in the queue! Half-a-dozen others were already there, most of them to my chagrin older than I was and a couple already in uniform. We eyed one another warily, like dogs who want to be friendly but find themselves in contention for the one and only bone. Nobody had much to say as we sat on a line of austere wooden benches and awaited our turn to be interviewed. But as each applicant came out through the door, we tried to read from his expression 'Has he got in?', and asked ourselves 'Shall I?' Suddenly I found myself at the head of the queue.

The interviewing officer turned out to be not the ogre I'd been afraid of, but a charming old man with a kind smile and gentle eyes: 'So you're J. A. Cunningham? And you are at

Charterhouse?'

'Yes, sir.'

'Play any games?'

'I'm in the First Eleven at cricket, sir. And I've got my colours for racquets.'

'Racquets, eh! So you should have a good eye?'

'Well, yes, sir. I suppose so.'

'How old are you?'

'Nearly eighteen, sir.' (Stretching the truth wasn't the same, I told myself, as breaking it!)

'Hmmm! . . . .' I could see he didn't believe me. 'Now suppose, Mr Cunningham, you are flying on a reconnaissance patrol. You're behind the enemy lines, and your engine fails. You make a forced landing. What would you do next?'

I hadn't the faintest idea what I'd do next! For a moment my mind went blank; then as a drowning man will clutch at a straw I battoned onto the first idea that came into my head: 'Destroy the plane, sir.'

'How would you do that?'

'Let out some petrol, sir. And set fire to it.'

'A bit drastic, don't you think?'

(Oh Lord! I must have given him the wrong answer. But I'd better stick to my guns.) 'Well, sir. Aircraft are worth their weight in gold. I wouldn't want the Huns to get hold of it. . . .'

'That's true. But don't you think it might have been better to repair the engine?'

'Yes, sir.' (Oh damn and blast it! Why hadn't I thought of that? Now he was going to turn me down.)

He was speaking again. 'Or perhaps you think repairing an engine wouldn't be your job? A bit too dirty perhaps?'

'Oh no, sir! Gosh, if I knew how to, I'd do it like a shot.'

He regarded me with more sympathy than enthusiasm. I could read his mind like a book; he thought I was too young. As in a nightmare I was powerless to prevent, I could see him striking my name off his list. 'I'm terribly keen, sir,' I blurted out. 'And I *have* done a bit of flying already.'

'What in?'

'A Maurice Farman Longhorn, sir.'

He looked at me with slightly more interest: 'What speed did you land at?'

'The approach at fifty, sir. The touch-down at forty-five.'

A pause that seemed to go on and on, a stare that seemed to go through and through me, then a slow smile: 'All right. I'll write to the OC at Brooklands. As soon as there's a vacancy he'll let you know.'

'Oh, thanks, sir! Thanks most awfully!'

By the time I left the War Office the mist had vanished, the sky was azure, the sun was gold as the eye of a lynx. It was a day to match my mood.

I imagined in my innocence that the OC at Brooklands would be looking forward eagerly to the arrival of keen young pilots like myself all wanting to 'take their ticket'. But as the days lengthened to weeks and the weeks to months and there was still no word from him, I became disillusioned. 'I reckon,' I said to Gavin, 'they've lost my application.'

'I doubt it. After all the forms you filled in!'

I sent a stone skimming first-bounce across the Helford. 'I bet Otto's not having to hang about like this.'

Gavin was philosophic: 'Confucius he say "everything comes to him who waits"!'

'He didn't say anything of the bloody sort! . . . . I had a rotten dream last night. I dreamed the war was over. Before I'd even taken my ticket.'

To another generation with another set of values it may seem strange that our greatest fear that autumn was that the war would be over before we'd had time for a crack at the Hun. I can only say that for ninety-nine out of a hundred of us that is the way we felt. Only the very occasional odd-man-out saw things differently. And when – as happened that evening – the rest of us met such a man, we didn't know what to make of him.

Gavin and I were riding back to the Pendowers' farm. As we skirted the dried-up bed of the Helford, we passed what looked

23

like a derelict cottage; only when I saw smoke coming out through a hole in the roof did I realise it was occupied. 'Who', I asked him, 'lives there?'

'Will Willcock. He used to be a mud-pilot. Till the river silted up. Look! There he is.'

We rode across to him.

The scene reminded me of a Constable painting: the tumble-down cottage with its walls of wattle-and-daub, the cider-apple tree with its cankerous arms, the ragged figure of the labourer dwarfed by an immensity of sky. 'Evening, Will.'

'Evenin', Master Gavin.'

'You found work yet?'

He gestured to the river: 'No water, zurr. No work.'

'You'll have to take the King's shilling!'

'Zurr?'

'You know. Join the colours. Fight for king and country.'

'Not me, zurr.'

'Why on earth not?'

The labourer shifted uncomfortably: 'I belong to be riverman. B'ain't much of a hand at fightin'.'

'You'd soon learn.'

Will Willcock was silent.

'What's the matter? Not afraid, are you?'

'No, zurr. It's jest that killin' folk don't seem properly right.'

'Good God man! You don't want the Huns over here, do you? Looting your cottage! Raping your wife!'

Will Willcock's eyes were puzzled: 'B'ain't no Germans here, zurr. Reckon my Jeanie won't come to harm.'

The man, I thought, was an idiot. I felt sorry for him, with his mean little croft and his mean little scruples. 'Come on,' I said to Gavin. 'Let's be getting back.'

As we wheeled round our horses, a shaft of sun broke through the clouds, bathing the scene in a golden almost ethereal light. I never saw Will Willcock again. I never expected to think of him again. I had no premonition that every detail of this our one brief meeting was to stay fixed in my memory, as a fly is fixed in amber, for the rest of my life. It was always the same scene that came back to me: the tumbledown cottage, the cankered cider-apple and the awkward figure of the mud-pilot. What changed was the way I interpreted it.

Next morning the postman brought me a special delivery. 'Report Brooklands', the telegram read. 'October 30th.'

Brooklands was a civil airfield about fifteen miles from London. It was surrounded by pine woods, a race-track and a sewage farm – the latter the scene of many a malodourous forced landing! I went there for eight weeks' training as a civilian cadet.

Being a civilian had its disadvantages in the autumn of 1914. It meant that we were fair game for the 'patriotic' busybodies who took it on themselves to roam the streets of London distributing white feathers. On our very first night in town we ran into one of them outside the Ritz. 'And why', trumpeted the formidable old lady, 'aren't you boys in uniform?'

I was tongue-tied with embarrassment. One of my friends, however, wasn't so lacking in *savoir faire*. He lifted his hat: 'Excuse me, madam. My mother warned me never to speak to strange women in the street.'

Of more concern to us that autumn than white feathers was the weather. It rained hour after hour, day after day, week after week. And how we cursed it. For it stopped us flying. . . . Flying in those days was surrounded by a good deal of mumbo-jumbo. Conditions, it was thought, had to be exactly right. Too much wind and the planes would be damaged or blown backwards; not enough wind and they would never get off the ground; flying in rain cloud or poor visibility was taboo, and aircraft spent most of their time grounded with recalcitrant engines. I doubt if we flew one day in five. We had instead to make do with lectures ('What a bore! Who cares about the *theory* of flight? Or the *layout* of a Renault engine?'), and with gazing hopefully at the Longhorns and BE2s in the hangars and trying to persuade our instructors to trundle them out. In three weeks I flew less than six hours. But at last I managed to go solo.

November 20th was the date of this epoch-making event. The

morning, as usual, had been grey and overcast; but by mid-day the sky was clearing, a watery sun was shining as though it couldn't believe its luck, and a pair of Longhorns were circling the airfield like dowagers performing a stately dance. I did twenty minutes' dual with Sergeant Parker, and when we had finished he taxied across to the hangars. 'You seem', he shouted above the tick-tick-tick of the engine, 'to have got the hang of it. You'd better go solo.'

I thanked him with mixed feelings.

'Take that one,' he pointed to a Longhorn which a little posse of mechanics were wheeling onto the tarmac. 'And Cunningham . . .'

'Sir?'

'If you want to stay alive, *don't* go into a daydream!'

'Right, sir.'

As I walked across to the Longhorn I had the quite ridiculous feeling that both it and the mechanics were eyeing me with trepidation. 'I'm taking this one up,' I said with what I hoped was an air of confidence.

The mechanics exchanged glances. 'If you say so, sir,' the corporal's voice had as much enthusiasm as an undertaker's.

I climbed into the cockpit and checked the switches. From behind my back came the creak of a turning propellor and a shout of 'Contact!'

For a moment I thought I was saved, that the engine wasn't going to fire; then it exploded into life; and like a boxer who feels the stool pulled from beneath him, I knew there was no escape. I tightened my safety belt, and with an air of bravado which I hoped impressed the mechanics waved away the chocks. But my bravado was short-lived. As the Longhorn with a sudden lurch lumbered forward, there was no getting away from the fact that I was more frightened and more alone than I had ever been in my life.

As I taxied with exaggerated care to the outermost limit of the landing strip I felt – quite erroneously! – that the eyes of everyone on the airfield were on me. When I was in position, I took a deep breath. I remembered all the pilots whose first solo had been their last, and told myself I must have been crazy to *volunteer* to fly! I looked at my hands and saw they were trembling, and was tempted to turn back and say there was something wrong with the engine. Then I thought of the way my friends would look at me, and smile . . . . I checked the windsock and swung into wind. (Last week Ted Carson had forgotten this, had taken-off *down*-wind and toppled arse over tit into the sewage farm! At least I wouldn't do *that!*) Now firmly forward with the throttle, and gently forward with the stick. A quick look at the air-speed indicator: thirty, thirty-five, forty. Ah, up comes the tail. Now don't pull her off too soon, or she'll stall. And not too late, or you'll end up like Buster Jackson in the pines – what a time to think of *that!*. . . . Bounce, clatter! Bounce, swerve! For God's sake hold her straight. . . . Forty-five, fifty. Now, back with the stick. Why's everything so quiet? We must be airborne. Of course we're airborne! Look at the pine trees floating past beneath us. Look at their branches rippling in the wind, like waves on the sea – I wonder if that's the last thing poor Jackson saw? . . . Six hundred feet: that's high enough. Now level off, and keep the horizon steady. All right so far. . . . Now a turn: a little rudder and a little stick, gently and together. That was rather good. Look, there's the airfield drifting backwards under the wing. How small it looks. The men ants, the hangars bricks, the river a snake: a tired old snake looping away into the evening haze. . . . God, what's happening? Why've the controls gone slack? Quick, we're stalling. Down with the nose! . . . Phew, that was *nasty!* Didn't old Parker warn me not to daydream. I'd better land before I kill myself! . . .

But *how* to land? (Nobby Clarke, on *his* first solo, had been too frightened to come down, and had flown round and round the airfield till he ran out of petrol and crashed. At least I'll have a go!). . . . Check the wind direction. Line up with the airfield. Nose down. Engine off. And start to lose height. How quiet it is without the engine. I can hear the wind in the wires. Sixty, sixty-five. A bit fast. Up with the nose. That's more like it. There go the pines beneath us. No need to juggle with the

27

engine; we're coming in just about right. The airfield's getting bigger and bigger. It's rushing towards us. Help, it's here already! Flatten out! Quick! Or we'll fly slap into the ground. Nose up – but not too much or we'll stall. That's it. Now hold it, hold it, hold it. Why on earth don't we land? We're floating on and on. Oh Lord, we're going to float right across the field and into the sewage farm!. . . . Rumble, bounce. Rumble, lurch. The rumbling fading to silence. The air-speed indicator subsiding to zero. And looking down I can see daisies in the grass, and the grass motionless, and the puffy white seeds of a dandelion floating gently past the nacelle.

I've made it! Now to taxi back to the hangars in style.

As I parked the Longhorn with a flourish, one of the mechanics ran forward to peer anxiously at the skids. 'No damage is there?'

'Nao! These old cows'll stand anything!'

His matter-of-factness failed to deflate my ego. I had gone solo. The sky was mine to play in. God was in heaven. All was right with the world. It wasn't difficult, I told myself, to be a pilot.

Within twenty-four hours I had been taught otherwise.

Next morning we were outside the hangars, being initiated into the mysteries of the Lewis-gun, when a strange-looking aircraft touched down and came taxying towards us. It was, we were told, our latest and greatest fighting-machine, a BE2C, straight from the Royal Aircraft Establishment at Farnborough, and this particular aircraft was about to embark on a series of demonstration flights all over the country. We clustered round it eagerly, admiring its dihedral wings and rakish lines. And even more eagerly we clustered round the pilot. He was good-looking and easy-going; his leather flying jacket was festooned with charms and badges; his scarf was multicoloured as Joseph's coat, and there seemed to be nothing about flying he didn't know; he had two hundred hours in his log book, he had flown over the Front, he had actually, it was whispered, shot down a German balloon.

He gave us a talk that afternoon in the hangar. A great deal of what he said was above our heads, but we were a captive audience. And as he spoke of vertical turns and spiral glides, of how to get out of a spin and of what machines it was safe to loop, we listened open-mouthed and goggle-eyed and dreamed of the day when we too might be masters of the air. At the end of the talk he and his observer clambered into their magnificent aircraft and prepared to take-off. We lined up on the tarmac to watch.

It was a lovely evening: bright sun, blustering wind, and in the west a great mountain range of cumulus. The BE2 taxied to the far side of the airfield. It swung into wind. For a moment it hung poised like a dragonfly for flight, the sun glinting brightly on its wings. Then its engine burst into a full-blooded roar. It came hurtling towards us. It rose gracefully into the air. As it passed over the hangars the pilot gave us a wave; he was so close that I could see the individual bands of red and gold on his scarf. We turned to watch, shading our eyes against the glare of the sun.

The roar of the engine faltered, picked-up, then faltered again. It coughed harshly, like an asthmatic fighting for air. Then it cut dead.

The BE2 was at about four hundred feet: well past the boundary of the airfield. Ahead lay the sewage farm, unprepossessing but safe.

No-one will ever know why the pilot turned back. Perhaps he was anxious not to damage his fine new aircraft, perhaps he underestimated the wind, perhaps he overestimated his skill.

We watched, full of admiration, as quickly and decisively he turned back towards the airfield. It looked at first as though he had plenty of time and plenty of height: as though getting back would be the simplest thing in the world. Then we noticed that he seemed to be coming towards us more and more slowly, that he was losing height more and more quickly, that his wings were trembling. What, I wondered, were the pilot's thoughts as it came to him that he wasn't going to make it?

He was moving so slowly now that he seemed almost to be

29

hovering, to be clawing desperately at the air. Suddenly his wing dropped. And the BE2 flicked over into a spin and fell deadweight out of the sky.

From behind the hangars came the most terrible splintering crash. The emergency klaxon let out a discordant wail.

'Keep back!' an instructor shouted.

But already we were rushing across the tarmac, intent on seeing what we knew in our hearts it would be better not to see.

As we rounded the hangars it was a terrible sight that met our eyes. On the very edge of the airfield the BE2 lay squelched out like an over-ripe plum flung violently to earth. Its wings were broken; its fuselage was shattered; its tail-plane was severed from its body; in its cockpits two figures lay limp as rag dolls. And as motionless.

But no! Not both were motionless. The pilot's arm was moving feebly, as though he was trying to lever himself out of the wreckage.

But as we rushed towards him there was a flicker of flame.

'Down!' someone shouted.

A line of yellow flashed fast as lightning through the wreckage – petrol igniting back down the fractured fuel pipe. The petrol tank exploded. A sheet of flame rose high as the highest pine. And a blast of heat too terrible to be endured sent us reeling back, shielding our eyes. Through my splayed-out fingers I could see the figures in the cockpits jerk like marionettes as the flames swept over them. They twisted and jerked, and jerked and twisted. Then, mercifully, they were still. Then they started to glow.

Men with fire extinguishers rushed forward; but they too were driven back; for foam had little effect on fifty gallons of fiercely blazing fuel. The bodies of the pilot and the observer began to disintegrate.

It was several minutes before the flames were brought under control. And when some of us with axes and fire extinguishers did at last hack a way through to the cockpits, there wasn't a great deal left for us to carry to the ambulance.

Long after we had drifted back to our quarters, numb with

shock, a thin column of smoke coiled up into the evening sky. It was a particularly lovely sky, with the setting sun flinging out great bands of red and gold. I couldn't to start with think what the bands of red and gold reminded me of. Then I got it. It was as though the pilot's scarf had been strung out like a multicoloured funeral shroud across the sky.

Next morning all cadets were summoned to the CO's office. I think that what we longed for most was reassurance: to be told that so terrible an accident had been due to some freak combination of circumstances and was never likely to happen again, and certainly never to us. We were in for a shock.

The CO spoke to us for less than two minutes; but they were two minutes I'll never forget. For it seemed to me that what he said was even more terrible than the accident.

There were, he told us, certain basic rules to flying which must never be broken. The pilot of the BE2 had known these rules. But he had broken them. So he deserved to die. 'You have been told,' he said – 'and that fool of a pilot had been told, again and again and again – *never* turn back. If your engine fails on take-off *always* land straight ahead. Better to smash your wheels, your skids and your propellor than burn yourself and your passenger to death. . . . Now I want to make one thing crystal clear,' he ended, 'that pilot broke the rules, so he roasted alive. You break the rules, and you'll roast alive too. Remember that.' He picked up his swagger stick and slammed it down on a desk as though something had made him angry, and stalked out of the office.

I thought him unbearably callous. And I said as much to Sergeant Parker as we walked that evening over the airfield. 'Another couple of yards,' I said, 'and the pilot would have made it, and we'd all be calling him a hero.'

Sergeant Parker sucked his teeth: 'Reckon I'd rather be covered in shit and alive than a hero and dead.'

I muttered that I supposed so.

Sergeant Parker came to a halt. He put his hands on his hips and looked me up and down as though I were about six inches high. 'Listen, sonny' – he only reminded me of my lack of years when I'd done or said something to displease him – 'Listen, sonny. You get your head out of the clouds, or you won't live long enough to take your ticket. Flying isn't a sport – like batting for the jolly old school. Flying's a battle: a bloody non-stop battle. And the only rule worth a tinker's cuss is "stay alive". Think you can remember that?'

I said I'd remember. But I said it, truth to tell, more out of politeness than conviction. For my head, in those my days of innocence, was still very much in the clouds, still as chockfull of romantic notions as Malory's *Morte d'Arthur*.

I left Brooklands in mid-December with sixteen hours in my logbook, the rank of second-lieutenant, and a smart new uniform, including a Sam Browne belt which I didn't know how to put on and a pistol I didn't know how to use. But I still hadn't got what I wanted most: my wings. These, provided I didn't make a fool of myself, would be sewn onto my tunic at the end of four weeks' final training at Gosport.

Gosport was fun. And here, even more than at Brooklands, I found myself in a world where my whole life – thinking and talking, eating and sleeping, working and playing – was orientated to the air. There were, of course, *divertissements*: walks on the Downs, theatres restaurants, girls – though none of the latter struck me as a patch on Jessica – but these were peripheral pleasures. What mattered most to me in those days was my growing infatuation with the air. I flew whatever, wherever and whenever I could. And it was here at Gosport that I first lost my heart to a plane: the diminutive Bristol Scout.

She had a radial engine, a square rudder and neat uncomplicated lines. I only managed to fly her once, for she was the one and only Scout on the airfield and as sought-after by her swains as Shakespeare's Silvia. I took her up one particularly lovely afternoon over the New Forest. . . . A couple of gentle turns, a couple of steep turns, a couple of near-vertical turns. (How wonderfully responsive she was!) A not very expert spiral dive. (A less accommodating plane and I'd have just about ripped the wings off!) A loop. (That was fabulous. Easy as falling out of bed!) Soon we were diving, climbing, looping, rolling, now falling like a leaf towards the earth, now soaring like a rocket towards the clouds. Never before had I enjoyed such a sense of one-ness with a plane; no manoeuvre seemed too difficult for us, no challenge too testing. I understood that afternoon what Sergeant Parker had meant when he'd told us: 'Flying a plane is like making love to a woman. Some'll do this. Some'll do that. Some'll do bugger all. And once in a life-time you'll find a thoroughbred you can do anything with. She's the one to hang on to!' If only, I thought, as we stooped and soared through a sky that seemed truly halfway to heaven, I could hang on to the Bristol Scout. . . . But too soon the fields were darkening, the fuel in my tank running low.

I landed her with reverence, said goodbye to her with regret, and dreamed that night of deeds of unbelievable audacity that she and I performed together over the Front.

A week later I had a very different experience in a very different plane.

I was flying a BE2 across the Solent at something like 4,000 feet. I wasn't concentrating as much as I ought to have been. As a matter of fact I was thinking of Otto – wondering if he'd got *his* wings yet and if he had, what sort of plane he was flying (I'd wager it wasn't a temperamental cow like the BE2!) – when, as if in retribution for my thoughts, the engine cut stone dead.

One moment the world was filled with a vibrating roar, next moment with silence. Absolute silence.

Fear pricked up the hair on the nape of my neck. I remembered another engine dying, another aircraft falling, another body disintegrating in the flames. It wasn't going to happen to me. Better, I told myself, to nosedive into the Solent than to lie trapped in a shattered cockpit burning to death.

I pushed the nose forward and turned for land. I checked the few things I was able to check – throttle lever, switches, petrol cock – but could find nothing wrong. So it was going to be a forced landing: something better pilots than I quite often failed to walk away from. . . . To my surprise I wasn't frightened –

perhaps because I was too preoccupied with the immediate mechanics of staying alive. . . . Now what had old Parker taught us? Maintain your airspeed: find the wind: pick a landing-site early: and don't change your mind. . . . My speed's OK. But how on earth do I find the wind? No sails on the Solent, no white horses on the sea, no smoke from the chimneys. But there, thank God, goes a streamer of smoke from a bonfire; almost parallel to the shore. So where do I land? The beach? – too full of breakwaters. The fields? – too far away. Oh Christ, there must be *somewhere*! I could feel the sweat in my eyes, and the incipient knot of fear in my stomach. Then I saw it, where the coast curved round towards Portsmouth: the triangle of grass, low scrub and heather, flanked by sand-dunes: small, but free of trees. It would have to be there.

I was so obsessed by what had happened at Brooklands, that I came in too high too fast too soon. As we neared the edge of the heath I was still at 200 feet. . . . What on earth would Parker have done? Of course. Sideslip. . . . I crossed the controls – stick one way, rudder the other. The plane slewed sideways. Slipstream poured into the cockpit. I lost 150 feet in less time than it takes to describe. The heath came rushing up at me. I lined up, knocked off the switches, and prayed that if we did go arse over tit we wouldn't catch fire. When the ground was so close that I could see the individual spikes of heather, I levelled off. And waited, and waited, and waited. But the wretched plane refused to land. It floated on and on: straight for the dunes. Then suddenly the tail dropped. There was a lurch, the faintest of bounces, a long-drawn rumbling sigh. We were down. Incredibly, I'd made a near-perfect three-point landing!

Relief left me breathless and weak at the knees. But the relief was short-lived; for we were still, at something over 40 miles an hour, careering straight for the dunes. Unable to break, afraid to swerve, I froze like a petrified rabbit. The dunes grew larger; they swelled up like gargantuan pumpkins; they filled the windscreen; they blotted out the sky. I shut my eyes. And the BE2 came to rest with its prop about eighteen inches from the wall of sand.

When I'd stopped shaking, I was brash enough to tell myself that I'd done rather well: that not many pilots could walk away from their first emergency landing without so much as a scratch on the plane.

But my instructor, when he appeared on the scene that evening, soon cut me down to size. He looked first at the BE2 then at the dunes and muttered, 'Better born lucky than skilful.'

All the same, he can't have thought me totally incompetent. Because a week later the station tailor was sewing on my wings.

We had been expecting two weeks' leave, but all we got was two days. They must, I told myself, be needing us jolly badly at the Front.

Two days wasn't long enough for me to visit both my family and Jessica – my father, perhaps I ought to explain, had been killed fighting the Boers when I was only a few weeks old; my mother had remarried, and though we got on well enough we weren't particularly close. It didn't take me long to make up my mind who I wanted to spend my forty-eight hours with. I telephoned Jessica and invited her to Southsea.

For a reason I couldn't understand at the time (but was soon to understand all too clearly) she seemed curiously loth to come. But I managed in the end to persuade her. And when that evening I met her at the station I was jolly glad I had; because she looked absolutely stunning, and I at last woke up to the fact that she was no longer the kid next-door but the sort of girl men turn to stare at.

Our last day together couldn't be called uneventful: a walk over the Downs, a box at the theatre, a champagne supper at the Queens and afterwards a *tête-à-tête* by the big coal fire in Jessica's bedroom. We had a lot to talk about: I telling her of my growing love affair with the air, she telling me of the battle she had had with her parents to let her start nursing. They, it seems, like a lot of their generation, thought that no girl of sixteen should get involved with anything as unpleasant as war.

Jessica, however, had always had a mind of her own; and to her parents' horror she had got a job scrubbing floors and sterilizing bandages at the local hospital. 'As soon as I'm old enough', she said, 'I'll start *proper* nursing. So watch out, maybe you'll see me at the Front!'

She was wearing a green velvet dress which impressed me enormously because it had no visible means of support. She looked very beautiful, and I reached for her hand. . . . Tomorrow I was going to the Front. I'd no idea what the Front would be like; I only knew it was a place a lot of people never came back from. I wanted, I suppose, some talisman, some memory to hold onto, something to remember and be remembered by. 'I'm going,' I said firmly, 'to kiss you.'

'No, Jack. Please.'

All girls, I told myself, put up a show of reluctance. I took her not very expertly in my arms.

She was about as responsive as a sack of potatoes. She clamped shut her mouth, screwed shut her eyes and held herself rigid. It wasn't at all what I'd hoped for! I stopped trying to kiss her, and ran my finger gently down the curve of her spine. Her eyes opened. I'll never forget the sequence that was mirrored in them. A flicker of surprise, a moment of excitement, then inexplicably a flood of fear. She shivered. Just for a moment it was as it should have been: her lips soft, her body yielding, our tongues exploring. Then she started to struggle. Violently. 'No! Please!'

I let her go with considerable reluctance.

She walked to the window, drew back the curtains and stood looking out across the Solent. Her voice was frightened: 'Please. Never kiss me like that again.'

'Well *I* enjoyed it!' I put an arm round her shoulder, but she shied away like a frightened animal.

'Steady on, Jess. There's nothing to be afraid of.'

'Oh, Jack! It's too late. . . . Please. Let's pretend it never happened.'

I stared at her: 'What do you mean, "too late"?'

She wouldn't look at me.

I had a thought I didn't care for. 'Is there someone else?'
She seemed less willing than ever to look at me.
'Jess?'
Her voice was so low I could hardly make out what she was
saying: 'I'm sorry. Very, very sorry. The last thing I want is to
hurt you. Especially now.'
'Is it someone I know?'
She closed her eyes as though in pain.
'Jess?'
She nodded.
I had a flash of belated intuition: 'Not Otto?'
Her head jerked up as though I had struck her. 'Yes. And
why not?'
I told myself I must have been blind: that it had all been hap-
pening in front of my eyes and I'd been too naive to take it in. I
took it in now. And as the full impact got through to me my
childhood dreams ebbed away like sand through a glass.
I suddenly realised that Jessica was talking: that the words
were tumbling out of her in a breathless not very coherent flood.
'Please, Jack. Try to understand. I'm very, very fond of you. I
like you very, very much. Always have. Always will. But I *love*
Otto. And he loves me. And we've promised to wait for one
another. Till the war's over. No matter how long it takes. . . .'
Our eyes met. Her voice faltered, and a slow blush suffused
every visible inch of her body. 'Jack! For God's sake. *Please*. It's
too *late* to look at me like that!'
I came-to with a start: 'Sorry.'
Silence. A log flaring suddenly in the fire, and crumbling as
suddenly to ash. Then she said awkwardly: 'Would you like me
to go?'
'Go? Go where?'
'I mean' – her blush deepened, and she started twisting and
untwisting her handkerchief – 'It's your last night of leave. Do
you want to spend it with someone else?'
'Good Lord, no!'
'Oh, Jack!' Inexplicably she burst into tears.
Never in all my life, I thought, would I understand women.

I was tempted to tell her that falling in love with a German could lead to nothing but trouble. But this she knew. And who was I to say "this is right" and "this is wrong"? I didn't stay with her much longer. Every time our eyes met I couldn't help thinking of all the things that might have been but never could be now. And I reckon she knew what I was thinking. As I was leaving she reached for my hand: 'Every night,' she said quietly, 'I ask God for two things. I ask Him for victory, and I ask Him to look after Otto. From now on I'm asking Him something else. To look after you.'

I remembered the poem:

'God heard the embattled nations sing and shout:
'Gott strafe England' – 'God save the King' –
'God this' – 'God that' and 'God the other thing – '
'My God,' said God, 'I've got my work cut out!'''

I was confused. I wasn't sure if I was flattered or embarrassed. But as I stared at Jessica, firelight in her hair, concern in her eyes, one thing I *was* sure of. Otto von Searle was a lucky man.

4

I'll never forget the thrill of seeing the squadron take off from Gosport that winter morning.

The BE2s lined up by flights in front of the hangars. Their pennants streamed bravely in the wind; their fabric glistened brightly in the sun; their crews, resplendent in leather coats sheepskin boots and sweetheart-knitted scarves, strapped themselves in; chocks were kicked under wheels, switches were checked, propellers were turned; cries of 'contact!' came faintly over the tarmac, and one by one the engines spluttered to life. For a couple of minutes the squadron warmed up, a deep pulsating roar, rising and falling as pilot after pilot tested his revs and his magnetos before throttling back. When everyone was ready the CO raised his hand, and the first flight taxied away in single file, to be followed by the second, then the third. In quick succession the aircraft swung into wind; the pilots rammed open their throttles and one after another the planes came charging towards us to rise like unwieldy partridges into the air. For a moment they swayed this way and that in slipstream and ground gust; then, as they gained flying speed, they came hurtling in line astern over the hangar. I can still hear the staccato roar of their engines. I can still smell the tang of half-burnt oil. I can still see the goggled aircrew each in turn leaning out of his cockpit to give us a farewell almost a ceremonial wave: a valediction to quicken the heartbeat, a 'hail Caesar, we who are about to die salute you'.

At two thousand feet they formed up over the airfield: three diamond-shaped flights of four forming the head of an arrow. Then they set course for France. We watched them heading south over the grey waters of the Solent, their silhouettes

39

growing smaller and smaller and the roar of their engines fainter and fainter until they were gone. And how we wished with all our hearts that we had gone with them. For this is the way that everyone would have liked to go to the Front: in style.

Reality for most of us was more prosaic. In my case I was told to report as spare pilot to Number Eight Squadron at Saint Genis-en-Lys; and when I asked what plane I could have to fly there, the Transport Officer said sourly that I could go to war like everyone else: by train, boat and shanks's pony!

I looked up Saint Genis-en-Lys on the map. It was on the Franco-Belgian border, not far from the much sung-of town of Armentières – so at least, I told myself, I shouldn't lack for feminine company!

But there was, alas, no sign of the celebrated Mademoiselles when, a couple of days later, I got out of the train at Armentières station. Nor was there sign of the transport which should have been waiting to take me to Eight Squadron. Nor for that matter was there anyone who seemed to have heard of Eight Squadron, much less who knew where it was. It was the first time I had been out of England, and I was standing in the main street of Armentières listening to the gunfire (which sounded too close for comfort!) and feeling distinctly homesick, when I saw coming out of a café a young officer with wings on his tunic. I hurried across to him. 'I say! Excuse me, do you know where Eight Squadron is?'

'Too bloody well!' His manner was languid but his eyes sharp. 'You the new pilot?'

I nodded: 'Jack Cunningham.'

He held out his hand: 'Chris Scott. Where's your plane?'

I told him I hadn't got one.

'Uncle *will* be glad to see you!' I must have looked discomforted because he added quickly: 'No offence, old chap. But pilots are two a penny. It's planes we're short of. How many hours have you done?'

'About thirty.'

'So you know all about it?'

I shook my head: 'I'm not *that* wet behind the ears!'

40

He laughed: 'Then maybe you'll live longer than the last chap. He knew *everything.* . . . Come on. Transport's the other side of the square.'

As we lumbered out of Armentières I studied my fellow pilot. Chris Scott was about the same height as I was (five feet, eleven). He had blond curly hair soft as a girl's, a great beak of a nose, and slate grey eyes that looked as though they wouldn't suffer fools gladly. Any sort of physical effort he appeared to regard as a fearful bore; but I got the impression he might not be so languorous in a crisis.

As we headed south the countryside seemed peaceful enough: gentle undulating fields, long lines of poplars, the occasional waggon pulled by draught horses straight out of a Morland painting, and a succession of canals half-choked with reeds. I asked how far it was to the Front.

'Four or five miles. Forget it. You'll see it soon enough.'

We turned into a deeply rutted track. The farms here had sandbags protecting their windows and doors, the lines of poplars had gaps in them, the fields were pock-marked with craters. There were more troops about; we passed a little group of Sikhs washing their clothes in a canal. The gunfire was louder now; it reminded me of the baying of hounds closing in for the kill. The transport ground to a halt.

I saw a small stone church, a farmhouse, a line of canvas hangars (each big enough to house just the single plane), a green meadow (airfield would be altogether too grand a word for it), and a row of barges strung out like beads along the bank of a slow-moving river. 'Welcome', Chris was saying, 'to the Ritz on the Riviera!'

It wasn't at all what I had expected. It was so beautiful: so peaceful. It was some time before I realised that the paraphernalia of war was there all right, only camouflaged: the officers' mess for example was in the flagstoned kitchen of the farm, the crewrooms were in a converted stable, my quarters were a cabin in a barge – when I looked out of my porthole I had an idyllic view of poplar and willow, bulrush and sedgegrass and long trailing skeins of water-lilies. It was hard to equate this

41

Arcady with the stories I had been told of the squalor of the Front.

And I was in for another surprise that evening when I met my fellow pilots and observers. It would be an oversimplification to say they were unfriendly; but they were – or so it seemed to me – inexplicably silent and reserved. It was as though each had built round himself a wall, a defensive barrier through which only the chosen few were permitted to enter. I couldn't make it out. I couldn't, I suppose, be expected to understand that first evening that friendships doomed to transcience are more emotionally distressing than no friendship at all, that the human heart can bear only so much bereavement, and there are times when it is best to pin a notice on it 'Private. Keep Out'. So in my naivety I thought the squadron (apart from Chris) a dull standoffish lot. I left them early. At least in my cabin I had a gramophone and a stack of the latest foxtrots.

Before turning in, I stood for a while on deck. It was a lovely night. In the west a hunter's moon was rising out of the poplars. In the east the sky was equally bright, but with a different brightness – the blink of gunfire and little clusters of calcium flares which soared half-way to heaven, hesitated, and then came drifting slowly back to earth. There was a good deal of noise: a duet of clattering rifles and machine-guns, while from behind the lines the big guns droned out a funereal accompaniment. It was a far cry to the quiet waters of the Helford. . . . I found myself wondering what Jessica was doing: playing bezique perhaps with her brother, or reading her *Manual of Nursing*, or was she lying awake in bed and thinking of Otto? And what, I wondered, was Otto doing? Could it be that he too had been posted to the Front: that he was listening to the same guns as I was, staring at the same flares, thinking the same thoughts about the same girl? Perhaps one day, high above the trenches, we'd meet? Perhaps, perhaps, perhaps. . . .

Next morning I was summoned to the CO's office.

Major 'Beelzebub' Bertram was seated behind a desk littered

with maps log-books and diagrams of aircraft. Neither his appearance nor his manner was calculated to put one at ease: a leonine head, a luxuriant jet-black beard, and big hairy hands splayed out on the desk like spiders about to jump. His eyes were very dark and very masterful, half hidden by the great tufted eyebrows which had given him his nickname. His voice was a muted bellow: 'So, you're J. A. Cunningham?'

'Yes, Sir.'

'How many hours flying?'

'Thirty-one, sir.'

'Christ almighty! How many crashes?'

'None, sir – yet!'

'A pilot who knows all the answers, eh!'

'No, sir.'

His eyes became slightly less intolerant. 'Then *learn* all the answers, Jack Cunningham. And learn them fast. Or we'll be burying you along with all the other young eagles who try to soar before they can flutter.' He looked at me thoughtfully: 'I suppose you want a crack right away at the Hun?'

I almost blurted out an automatic 'Yes, sir'. I don't know what it was that made me instead say guardedly: 'When I'm ready.'

For a moment I had his interest. But for a moment only. Then the brusque uncaring mask was back in place. Years later I was to play the same game myself: sitting behind a desk and watching the keen young pilots quickly come and quickly go, and every now and then spotting a potential survivor but telling myself not to start caring, not to get involved, because no matter how good he was and how lucky he was, he wasn't likely to survive for long. 'What planes', he grunted, 'have you flown?'

'Longhorns and Shorthorns, BE2s and Bristol Scouts.' I hesitated. 'Any chance of flying a Scout, sir?'

He shook his head: 'We've Shorthorns, BE2s and Nieuports. You'll start with a Shorthorn.'

My disappointment must have been obvious, because his eyes darkened and his fingers drummed threateningly on the desk. 'Shorthorns not good enough for you, Jack Cunningham?'

'I didn't say so, sir.'

'Don't try to run before you can crawl. You fly the bloody Shortarse. You fly it all day and every day. And you break so much as a strut, I'll have your liver for breakfast. Understand?'

I said that I understood. Then, since the conversation appeared to have ended, I saluted hastily and made a not very dignified exit, half-tripping over the doormat.

Chris was waiting to ask how I'd got on.

'No wonder,' I muttered, 'you call the old devil "Beelzebub"!'

He laughed. 'Uncle's all right. Wait till you see him at a drunk! And he's a damn fine pilot. . . . By the way, you're flying this evening.'

This cheered me up. I had visions (half wishful thinking, half fantasy) of Fokkers and Taubes scattering in terror as I dived on them while the Poor Bloody Infantry in the trenches brandished their rifles and cheered. . . . Imagine my disgust when it turned out that I was flying not as pilot but observer. For apparently it was one of Uncle's rules that newcomers were taken over the Front as passengers before they went on patrol.

My pilot for this inaugural flight was the squadron's second-in-command, Dick Sheppard, known as The Good Shepherd — and not only because of his surname, for he was indeed the most gentle and Christ-like of persons. Soon from 6,000 feet we were peering down on Armageddon.

I'll never forget my first view of the Front. It ran roughly north and south, as far in either direction as the eye could see: a swath of earthworks plastered like a suppurating weal across the fields of Flanders, Picardie and the Aisne. The earth-works were complex. There were frontline trenches (ours and the Germans' in places so close that they seemed almost to be touching), secondline trenches, thirdline trenches, support-trenches, communication trenches, decoy-trenches, machine-gun-positions, bunkers, saps and redoubts, and behind these a proliferation of depots, store-dumps and artillery ranges: an obscenity of excrement overlaid with mud and wire. It was an eyesore. But, from the air, nothing more.

Later I was to spend some time in the trenches. I was to smell the corpses, sink up to my thighs in the mud, see men blasted to pulp in front of my eyes and feel the rats scurrying over me in the dark. But of these things one had no cognisance from 6,000 feet. Which is probably why airmen tended to view the Front with detachment. It was another world: a world which we of the air were affiliated to and yet not part of. We felt as Dante and Vergil might have felt as they gazed trembling into the inner circles of the Inferno – an incredulous horror, a vicarious pity, a feeling of 'thank God that such a punishment hasn't been meted out to me'.

My day-dreaming was shattered by a resounding crash, a stench of cordite and a mushroom of yellow smoke about fifty yards behind us. We were being fired at!

The Good Shepherd didn't seem unduly perturbed, though he did, I noticed, gain height and alter course; and the next salvo burst well below and to the right of us. It was funny how the balls of smoke, like puffs of cotton wool, appeared as if by magic in the sky to be followed a moment later by a flat unecho-ing report. So this was the dreaded 'Archie'. It didn't seem very dangerous.

Our whole flight in fact turned out to be far less dangerous than I had anticipated; for apart from those few bursts of ack-ack not a shot was fired at us. It was a bit of an anti-climax. Too soon – at least to my way of thinking – we were heading back for Saint Genis.

The demarcation-line between the Front and the sur-rounding countryside was, from the air, surprisingly clear-cut. One moment we were peering down on a little corner of hell; next moment there unfolded beneath us a vista of Arcadian tranquillity: mile after hundred square mile of rolling country-side: well-tended fields and little patches of woodland, inter-sected by the shallow valley of the Lys. And what a beautiful valley it was! The river winding, looping and doubling back on itself through copses of poplar and willow, now running strongly between steep-sided banks, now flooding into a meander of marshes. And rising apparently out of the very centre of these marshes the spire of Saint Genis.

This was the womb that we who were lucky returned to: a haven of tranquillity, infinitely peaceful, infinitely at variance with the horror of the Front. It always reminded me of the Helford: a little corner of England grafted as by some miracle onto an alien shore.

Such were the contours of the earth I flew and fought over for the next two years.

But it was some time before I did any fighting. For next morning, to my fury, I was given the oldest Shorthorn in the squadron, and told to stay well clear of the Front and improve my flying. It was a discipline I didn't take to kindly at the time, though I can see now that it probably saved my life. For I was so piqued at what I took to be a vote of no-confidence in my ability, that I made up my mind to fly whatever plane I was given with more skill, precision and panache than it had ever been flown before. I'd show them I was up to it!

Now a Shorthorn isn't the most exciting of aircraft. But in the spring of 1915 I regarded *all* flying as a labour of love. For no thrill in life, it seemed to me, could compare with the thrill of taking a plane into the vast open reaches of the sky and putting it through all manner of dives, climbs, spins, stalls, loops, rolls and split-arse turns. The exhilaration, the rapport between pilot and plane, the satisfaction one got from a well-executed manoeuvre: these meant more to me, I think, than the love of women (about which I was abysmally ignorant!) or the friendship of men (which I was soon to discover could end only in heartbreak). So I didn't need to be *told* to fly the Shorthorn; the difficulty was keeping me long enough on the ground for the plane to be serviced! And every time I went up I tried something new. Taking-off, I'd experiment with lifting clear at different speeds and climbing at different angles. Landing, I'd pick a spot on the airfield and put down on it, wheels and tailskid together, from different heights and directions, again and again. I'd practice emergency landings, switching off the

46

engine and making it a point of honour not to restart it until my wheels were feathering the field I'd decided to put down in. I'd climb to seven, eight and even nine thousand feet, the Shorthorn clawing at the rarefied air and my goggles white with rime. I'd fight with imaginary Fokkers, play with cottonwool clouds, and enjoy every moment of it.

I didn't think anyone noticed what I was doing, much less cared. But in this I was wrong. For after about ten days The Good Shepherd sent for me. 'You seem', he said with a smile, 'to have got the hang of the Shorthorn. How about trying a Nieuport?'

'I'd like to, sir. Very much.'

'You can have mine. Tomorrow.'

'Thanks awfully, sir.' I hesitated. 'Any chance of my going on patrol soon?'

'Why?'

'I feel a passenger, sir. The rest of you going after the Hun. While I lark about behind the lines.'

His hand rested for a moment on my shoulder. 'Ride your luck, Jack Cunningham. And thank God you've a CO who *cares*. In nine squadrons out of ten new pilots are thrown in the deep end – and get themselves killed in the first couple of weeks. Learn what you can, while you can. Your turn will come soon enough.'

It came sooner than I expected. For the very next afternoon, while I was flying The Good Shepherd's Nieuport, one of our BE2s crashed and burned out in no-man's-land.

From the reports we managed to piece together we gathered that the plane's engine had failed when it was patrolling on the German side of the Front, that the pilot had tried to glide back across the lines, but had been hit by rifle fire and spun in.

'Who', I asked Chris, 'was flying it?'

'I'm afraid', he said, 'it was The Good Shepherd.'

I went for a walk that night by the river. I told myself I wasn't *really* responsible for The Good Shepherd's death; but I couldn't get it out of my head that if he hadn't lent me his Nieuport he'd never have been flying that ill-fated BE2. I

47

remembered his gentleness; I remembered his kindness – his hand on my shoulder; and I remembered the saying of Philocrates that 'war never chooses an evil man, but the good'. I stared at the river, lacquered gold in the light of the moon; and suddenly to my horror it was as though the Lys had been metamorphosed to a river of fire, and in the flames lay the wreckage of the BE2 disintegrating (like the one at Brooklands) in the heat. The hallucination lasted a second only; but for that second it was unbearably real. I could see the pilot's body jerk and twitch; I could feel the heat of the flames. I screwed shut my eyes and prayed that The Good Shepherd had been dead before he hit the ground.

Next morning I flew my first patrol.

It was a defensive patrol. All I had to do was fly parallel to the Front and keep an eye open for German aircraft trying to cross onto our side of the lines, a thing they hardly ever did. Not the sort of patrol that was likely to lead to action. My observer and I, however, were spoiling for a fight – hadn't God Himself condoned the taking of an eye for an eye? I scanned the sky methodically in search of an enemy plane, while my observer sighted and resighted a fearsome-looking carbine so heavy that he could hardly shift it from one side of the cockpit to the other. Nothing would have given us greater pleasure than to send a Fokker or Taube hurtling to destruction. But none materialised.

That is the way it was. You could court death, and he'd be elusive. You could be daydreaming without a care in the world, and he'd sponge you off the face of the sky as though you had never been. My first patrol, like so many of those that followed, was without incident.

It didn't take me long to find my niche in the squadron: that of a dogsbody, willing, and indeed anxious, to fly anything, anywhere, any time. My enthusiasm was a source of amusement to the more experienced pilots, and I got the reputation – quite undeservedly – of being a bit of a fire-eater. I say 'undeservedly' because, truth to tell, it was flying that turned me on, not fighting. My idea of the perfect dawn patrol wasn't to gobble up

48

a couple of Taubes before breakfast, but to watch the sun come bursting out of the valley of the Rhine like a catherine wheel of the gods. On contact patrol, instead of 'diligently seeking out the enemy' I'd climb up and up till I came to that vast and beautiful world above the clouds, man's first staging post on his journey to the stars. And at the going down of the sun instead of flying low to take pot shots at men in the trenches I'd linger, long after others had landed, among the battlements of cumulus, watching the cloud tops change from white to copper, copper to saffron, saffron to pink and pink to mauve until they were submerged by the advancing canopy of night. The wonder and the beauty of these lonely vigils made me feel somehow close to God.

I had been with the squadron for almost seven weeks before I had my first real taste of action. In those seven weeks I had been fired on only occasionally and had seen no more than a handful of Fokkers and Taubes. Then one misty April morning, as I was taking photographs of Ronchin, everything happened at once.

Ronchin was the German-occupied aerodrome on the outskirts of Lille, no more than a dozen miles from Saint Genis. You might say that we and the pilots of Ronchin were neighbours; and we were therefore none too pleased to get an Intelligence report that a squadron of sleek new Fokker monoplanes, had been flown into the airfield. 'We'd better', Uncle said, 'see what we're up against.' So early one morning I found myself heading east in a BE2 with a big mahogany camera box lashed to my fuselage and a glum-looking sergeant-observer in the front cockpit. (No doubt he was cursing his luck at being paired with an inexperienced pilot.) All was peaceful as we crossed the lines and headed for Lille; the sky was empty, the Front quiescent, as though everyone had grown suddenly tired of fighting and decided to stay asleep. Soon we were nearing the airfield. Now came the tricky bit. I had to keep the plane straight and level with my left hand, peer over the side and get the area I wanted to photograph in the centre of a ball-and-crosswire sight, then lean out into the slipstream and push the camera handle backward and forward to change the plates, pulling the string individually for each exposure. (In a normal plane all this would have been done by the observer; but in a BE2 the observer couldn't see beneath him because of the wings.) I was getting everything nicely lined up when three little puffs of yellow appeared as if by magic ahead of us.

The observer pointed: 'Archie!'

I knew very well it was Archie, but there didn't seem to be anything I could do about it. I held course and went on cranking away at the camera.

The next salvo was closer. They'd got our height this time, and were less than fifty yards behind us.

I was frightened. And I didn't know what to do. It seemed to me that if I held course I'd be blown to bits, and if I broke away I'd be branded a coward. A terrible scene flashed through my mind: a court martial, and my judges Jessica and Otto, and the tears in Jessica's eyes and the contempt in Otto's. . . . I went on cranking away with a sort of numb despair at the camera. I did, however, ease back on the stick so that we gained about fifty feet. And it was as well I did.

There was a terrifying crash, far louder than thunder, and the plane was flung violently upwards. If I hadn't gained that bit of extra height it would have been a direct hit. As it was, I thought we were done for. Great rents appeared in the wing where shrapnel had sliced through it. The engine set up the most fearful clatter as though it was about to disintegrate. And the observer waved his arms and hammered frantically on the fuselage: 'Break away!'

I rammed down the nose and spiralled earthwards like a falling leaf, twisting and turning first one way then another. For a terrible moment it seemed that whichever way I turned Archie followed. Then mercifully the gunfire grew more and more sporadic, until finally it petered out.

My mouth was dry. My hands were trembling. And the worst of it was that I'd photographed less than half of Ronchin, and I knew I had to go back.

I had my first intimation that morning of why pilots crack up. It was the strain: the strain of having always to fight down and hide the fear which we could never openly admit to, the strain as von Richthofen put it of 'having always to overcome the inner *schweinehund*'. So we gained a victory over ourselves. We defeated the *schweinehund* again and again. But there was always another victory to be won on the morrow. The strain never ended. Nor was it like a physical strain from which one could in time recover; it was more like a permanent damage to the very fabric of one's being. Nobody who flew for long over the Western Front was ever quite the same again.

So when I'd checked that my observer wasn't wounded and the plane wasn't too seriously damaged, I headed again for the airfield.

Only this time I approached it with discretion, altering height and weaving from side to side to make it difficult for the gunners to get our range. To start with it worked. The ack-ack was sporadic and inaccurate. But when it came to actually taking the photographs I had no option but to fly straight and level; and then the salvos once again burst terrifyingly close. It was the first time I'd been under heavy fire. And I didn't like it. . . . I tried to concentrate on getting a continuous mosaic of pictures along the perimeter track – even from 6,000 feet I could make out the aircraft dotted at intervals along the tarmac; though whether they were Fokkers or Taubes, old or new, only an expert with a magnifying glass would be able to say. . . . But what was happening to Archie? At the very moment one would have thought that every gun on the airfield would be blazing away at us, the shell bursts faded to no more than a solitary explosion. My brain must have been addled by noise and fear, because I remember thinking how very convenient that at the crucial moment the guns should all have run out of ammunition!

I was about to pull the string for the last exposure when my observer let out a frightened shout: 'Fokker!'

So *that* was why the guns had stopped firing! I jerked round and saw the thin silhouette of the monoplane ghosting down on us out of the sun.

The Fokker, haloed by sunlight, looked frail and ethereal,

more beautiful than dangerous. Only when it swung parallel to us and opened fire did fear hit me like a kick in the stomach.

I hauled the BE2 into a tight turn.

The Fokker followed, like a venomous insect. I could see the great black crosses on its wing. I could hear the crack-crack-crack of its bullets whistling past my head. Then came an even more fiendish clatter as my observer opened up with *his* gun. I hoped he knew what he was doing. His cockpit was so hemmed in by struts and wires that the most likely thing for him to hit was his own plane – or even his own pilot!

The Fokker broke away, climbed, hesitated, then came at us again. He must have been an inexperienced pilot, for he opened fire too soon. I started to turn one way, swung suddenly the other, and yanked the protesting BE2 into a stall turn. The Fokker, surprised, hesitated. Then tried to follow. And as he flashed past, below us and ahead of us, we almost had him. In fact I reckon we *would* have had him, if the observer's gun hadn't chosen this most inopportune moment to jam. I could see the sergeant yanking away at the trigger and nothing happening. I could see him pounding the fuselage in frustration and despair. Then, as the Fokker turned towards us, he signalled me to run for it.

I didn't need to be told! It took me about two seconds to get my bearings. Then, like a rabbit to its burrow, I was scurrying for home.

If the Fokker pilot had had his wits about him he'd have followed us down. But his inexperience saved our lives. The last we saw of him he was still at 6,000 feet, still hovering over the airfield, like a bird well-pleased with itself at having driven a rival from its territory.

The sergeant, when we landed, was beside himself with fury. He heaved the Lewis-gun over the side. 'Bloody double drums! Jam, jam, jam! God damn it. We had him cold!'

'At least', I said mildly, 'he didn't get *us*!'

His anger evaporated a little. 'No, sir. You did well.' He hesitated, and I could see that he wanted to say something but wasn't sure if he ought to.'

'What is it, sergeant?'

'About the Archie, sir. If you don't mind a tip?'

'Go on.'

'Never stay on course, sir, while Jerry's ranging you. They're methodical bastards. On the third or fourth salvo, they'll get you.'

It was I who hesitated now. 'That makes sense. It was just . . . well, breaking away seemed a bit like running away.'

The sergeant scratched his ear. 'If you *hadn't* broken away, sir, you'd have been disobeying orders, wouldn't you? Dead men can't take photographs!'

When the sergeant had gone I took a closer look at the BE2. She was damaged all right: great rents in her wing, burnt oil all over her cowling, and slicing diagonally across the tailplane a neat little line of bullet holes – I'd no idea the Fokker had actually hit us! This, I thought, was Action with a capital A. But I'd survived. And I reckoned the photographs ought to be good.

It rather took the gilt off the gingerbread when the chap developing the photos told me that evening that the plates were blank. They had been loaded into the camera upsidedown. Next morning Ronchin had to be photographed all over again.

This, however, didn't worry me. For to my surprise and delight I was given two weeks' leave.

I spent the first week with my mother and her Geordie husband in Newcastle, and the second week with the Pendowers. The latter was fun. Gavin, a young-looking sixteen, was on holiday from Charterhouse. He was still very much a schoolboy, and it was, I suppose, only to be expected that he should be forever reading books on aerodynamics and asking me what it was like to be a pilot. As for Jessica, she had graduated, if that is the right word, from bandages to bedpans, and had now, much against her parents' wishes, left home and was working in the wards.

'Isn't it pretty unpleasant?' I asked her.

'From what I've heard, it's not half as bad as the trenches!'

'I dare say. But it's different for a girl.'

Jessica looked at me thoughtfully: 'Why? You don't really think, do you, that while all the men are dying at the Front, all the women ought to be sitting at home: knitting socks?'

'I suppose not. It's just . . . Well, I'm very fond of you, Jess. I don't like to think of you with no home. And having a bad time.'

She smiled: 'I'm very fond of *you*, Jack. But I don't think it strange that *you've* left home. And become a pilot.'

I began to realise there was more to Jessica than a cascade of auburn hair. I saw a lot of her that leave. She never disguised the fact that her heart, at least for the duration, belonged to Otto; but we had been childhood friends, I was happy and at ease with her, she seemed to grow more beautiful each time I saw her, and it is in man's nature ever to hanker after the unattainable. . . So there we were, on the penultimate night of my leave, having dinner in the old Red Lion in Truro. The waiters obviously thought we were lovers. They gave us a secluded table, soft candlelight, ice-cold champagne and conspiratorial smiles. Perhaps it was the champagne that made Jessica unguarded. We were talking of Otto, and I'd just remarked that he must surely by now have got his wings. 'Oh, yes,' she said brightly. 'He got them before Christmas.'

I stared at her.

Her hand flew to her mouth.

'How the devil,' I said slowly, 'do *you* know?'

She took a gulp of champagne: 'Promise not to tell anyone? What I tell you?'

I shook my head.

There was a long silence.

'What are friends for,' I said, 'if you don't trust them?'

Her head jerked up as though I had struck her. 'I *do* trust you.' She took a deep breath and looked at me very straight. 'I know Otto's got his wings because I had a letter from him.'

'But that's impossible!'

'You remember about a week ago: there was a zeppelin raid on Yarmouth and King's Lynn?'

'Go on.'

'Well, as far as I can make out Otto knew one of the zeppelin captains – I think they were some sort of relatives. Anyhow, he wrote me a letter. Stuck a British stamp on it. And gave it to this captain fellow. When the zeppelin was over King's Lynn the captain tipped out the letter and his bombs at the same time. Next morning a farm-worker found it in a hedge. I suppose he thought someone had dropped it out of a car or something. Anyhow, he posted it. I got it next day. . . .'

It was an innocent enough story. But I didn't like it. There was a lot of anti-German feeling about: a lot of witch-hunting. If people knew Jessica had been getting letters from a German pilot they could make life jolly unpleasant for her. 'You'd better keep quiet about this,' I said slowly, 'or you'll end up in the Tower!'

Again her head jerked up. 'Otto and I have done nothing wrong. Do you think it's wrong to fall in love? Something to be ashamed of?'

She looked more beautiful than ever when she was angry; and I couldn't help wishing it had been on *my* behalf that her eyes were bright and her cheeks flushed. I muttered that some people would say corresponding with an enemy officer was treason.

'Not our sort of corresponding. I don't want to hurt you, Jack. But Otto's letter was a *love* letter. He only mentions the war once.' She handed me an envelope. 'Read it.'

'What good will that do?'

'I want you to see we're doing nothing wrong. Please.'

Well, I didn't want to read it. But how, when she was asking for reassurance, could I refuse?

She had told me it was a love letter. And that's exactly what it was: utterly innocent, utterly innocuous. There wasn't even a mention of war until the last page. But that last page . . . looking back, I suppose there was a sort of tragic inevitability about it.

'I have not on purpose mentioned war,' Otto had written, 'because this is something I know we would both forget. I try very hard to forget. Often in the night and not so often in the day I shut my eyes and think of you, and it is then as though

55

there were no more war and we were again together. You must try that, my Jesse. All you have to do is close your eyes. . . . But because I believe you might wish to know what I have been doing, I would tell you that in December I was awarded my wings and sent to a *Feldfliegerabteilungen* in Saxony. This is a beautiful part of our country, in places every bit as lovely as your Helford River. Now, however, we are in a part of the country that is not so beautiful. For our *Feldfliegerabteilungen* has been sent to the Front, to an airfield known as Ronchin. . . .'

I handed the letter back.

Jessica was looking at me curiously: 'What's up?'

'Nothing.'

'Please, Jack. What is it?'

I shook my head.

Her eyes were hurt: 'You said it yourself. What are friends for, if you don't trust them?'

I said angrily that it was nothing. It was as though I had some terrible premonition: as though my every instinct was screaming Jessica must never know that Otto and I were divided by only a few miles of war-torn earth, only a few minutes' flying time of soon-to-be-bitterly-contested sky.

5

In the fortnight I'd been away spring had come to Saint Genis. The willows lining the Lys had been transformed to cascades of gold, a new generation of waterfowl was at play in the reeds, and we of the air were enjoying a final taste of flying as it had been once, should have been always but was never to be again.

One episode in this the Indian Summer of our innocence, I remember with special affection: my last patrol in a Shorthorn.

For three months I had flown my ancient Shorthorn almost every day, sometimes twice a day. She had never let me down. But the powers-that-be had decided she was too vulnerable to the improved ack-ack and the faster Fokkers. Tomorrow she was being flown to Saint Omer to be broken up.

It was a lovely evening as we took-off for the last time: to the east a sky washed clean by rain, to the west a majestic mountain range of cumulus. I made for the cumulus and climbed up and up through its swirling walls of white, until I emerged into the solitude of that other world where not only is there no trace of man but no trace either of his planet Earth. I levelled off some two or three hundred feet above the top of the clouds, and thought that never in all my life had I seen anything so beautiful. Normally cloud-tops are pure white; but on this occasion the sun was sinking through a distant veil of cirrus, and the cloud banks in the east were metamorphosed to great drifts of gold: a gold in some places deep as orange, in others pale as champagne: twenty-thousand square miles of auriferous plateaux. No traveller in the desert, no voyager to the pole, had ever set eyes on so magnificent a panorama: only we lonely threshers of the sky. I was flying contentedly along the top of the clouds, when I became aware of movement ahead of me. I stared and stared again. It was some seconds before I realised that I was witnessing the birth of a cloud.

One moment nothing; next moment a patch of white the size of a man's hand; next moment the patch swelling up, budding, and bursting into a gargantuan many-petalled flower: a flower which swiftly proliferated, throwing out head after head like a hydra, until it was no longer a flower but a magnificent edifice, a cathedral of the sky, a marriage of light and moisture, nurtured by the sun, drifting elegantly across the heavens. Fascinated, I flew towards it. Wondering, I circled it, marvelling at its ever-changing shape and colour – white and grey, pink and gold, saffron and rose, and deep in its heart a mysterious kaleidoscope of shadow.

Suddenly to my horror I saw coming out of this shadow another plane. Only no ordinary plane. A nightmare monstrosity, jet black, ringed with flame, three times the size of the Shorthorn, leaping at me from the maw of the cloud like a great eagle from its eerie.

I flung the Shorthorn aside.

And the plane vanished.

I stared this way and that, moistening my lips, trembling, expecting any second to see it coming at me again, guns clattering. But it had vanished: sponged as if by magic off the face of the sky. And suddenly I understood. It had been a shadow: my own silhouette, magnified by refracted light and haloed by parhelion, reflected against the whiteness of the cloud.

I knew that's what it must have been. It couldn't have been anything else. Yet wild horses wouldn't have dragged me back to that beautiful but sinister cloud. I found a rift in the cumulus, dived through it as though Lucifer himself were on my tail, and headed at full throttle for Saint Genis. And how glad I was to get back to the warmth, companionship and normality of the mess!

Next morning my Shorthorn was ferried to Saint Omer.

I stood on the tarmac and watched her grow smaller and smaller and fainter and fainter, until she merged into a distant belt of rain. It was silly, I told myself, to get so devoted to a *plane*.

Chris must have read my thoughts. He tossed me my helmet 'Come on! I'll show you how to fly a Nieuport!'

For an hour we wheeled and cartwheeled about the sky. Chris was a better pilot than I was, *and* he was used to Nieuports; no matter how I twisted and turned I couldn't shake him off my tail. All the same I had to admit that the Nieuport handled sweetly enough, especially close to the ground. And it was nice to be on one's own: not to have an observer ever hammering on the fuselage and threatening to shoot away one's propeller!

Over the next few weeks I settled into a routine of flying BE2s and Nieuports alternatively: the former on artillery spotting, the latter on contact patrol.

Some pilots regarded contact patrol as a waste of time; but I enjoyed it; for although German aircraft seldom put in an appearance, the Front itself was always interesting. Flying over it four or five times a week, I soon got to know the section from Ypres to Loos rather better than the back of my hand. I could tell at a glance which saps had been pushed forward overnight, which gaps had been strengthened with wire, which batteries had been resited, and which troops were moving up and which falling back. By making a note of these small changes it was usually possible to piece together a useful Intelligence Report. And if this sounds unspectacular and unrewarding work the fact was that aircraft, in the spring of 1915, were still regarded as little more than observation platforms, both the British and the German General Staff agreeing that in the words of the latter 'it is the duty of the aviator to see, not to fight'.

So as the armies beneath us lay deathlocked in mud and wire, we observed; we advised; but we didn't as yet participate. On the rare occasions we did lose a plane it was more likely to be through accident than through enemy action – as I to my cost found out.

I was coming in to land in the squadron's one and only Parasol (a fine aircraft, but the very devil to land – if you didn't do it exactly right you bounced like a ball and the wind got under your wingtips and flipped you onto your back). Now there were two ways you could land at Saint Genis. The proper way was to come in parallel to the poplars lining the Lys; the improper way to sideslip over the poplars and touch down in the direction of the sheds. Experienced pilots favoured the latter; you ended up beside the mess, and avoided a long wet tramp over the airfield. I'd often landed this way in Shorthorns and Nieuports. Why not, I asked myself, in a Parasol? . . . As I came drifting over the poplars it did occur to me that I'd be touching down a bit crosswind. It occurred to me also that I'd only landed the Parasol once before and that I ought to be careful. But I told myself if others could do it so could I. . . . The crosswind hit me just as my wheels were about to touch the grass, so I gave the Parasol a burst of throttle and pulled up her wing. The burst of throttle gave her added lift; instead of landing she drifted on and on. Straight for the sheds. I hauled back on the stick to get her to stall. But she had too much flying speed. She reared up like a terrified horse. And the wind got under her wings.

I knew what was happening, but there wasn't a thing I could do to prevent it. As in a slow-motion nightmare too terrible to be believed I felt the nose rising, rising, rising. I remembered that pilots who flipped over backward very often broke not only their aircraft's back but their own. I knocked off the switches. Shut my eyes. And prayed.

For a second that seemed like eternity the Parasol hung near-vertical, her propeller clawing at the sky. Then she fell.

But by the grace of God she fell forward.

There was a terrible splintering crash. The undercarriage disintegrated. The propeller disintegrated. The engine cowling disintegrated. Just about everything disintegrated. And we came to rest squelched-out like a rotten plum with petrol trickling out of the fuel tank.

I remember thinking I'd better get out quick, in case she caught fire. I remember pain knifing across the back of my neck as I struggled with the straps. The next thing I remember is Chris half-dragging me, half-lifting me out of the cockpit, while the crew of the fire-tender sprayed foam all over the Parasol.

He laid me out, very gently, in the grass. 'Keep still.'

'I'm all right,' I muttered, and tried to sit up. For a moment the airfield gyrated like a top. Then my head cleared.

'Is your back OK?' Chris was looking at me anxiously.

'It's fine.' I tried to stand up. And at the third attempt made it.

When he realised I wasn't all that badly hurt, his eyes lost some of their sympathy: 'That was a bloody silly thing to do!'

'You don't have to tell me.'

The first aid party came cantering hopefully up with a stretcher. 'You'd better', Chris said, 'let them have a look at you.'

. I tried to shake my head. But pain seared a second time across my neck. And I blacked out.

I came-to in the squadron's casualty room with my neck in a sort of plaster cast, a splitting headache and a foul taste in my mouth – years later I discovered I was allergic to morphia. The doctor was afraid at first that I'd broken my neck. But it turned out I had only temporarily trapped a nerve. After twenty-four hours the plaster was off. After thirty-six hours I was up and about. And after forty-eight hours I was knocking anxiously on Major Bertram's door.

Anxiously, because it would be an understatement to say that our Commanding Officer didn't suffer fools gladly. And a fool is what I had very definitely been.

There were, however, no signs to start with of the wrath I had feared. Beelzebub told me to stand at ease; he offered me a chair – which I had the sense, thank heavens, to refuse; he enquired after my neck. But I wasn't deceived; his eyes were dark with a banked-down anger which made me remember that volcanoes were the more dangerous when they *weren't* belching smoke and flame. I was prepared for a dressing-down. What I wasn't prepared for was the bombshell he dropped almost casually. 'I'm thinking', he said, 'of having you transferred to another squadron.'

As the words sunk home I realised for the first time the depth of the pit I had dug for myself. 'I very much hope you won't, sir.'

He fixed me with his disconcerting stare. 'You seem young

and in good health. Would a walk of some 150 yards have inconvenienced you?'

'No, sir.'

'You seem to have a pair of good strong boots. Would a walk through a little damp grass have harmed you?'

'No, sir.'

'Then tell me: why did you land crosswind? Towards the sheds?'

'I promise you, sir. It won't happen again.'

'That I am sure of.'

There was a silence that went on and on. Then his fist smashed suddenly onto the table. 'You young fool! Try to run, would you, before you can crawl!'

My wits deserted me. I stared at him like a mesmerised rabbit.

He was speaking again. 'Now listen to me. And when I've finished give me one good reason – if you can – why I shouldn't have you transferred. Every other squadron in France has crippling losses. The "Stuffed Shirt" has lost a third of the pilots in his squadron, the " 'Beardless Wonder" half, and the *real* fighting hasn't started yet. Now in *my* squadron I won't accept those sort of losses. So I can't afford accidents, you understand? Least of all can I afford accidents due to a pilot's vanity and sloth. Your accident *was* due to vanity and sloth, Jack Cunningham?'

'And to inexperience, sir. But I've learned my lesson. It won't happen again.'

He stared at me. For a long time. As though trying to see into the very core of my being. 'Tell me', he said unexpectedly. 'Have you a girl?'

'No, sir.'

'Your friend Chris Scott has a girl, hasn't he?'

I couldn't think what he was getting at: 'Chris is married, sir.'

'Exactly. And do you see *him* showing off? Larking about? Landing cross-wind?'

Now that I came to think about it, I never had. Chris was a fine pilot. I'd seen him take risks. But never an unnecessary one.

Beelzebub was watching me. 'Do you understand what I'm saying?'

'That Chris has a special reason for wanting to stay alive?'

He nodded. 'We all want to live. But those with a special reason work at it hardest.'

'Let me stay, sir. And I'll get myself a special reason!'

The anger which up to now hadn't left his eyes gave way to a flicker of amusement. 'A girl', he grunted, 'might be the answer. Bring you down to earth.'

I didn't know what to say to that, so I said nothing. And at the end of another long silence and even longer stare, he muttered that he didn't know why he bothered with me, but much against his better judgment he'd give me one more chance. 'But one only,' he added with a touch of his old acerbity. 'Break so much as a landing wire, and you'll be out on your ear.'

'Oh gosh, sir! Thanks!' The old devil, I told myself, was quite human really. I wasn't sure whether to get out of his sight as fast as I could before he changed his mind, or ask him something that puzzled me. 'Sir. . . .?'

'You still here!'

'What made you say the *real* fighting hasn't started yet?'

Major Bertram walked to the window and stood looking out across the airfield. It was a peaceful scene. 'Up to now', he said quietly, 'the old men who run the war have thought of aircraft as toys: novelties: more dangerous than useful. But they're beginning to learn. One day they'll discover what their "toys" are capable of. And when that happens, Jack Cunningham, God help you. God help us all.'

They had nicknamed him the devil. But he seemed to me more like a prophet: a voice crying in the wilderness: a harbinger of the Armageddon to come.

That spring, as though the 'old men' on the General Staff had been eavesdropping, there was a sudden increase in aerial activity. By the end of April we were making contact with our friends from Ronchin almost every day – though we were still as

63

likely to greet them with a wave as a bullet. There was a sharp increase too in the effectiveness of Archie. Artillery spotting became decidedly unpleasant, and it was only a matter of time before we lost another BE2.

No-one was certain how it happened. Some said the plane was hit by Archie and plunged into the trenches in flames, others that it crashlanded behind the German lines. What *was* certain was that it didn't return. We stayed up late that night, peering anxiously into the darkening sky and dashing hopefully to the telephone each time it rang; but hope ebbed with the hours; by midnight we were resigned to the inevitable. For a couple of days the squadron was conscious of loss – two empty seats in the mess, no fishing-rod slung out of the penultimate cabin in the barge, no baritone among the after-dinner singers round the piano. But death was something we were becoming accustomed to. It would be wrong to say that by the third day we had forgotten the pilot and observer of the BE2; but most of us had stopped remembering them – until our memories were given an unexpected jolt.

It was dawn, and the sun was climbing out of the trenches like a disc of blood. Most people on the airfield were still asleep; but I happened to have got up early because I liked sometimes to go for a walk by the river before the morning barrage made a nonsense of its serenity. I was walking along the towpath; wondering whether a post-like object on the opposite bank was *really* a post – or could it be a heron? – when I heard the roar of aircraft.

There were two of them. And the moment I saw them I flung myself on my face in the reeds. For they were Fokkers.

Talk about surprise! They came in down the path of the sun without a shot being fired at them. I expected them to start machine-gunning our aircraft and hangars. Instead they flew low and straight over the centre of the airfield. The leading plane dropped something. They waggled their wings. Soared skyward as though in a ceremonial salute. And were halfway back to Hunland before a gun opened up.

All over the airfield men were tumbling out of huts and tents, rubbing the sleep from their eyes. I could see Beelzebub in a bright red nightshirt berating the gun crews – when the alarm klaxon set up a discordant clatter long after the planes were out of sight, I thought he was going to have a fit! Several people had noticed the little black object, about the size of a hold-all, lying in the middle of the airfield. A group of mechanics were running towards it when they were halted by a bellow from Beelzebub. 'Keep back! It may be a bomb!'

He pushed past the mechanics, his nightshirt billowing about him like a great red sail. He walked right up to the object and stood very still, for several seconds, staring down at it. Then, almost reverently, he picked it up and carried it back to the mess.

For the next forty-eight hours the wreath and the letter were laid-out side-by-side for all to see and to read.

Pinned to the wreath was a card. It read: 'To the memory of Jimmy Padmore, observer R.F.C. Our brave and chivalrous opponent. *Feldfliegerabteilungen* 15'.

The letter was from Jimmy's pilot. It told us that the missing BE2 had indeed been hit by Archie and had crashed behind the German lines: that the observer had been killed, but that he (the pilot) had been hauled out of the blazing wreckage with back injuries and taken to hospital. It told us that he was being well, and indeed most hospitably, treated by his captors. . . . One sentence in particular made me think. It seems that several of the German pilots from Ronchin had visited their opposite number in hospital: had brought him fresh fruit, and smuggled in a bottle of schnapps. 'Our friends the enemy', the BE2 pilot wrote, 'are doing all they can to cheer me up. They're jolly sporting chaps.'

It was something none of us doubted. German pilots flew under a cross, we under a circle; but that was about the only difference between us. We were brothers of the sky: bound one to another by youth, a common love of adventure, and a common disregard for danger and convention. We were the young eagles, flexing our wings together as we reached for the same far-distant stars.

Yet the implications had me worried. For if the Huns were really such sporting fellows, why were we trying to kill them?

A scene came suddenly and unexpectedly to mind. Two horsemen – Gavin and I – in a sunlit clearing: a tumbledown cottage, a cankered apple-tree and the awkward figure of the mudpilot. 'It's jest', Will Willcock was saying, 'that killin' folk don't seem properly right.'

A couple of days later I was flying a Nieuport on dawn patrol when, in the pale half light that ushers in the sunrise, I spotted a Fokker. And what a nerve! The wretched fellow was photographing our trenches!

Now the Nieuport was a single-seater, my only armament was a rifle, and I knew it wasn't going to be easy to fly and shoot at the same time. However, I manoeuvred myself hopefully into the sun and proceeded to stalk the Fokker. Or rather I tried to stalk him; since he was flying at seventy-five and my top speed was no more than eighty-five there were obvious difficulties! And to add to these difficulties the Fokker pilot had his wits about him; for just as I was getting nicely into position he turned away and put down his nose to gain speed. I did the same, trying to head him off; but he went belting down and down, faster and faster. Suddenly, to my astonishment, he went into a loop. Only this was no ordinary loop. He half-rolled off the top of it, and ended up 500 feet above me flying in the opposite direction. From here he calmly went on photographing the trenches. It was a spectacular and most effective piece of flying.

Feeling none too pleased at being outmanoeuvred, I plodded after him. It took me the better part of ten minutes to get into position again; and he must have been watching me all the time; because just as I was about to reach for my rifle, he went into a tight turn. He obviously expected me to follow. But if he could be clever, so could I. I turned in the opposite direction, hauled the Nieuport into a stall turn, and ended up above and behind him. Much to my satisfaction, as I came out of the turn, I could see him peering this way and that, wondering where on earth I'd got to. I grabbed my rifle, and took a snap shot at his propellor. I can't have been far off target, because he flinched and rolled over into a spin: down and down, round and round, like a falling leaf. For a moment I thought I'd got him – and didn't know whether to be elated or appalled. But after about a thousand feet he levelled off, turned parallel to the trenches, and damn me if he didn't start cranking away again with his camera! He was a cool one!

I was conscious of a rapport between us: an almost physical bond. There is of course a special affinity between two men who are matched one against the other in single combat; and this is especially true when the men are alone, the terms are equal and the stakes are life and death. It is a ritual old as time: two cavemen with clubs and the carcass midway between them, two knights with lances in a chivalrous but deadly joust. . . . I found myself eying the Fokker pilot appraisingly, calculating the performance of his plane, assessing his character and skill. I decided to test his nerve.

I flew straight at him.

Now I had, I need hardly say, not the slightest intention of ramming him – *that* sort of courage was altogether beyond me. But I intended to frighten him: to make him break away.

But instead of breaking away he turned and flew straight at *me*!

At a combined speed of over a hundred and fifty miles an hour Nieuport and Fokker tore at one another like angry eagles.

We didn't have time to think. We both kept coming till the last possible fraction of a second. Then simultaneously we flung our aircraft aside.

We missed by no more than a couple of feet! We were so close that the blast from one another's slipstream slammed into us like a physical blow. So close that for a split second we could see one another clearly.

His face (like mine) was turning away, flinching, as he thought he'd left it too late. His eyes (like mine) were wild with exhilaration and fear.

And they were eyes that I recognised: very blue and very

wide apart.

Otto's.

For about ten seconds I simply kept on flying. My mouth was dry, my heart pounding, my hands shaking; it was the nearest I'd ever been to death. Then, slowly, I turned to look for the Fokker. He was about a mile away, also turning, probably, I told myself, as shaken as I was. We came back towards one another: hesitantly, like two dogs who want to play but fear one another's teeth. And as we closed, I began to have second thoughts. Had it *really* been Otto? Had he recognised me? And if he had, did he still feel about me the way that I still felt about him?

Then I saw that he was waggling his wings.

Relief washed over me like a wave of the sea. Though adversaries, we could still be friends. I waggled *my* wings, and waved. He waved back. And as though by mutual consent we turned and flew near-parallel to one another. Soon we were separated by no more than the wingspan of our planes.

I could see him as clearly as though he were on the opposite side of the monitors' dormitory, grinning all over his face. We gave each other the thumbs-up. We took off our helmets and waved them over our heads. If only we could have had five minutes together to talk! Or even five seconds to shake one another by the hand!

At five thousand feet we flew side by side over the trenches. What those below us must be thinking we neither knew nor cared. We were comrades, bound by ties that transcended the pettiness of war.

Yet the war was something we weren't able to forget. Away to the south allied artillery was starting its usual morning barrage; away to the north I could see German lorries heading in a haze of dust for the Front – *that* would have to be reported. And why was Otto gesticulating first to his camera then to our trenches? I shook my head.

He ignored me and lined up his camera.

I waved him away.

He took no notice. He started taking photographs of the

68

trenches. The war became suddenly all too real.

I didn't know what to do. But two things I was sure of: I couldn't let him get away with it, and I couldn't kill him. I reached for my rifle. I sighted it well above and behind the Fokker's tailplane. And fired.

Otto's head jerked up. He was so close that I could see the surprise in his eyes. Then the sadness. Then the anger.

I edged as close to the Fokker as I dared. I pointed to the trenches and shook my head.

Otto glared at me.

We were now flying with wings interlocked, within a hairs-breadth of touching. The slightest error of judgment, the slightest air pocket, even a not-too-distant burst of Archie, and we'd have been flung together, to fall, a twisting ball of flame, to our death. I could feel the sweat running cold and salt into my eyes. Why in God's name didn't he get the message?

As though in answer to my prayer, the Fokker pulled fractionally away from the trenches. Our wings disengaged.

I gave Otto the thumbs-up. And, thank heavens, he seemed to realise in what a predicament his penchant for photography had put me, because he replied with a wave and a smile. For a few but how wonderful moments we were again flying side-by-side, not adversaries but friends. I was conscious of a glow of well-being. Good had triumphed over evil, love over hate; if only, I thought, the politicians could settle their differences in such a civilised manner!

Suddenly to my amazement I realised that the sky was changing colour. For a moment I couldn't think what was happening. Then I saw the sun coming up like an oriflamme out of the trenches, turning the clouds around us from mother-of-pearl to gold, and the sky from grey to a pink. It was a dawn to match our mood.

One moment Otto was beside me. Next he was rolling off the top of a loop and trying to get on my tail. Like dolphins at play we twisted and turned, dived and soared through the playground of the sky. We jinked in and out of the bastions of cloud; we spun like leaves towards the gyrating earth; we climbed a

69

little way together toward the stars.

Bliss was it in that dawn to be alive.
But to be young was very heaven!

Not until fuel was low in our tanks did we give one another a reluctant wave. Then he was heading for Ronchin and I for Saint Genis-en-Lys.

6

I wasn't surprised, next morning, when Uncle sent for me. What did surprise me was that he seemed to take a harmless escapade so seriously. 'I have reports', he said curtly, 'that you were seen "larking about" with a German aircraft. I must warn you, 2nd Lieutenant Cunningham, that fraternising with the enemy is an offence punishable by court martial.'

If he was trying to frighten me he certainly succeeded.

He was speaking again. 'Now I have to report on this. What goes into my report must be the truth. But it needn't be the whole truth. Do you understand?'

'I'm not ashamed', I blurted out, 'of what happened.'

His fist crashed onto the table. 'God in heaven, boy! I don't care a fig for your feelings. What I want are facts. Facts for my report. Facts to stop a court martial. And you blindfold in front of a firing squad. *Now* do you understand?'

It came to me that the trouble I'd been in before was nothing to the trouble I'd got myself into now. I moistened my lips. 'Would you advise me, sir? What to say?'

'You really need a wet nurse, don't you!'

'No. Just a friend.'

For a moment he stared at me as though I was an insect he was about to dissect; then, grudgingly, his eyes softened. 'All right,' he grunted without enthusiasm. 'What happened?'

I told him everything: not only what had taken place above the trenches, but how I'd known Otto at school, how he had become my closest friend and how I could no more kill him than I could kill my brother. Once or twice, I saw his fingers drumming the top of his desk as though he didn't care for what he was hearing; and when I'd finished he got to his feet and began

71

to pace the room, hands clasped behind his back, beard thrust forward like the prow of a ship. 'If you value your life,' he muttered, '*never* tell anyone else what you've told me'. More pacing up and down; then he seemed suddenly to come to a decision. 'I'll help you, lad, provided you'll help yourself. Provided you'll wake up to the fact that this war isn't some sort of jolly sporting game.'

'I realise that, sir.'

'Right. So you give me the facts I need. And I'll give you a piece of advice. . . . Now you saw this Fokker photographing the trenches. So what did you do?'

'Manoeuvred into the sun, sir. And stalked him.'

'Then?'

'As soon as he came within range, I opened fire.'

'What with?'

'My rifle.'

'And a rifle was the only weapon you had?'

'Yes sir.'

'How many shots did you fire?'

'Just one, sir.'

He looked at me very straight: 'And you only fired once because after your first shot the rifle jammed?'

I didn't like it. But I realised he was throwing me a lifeline. I muttered a reluctant 'Yes, sir.'

He gave a grunt of approval. 'And then? When you found you couldn't fire: what did you do?'

'Flew as close to the Fokker as I dared, sir.'

'Why?'

'To try and force him away from the trenches.'

'And did you succeed?'

'Yes, sir.'

'And then?'

'I tried to get on his tail, sir.'

'Knowing that if you kept him occupied he'd run out of fuel? And have to go back to Ronchin without his photographs?'

I muttered, 'That's right.' And wondered why I felt like Judas.

He pushed aside the pad on which he'd been making notes. 'So you're in the clear. They might even give you a medal! But another time, Jack Cunningham, you won't be so lucky. So let me give you some advice.' He walked to the window and stood staring out over the airfield. 'Have you ever', he said unexpectedly, 'been in the trenches?'

'No, sir.'

'You ought to. See how the other half live. Know what it's like to sink up to your knees in mud. Hear the shells thudding closer and closer and knowing the next lot'll land in *your* trench and wondering if one of them's got your number on it. Lie awake all night and hear men moaning in agony as they hang in the wire. War in the trenches, Jack Cunningham, is pure undiluted hell. And how', his eyes darkened, 'how do you suppose the poor devils down there feel when they see airmen larking about? Playing games? Fraternising? I tell you, there's enough ill will against the Flying Corps without young fools like you stoking the flames. Do you understand me?'

'Yes, sir.'

'Then understand this. Next time you meet your friend Otto-whatever-his-name-is, kill him.'

I'd known in my heart that this was what he was leading up to; but it was still a pretty unpleasant shock to hear it put into words. I may not have had a great deal of sense in those days, but I knew when to keep my mouth shut. 'Right, sir.'

His eyes were black as marble, and as cold. 'And mind you *get* it right, Jack Cunningham. Or by God I'll have you crucified. In front of a firing squad.'

I knew he meant it; and I wanted, suddenly and almost desperately, to get away from him. 'Is that all, sir?'

'That'll be all. So long as you obey orders.'

I saluted, and fled.

I was grateful to him for helping me, but I'd not the slightest intention of doing as he said. The war, I told myself, might have made *him* hard and callous. But it wasn't going to happen to me. . . . I was pretty immature in those days. And a bit of a prig.

That evening I took my problem to Chris. 'I ask you. Could

73

you kill your best friend?'

'I could kill you cheerfully at times!'

'No seriously! Could you? And live with it?'

For a long time he didn't answer, then he said carefully: 'I don't think you've any alternative. Say you come across your friend when he's artillery spotting: and say you *don't* kill him, and because of the reports he sends back, Jerry gets the range of our trenches. You could be responsible for hundreds of men being killed. Our own men. Men with wives: families. Could *you* live with that?'

I was very much afraid he was right; but perversely I went on arguing: 'I got him to clear off once, without killing him.'

'He may not *want* to clear off next time.'

'That's a bridge I'll cross', I said, 'when I come to it.'

Chris was looking at me thoughtfully: 'War isn't all beer and skittles, you know. We all have to give things up.' His voice was unexpectedly bitter.

'What have *you* had to give up, Chris?'

'Forget it.'

'No, please tell me.'

'If it hadn't been for the war,' he said shortly, 'Claire and I would have started a family.'

'You mean you think it's wrong to have children? In wartime?'

'If I survive,' he said, 'there'll be time enough *after* the war. If I don't survive, I don't want Claire lumbered.'

'She mightn't think of it as being "lumbered".'

'It could make it hard for her,' he said, 'to remarry.'

'She mightn't *want* to remarry.'

'Oh, Jack! You're an incurable romantic!'

'Some women might not. Especially if they have a child.'

His eyes closed, as though in pain. Then, almost angrily, he pulled a photograph out of his wallet: 'Can you see *her* an old maid, for the rest of her life?'

She was a stunner all right, though I suppose a purist would have said she was pretty rather than beautiful: blue eyes, a wide mouth, a turned-up nose and a mass of dark curly hair. Across

74

the photo she had scrawled in big childish handwriting in lipstick: 'Johnny – till the sands of the desert grow cold'.

'She calls me Johnny', he explained, 'because her sister's a Chris. She thinks of it as a girl's name.'

I handed back the photo: 'Lucky man!'

'So long as I'm alive.' Unexpectedly, he shivered. 'Silly, isn't it. I'm not afraid of dying. For myself. But oh God, am I afraid for her.'

I didn't know what to say to that. But Chris was my friend and I wanted to help. 'If anything happens to you,' I said, 'I'll keep an eye on her. If you like.'

'Thanks.' His hand rested for a moment on my shoulder. 'I'd like that more than anything in the world.'

That night we got drunk in a café in Armentières.

'*Garçon!*'

'*M'sieu?*'

'*Deux fines, et encore deux fines et toujours deux fines!*'

We toasted Claire: 'Here's hoping', I said, 'I never meet her!'

A couple of days later Saint Genis was visited by a high-ranking officer: a brigadier-general with a great booming voice that made Uncle's sound like a falsetto squeak. The pair of them did a whirlwind tour of the airfield. The brigadier-general didn't seem interested in the usual parades and inspections. Instead he waved his shooting stick at the poplars lining the Lys: 'Damned inconvenient, I'd have thought.'

'They are, sir.'

'Have 'em down.'

'I don't think,' Uncle ventured, 'they're inside the airfield.'

'Use some initiative, man. Like arsenic round the roots.'

The brigadier swept through Saint Genis like the proverbial dose of salts. And next morning Uncle summoned us to the crewroom. Our visitor, he told us, had been none other than '*Boom*' Trenchard, the newly-appointed head of the Flying Corps. Trenchard, he went on to explain, had the ear of the General Staff, and had managed to persuade them that aircraft were capable of great things: not only reconnaissance but fighting. So the war in the air was about to be hotted up. From now on there'd be non-stop offensive patrols over enemy territory, attacks on German trenches, and bombing raids on supply dumps, troop concentration and railways. He made it sound jolly exciting. Only at the very end did he add a note of warning. 'Now don't imagine Jerry is going to take this lying down. He'll be up there after us. And we think he may have something new up his sleeve – an improved fighter is the most likely bet. So watch out. And remember a good pilot completes his mission *and* gets back to base.'

There were two schools of thought that evening in the mess. Some reckoned our aerial offensive would be a seven days wonder. Others saw the writing on the wall.

As is the way with new brooms we set to work with a will, full of grandiose ideas of sweeping Jerry out of the sky. But the spectacular air battles we half-expected failed to materialise. What *did* materialise, however, was that the more we flew the more casualties we suffered. These casualties, to start with, were more niggling than crippling – a Nieuport caught in a thunderstorm and crash-landing in a field, a BE2 hit by rifle fire from the ground and ending up minus both its wings in a wood – but they were cumulative, and it wasn't long before the squadron was suffering the sort of losses that Uncle had described as unacceptable. On the other side of the coin we did begin to achieve results. After long sessions of struggling with our Heath Robinson bomb-sights we actually managed to blow up the railway line between Cambrai and le Cateau; after half-a-dozen inconclusive skirmishes we managed to hit a Taube in the engine and send it spinning earthward to crash between the lines; after hours of patient reconnaissance we managed to direct our artillery onto something worthwhile, a German ammunition dump.

Then, one morning when the water-lilies on the Lys were opening into great drifts of white and gold, I made my own small contribution to the offensive.

Sergeant Johnson and I were patrolling north of Vimy when

we noticed that below us Jerry was mounting a creeping barrage against our forward trenches. His artillery seemed to have got the range with uncanny precision. And I soon saw why. Half-a-mile behind the German lines, at about 5,000 feet, there floated what looked like a gargantuan grey-green sausage: an observation balloon: an evil eye surveying the slaughter over which it presided. Johnson lifted his Lewis-gun onto its mounting. We gave one another the thumbs-up.

Now I'd always thought of balloons as ripe for the plucking – didn't the ones we played with at Christmas go pop at the slightest provocation! But as we neared this one, Archie opened up from more than a dozen emplacements. The guns of course had been specially sited to discourage attacks such as ours and they soon got our range. The explosions became louder, sharper, increasingly violent. There was a highly unpleasant clunking as shrapnel thudded into our wings and fuselage. The BE2 shuddered. I rammed forward the throttle and increased our angle of dive. But at anything over eighty the wretched aircraft rattled and shook as though about to fall apart at the seams, and we came droning in to the attack with about as much *élan* as an exhausted snail. Johnson was waving at me to break away. But I pretended not to understand, and kept heading into the holocaust. It was terrifying. The crack of the explosions was like a continuous ripping of calico; the air reeked of cordite, and the whole sky seemed to be trembling and in places disintegrating. But by a miracle none of the shells registered a direct hit. And suddenly the balloon loomed up in front of us, improbably near. For a moment it disappeared behind the flash of an explosion. Then it was so close I could see individual men in the basket, one throwing himself flat on his face, another aiming his rifle, straight at my eyes. I flung the BE2 into a tight turn. As we flashed by Johnson opened up with his Lewis. I could see the bullets thudding into the fabric, slicing diagonally through the big black cross. I expected it to go up in flames. But the bullets had no visible effect. (I learned afterwards that the balloons were inflated to such a low pressure it was difficult to give them more than a slow puncture). So we spun round and

77

round in a tight circle, pumping lead into our unfortunate adversary from so close a range that the German guns didn't dare to fire for fear of hitting their own balloon. After a few seconds I found myself having to push the nose of the BE2 further and further forward to enable Johnson to fire. And it suddenly dawned on me – a bit belatedly! – that the balloon was being hauled in: a fact brought home by a sudden burst of rifle-fire from the ground. I looked down and saw to my horror that we were at no more than two thousand feet. And in trouble. For the second we pulled away, the guns would get us.

I found myself weighing up the possibilities with a detachment that surprised me, almost as though it was somebody else whose life was hanging in the balance. There was, I decided, only one hope. I waited till the balloon was no more than a couple of hundred feet from its moorings, picked the avenue of escape down which there seemed to be fewest guns, and dived for the comparative safety of ground level.

The second I broke away it seemed as though every gun between Ypres and Loos opened up at us. For perhaps five seconds the BE2 was at the centre of a maelstrom. Shrapnel pitted into us like hail. One blast tossed us high into the air, ripping off half the undercarriage; another slammed us almost into the ground, punching a hole in the wing not a dozen feet from my head.

From behind us came a sudden roar, and a spectacular lightening of the sky. I looked back. And what I saw will stay in my memory till the day I die.

The balloon was in flames. It hung like a tattered tapestry in the sky: a tapestry all leaping tongues of red and gold, and dripping little gouts of fire like an opened stomach blood. And beneath it hung the observation basket, glowing white-hot like a brazier. And diving out of the brazier three figures of red and gold, figures which for a moment sailed through the air, then fell to earth jerking and quivering like ignited squibs.

I shut my eyes. Only for a second. Then some instinct must have screamed warning. I came-to. And found we were hurtling straight for a ridge. The ridge was dotted with trees. The trees

78

were so close I could see the individual leaves on their branches. I hauled back the stick. And the BE2 skimmed the ridge as a stone skims the crest of a wave. We were so close I could feel the fuselage shudder as our tailskid scythed through the upper branches of one of the trees.

We weren't safe – or anything like it. But on the far side of the ridge we were screened for a moment from the worst of the gunfire. We had a breathing space in which to gather our scattered wits, before deciding how to try and get back across the lines.

I never thought we'd make it. The engine was coughing like an asthmatic, the controls were slack and the wings so colandered I expected them any second to drop off. But we were lucky. Half-an-hour and half-a-dozen near deaths later we limped back to Saint Genis and crashlanded in the long wet grass at the side of the Lys.

For once I'd done something right! Heaven knows how many times that evening I was greeted with 'Hear you roasted a sausage, young fellow! Well done!' But I wanted no part in the after-dinner celebrations in the Mess. I shut myself up in my cabin.

To forget. Or rather to try to forget.

There was, I told myself, only one way to look at it. Johnson and I had been lucky: the men in the balloon had been unlucky: that was war. It was no good being sentimental about it. Every second of every minute of every hour of every day of every week of every month of every year, someone on the Western Front was squeezing a trigger or thrusting a bayonet or lobbing a grenade or firing a shell and someone else as a consequence was dying. You'd go out of your mind if you thought about it. You had to pretend that those you were killing weren't men like you, weren't flesh and blood but some faceless and amorphous Enemy with a capital E. All this I told myself. But still the horror of the death I had meted out to my fellow airmen precluded sleep. I tried to concentrate my thoughts on other things: things that mattered to me: on God, my mother, Charterhouse, flying, the Helford River, Jessica. All of them brought a transitory comfort. But the image of only one of them stayed in my mind bright enough and long enough to blot out the flames. She was the one rock in a tempestuous sea to which my thoughts would anchor.

And at last, thinking of Jessica, I dropped off to sleep. And once again the two of us were walking hand in hand through the woods and beaches of our childhood – strange how the sun, in those days, seemed always to be shining. And everything was wonderfully quiet, and wonderfully peaceful and wonderfully happy. Until, as is often the way in dreams, things began to get mixed up. One moment I was with Jessica; next moment I was with Gavin; and we were riding into a clearing. It was a clearing I recognised: the dried-up bed of the river, the cottage, the cider-apple, the mud-pilot. I was telling myself that I'd seen it all before, when I realised this time there was somebody else in the clearing, a girl shading her eyes against the glare of the sun as she stood staring at us from the door of the cottage. She must, I thought, be the mud-pilot's wife. Then I saw her face: blue eyes, wide mouth, turned-up nose and a cascade of dark curly hair. It was Claire Scott. And she was pregnant.

Those who had said our offensive would soon peter out were now made to eat their words. There was no let-up in Trenchard's policy of continuous patrolling. And suddenly our losses became catastrophic. In the whole of June we lost two planes; then, in the first week of July, we lost three. Our first reaction was that we'd been unlucky. Then we learned that the squadrons north and south of us had suffered even heavier losses: that our planes were tumbling out of the sky like leaves at the first frost.

Uncle called us to a special briefing. He seemed, I noticed, to have grown suddenly older; his voice had lost its banter: 'We warned you,' he said, 'that Jerry might have something up his sleeve. Well, we don't *think* it's a new plane, because all our sighting reports have been of the same old Fokkers and Taubes. So we reckon it must be a new gun – something with a longer range perhaps, a better rate of fire, heavier bullets, incendiary bullets? Anyhow, we've *got* to know what it is. From now on you'll be flying in pairs. And if anything happens to one of you, the other's job is to get back and report. Do you understand that? No scrapping. No heroics. Just get back alive.' He went on to outline our new programme – which wasn't at all to our liking since it just about doubled the time we had to spend in the air.

A couple of days later Chris and I were on patrol between Ypres and Neuve Chapelle. It was a nondescript sort of day, with the cloud base at five thousand feet and light drizzle. We flew – as we'd been told to fly – side by side about a hundred-and-fifty yards apart, keeping an extremely wary lookout. Apart from the occasional inaccurate salvo, Archie didn't bother us; and I remember thinking it was such a miserable morning the gunners were probably loth to leave their dug-outs.

We were coming up to Lille when we spotted the Fokker. Chris saw him first, waggled his wings and pointed, and I was just in time to catch sight of the spindly high-wing monoplane as it disappeared into cloud. Thinking he might try to pounce on us from cloud cover, we lost height and altered course. A couple of minutes later the Fokker reappeared, dead ahead, coming straight at us. This suited us fine; for we knew the pilot wouldn't be able to fire at us head on. We waited, keyed up, expecting him any moment to turn. But he didn't. He came on and on. Straight at us.

A flicker of orange, like the flame of a match, appeared briefly from beside the Fokker's propeller. And Chris's plane gave a sudden lurch and flicked over into a spin, pouring smoke.

It happened so fast, I couldn't believe it. That couldn't be Chris, twisting and turning, round and round, down and down: slowly: like a falling leaf.

A tongue of flame leapt out of his engine, wavered for a moment like an unfurling flag, then wrapped itself round the wing. 'Please God,' I whispered. 'No!' But God didn't seem to be listening. The flames, whipped up by the slipstream, lengthened and spread. They curled back onto the fuselage, over the cockpit.

I closed my eyes and prayed that Chris was already dead.

Then I remembered the Fokker.

He had flashed past me, and was turning through a hundred-and-eighty degrees, coming back to deal with me as he had dealt with Chris. I reached for my rifle. I'd get the bastard. If it was the last thing I did on earth, I'd get him.

I was suddenly conscious of a strange booming in my ears. I couldn't for a moment think what it was – something wrong with the engine, the blood pounding in my temples? Then I realised it was Uncle's voice – 'No scrapping. No heroics. Just get back alive.' It was almost frightening. It was as though I became in an instant another person; ice cold; my grief for Chris, my fury with the Fokker, even my fear were sponged clean away, and every fibre of my brain and body became focused on the one thing that mattered, staying alive. . . . So the Fokker had a forward-firing machine-gun, a machine-gun which seemed to fire, incredible as it sounds, *through* its propeller. . . . He was coming at me a second time, head-on. I started to turn to the left, then a split second before I reckoned he'd fire, flung the Nieuport hard over to the right. I heard the staccato crack of his gun. I felt the stick shudder as bullets sliced through the tip of my tail. I rammed the nose forward, and the Nieuport went hurtling down, faster and faster till the wind in the wires was a frenzied high-pitched scream. Out of the corner of my eye I saw the Fokker starting to follow. Before he had time to get on my tail, I hauled the Nieuport into a loop. Up and up, slower and slower, clawing desperately for the safety of cloud. I did a half roll off the top of the loop, and as the plane shuddered near-stalling onto an even keel, took a quick look round. And saw, in the fraction of a second, that the cloud was mercifully close, the Fokker was mercifully far away and Chris was dead. At the very moment I looked down, his Nieuport scythed into a line of poplars. For a second the flames burned more brightly than ever; blazing fragments were tossed high into the air, then there was nothing. Nothing but memories and the promise of all that might have been but never would be now.

"ὦσ ὁ μὲυ ἔυθ απόλωλε, φἱλαιοι δέ κηδέ ὁπιοσω
πᾶοιυ ἐμοὶ δ ἐ μάλιοτα, τετεύχαταὶ."*

('So he fell in a far country: to the never-ending grief of his
friends, especially me.' (*Odyssey*)).

And how many other lives, I asked myself, would be snuffed
out the same way, if I didn't get back with my report? I fled for
the protecting canopy of cloud.

As the first coils of vapour came drifting past the tip of my
wings, I felt like a hunted animal who creeps heart-thudding
into the safety of a thicket.

For the next few minutes I was hard pressed to keep the Nieuport under control. For flying in cloud is like walking in a white-
out, a world without a horizon. An airman flies by his horizon;
take it away, and he can't tell if he is on an even keel, diving,
climbing or turning; sensation isn't to be relied on, and our only
instruments in those days were a rudimentary speed indicator
and a lateral bubble. So I had to concentrate just to hold course
and height. I had no time to think.

It wasn't until I landed at Saint Genis and saw the barge
where Chris had slept and the farmhouse where he had eaten
and the crewroom where the two of us had so often talked away
the hours, that the full impact of what had happened hit me.
And even then I was for some time too busy with my report for it
to sink in.

For Uncle made me tell my story again and again, urging me
each time to recall some small additional detail – had I actually
seen the machine-gun on the Fokker; had the spurt of flame as it
opened fire been in the centre of its propeller boss or to one side
of it? And at the end of it all, just as I was about to turn in, I had
to go through the whole performance again in front of a French
Intelligence Officer. 'Without doubt', the latter said when he
had heard my story, 'this Fokker pilot was using the device of
our Roland Garros: deflectors on the blades of his propeller.'

Uncle shook his head. 'No, sir. Your Garros was a hero. But
he was also a gambler. Each time he fired through his deflector

83

blades, he risked his life. Now I know the Hun. He's every bit as brave as we are. But he's *not* a gambler. German planes would never be fitted with a device that put their pilots at such a risk.'

The Intelligence Officer nodded: 'That is well reasoned.' And the pair of them embarked on a highly technical discussion. From what they were saying I gathered that earlier in the year the French ace Roland Garros had shot down several German planes by firing a machine-gun through his propeller, the bullets being deflected (hopefully!) from the blades by protecting-plates of specially toughened steel. Garros was a brave man; for he stood about as much chance of destroying himself as his enemy! And it wasn't long before the inevitable happened; he shot himself down over German-occupied territory, and his plane, in spite of his efforts to burn it, was captured. 'I suggest' – the Intelligence Officer looked at his watch – 'that the Germans got the *idea* of firing through a propeller from Garros's plane. And have now discovered a way of doing this safely.'

Uncle's voice was grave: 'If you're right, it means a revolution in aerial warfare. And one we're ill-prepared for.'

The Frenchman reached for his swagger-stick. 'We have fine new planes, m'sieu. And', he favoured me with a careless smile, 'brave young pilots. Together we shall drive the Bosch from the sky.'

'But at what cost?'

When the Intelligence Officer had gone, Uncle seemed loth for me to go too. 'What do *you* reckon we should do about these Fokkers, young Cunningham?'

I took so long to answer that he looked at me curiously. 'Spit it out, lad. I shan't eat you!'

'I think', I said slowly, 'we ought to cut down on our patrolling. Until we've a plane as good as their's.'

He nodded. 'You're right. But there's not a hope in hell of it happening. So what's the short-term answer? For us?'

'Flying in formation perhaps?'

'Damned wasteful. Half-a-dozen planes for a single recce.'

I would have liked to come up with something bright, but inspiration didn't seem to be forthcoming. 'All I can say, sir, is the sooner we get a forward-firing gun like the Fokkers the better.'

'A forward-firing gun. Hmmm!. . . .' My suggestion evidently triggered off a train of thought, for he walked to his desk and started ferreting through a stack of papers. After a while he must have found what he wanted, for he started to read. He read on and on, as though he'd forgotten I was in the room. I was about to ask if I could go, when he said, without looking up: 'I want you to fly to Farnborough. Tomorrow.'

'Right, sir.'

'Report here at nine. Ready for take-off.'

'Right, sir.' The idea came to me as I was turning for the door: 'Could I have twenty-four hours' leave? While I'm over there?'

'No.'

'Sir?'

He stared at me, as though whatever it was I was going to say he didn't want to hear it. I wasn't, however, going to be intimidated. 'Chris lived not far from Farnborough. . . .'

The anger ebbed slowly out of his eyes. 'You want to visit Claire?'

'It was a promise, sir.'

'Why not?' he said slowly. 'The bloody war can wait. Aren't kindness and decency the things we're supposed to be fighting for? Tell Claire her husband was a brave man, and that he didn't die in vain. It won't help her now. But it may bring her comfort one day.'

I thanked him. Within five minutes of leaving his office I was in bed. I was dog tired, but I couldn't sleep. For every time I shut my eyes Chris's face came welling flame-wrapped out of the dark. I learned that night why it is better for a pilot at the Front to have acquaintances rather than friends.

The Royal Aircraft Establishment at Farnborough was *the* place for aeronautical research and development. I expected to find it a bit overpowering; but luckily for me Uncle seemed to be well known there, and as his emissary I was given favoured treatment. I delivered the letter he had given me to his friend Major Tabor, a fat little man who looked like a cross between a jovial monk and a mature Billy Bunter. And Tabor certainly got things moving. Within an hour of my arrival I was seated at the controls of a strange experimental plane: a single-seater 'pusher', with the engine at the back of its fuselage and the pilot stuck out at the front as though on the bowsprit of a ship – about the only thing ahead of him was a swivel-mounted Lewis-gun. This was the DH2, soon to be unkindly dubbed 'the spinning incinerator'. It was not so much a plane as a flying gun-platform: a platform capable of firing dead ahead. I took it up that afternoon. It was an odd aircraft to fly, all lopsided because of the torque from its engine; to keep it level one had to hold both the stick and the rudder to one side, and when I 'blipped' it coming in to land the wretched thing canted almost onto its wingtip. But it had pros as well as cons. The pilot had a magnificent view, and a forward-firing gun – a Fokker coming straight at it would certainly get a hot reception. I began to realise why Uncle had sent me to Farnborough.

By the time I got down it was, I decided, too late that evening to go and see Claire Scott. But first thing next morning I borrowed a motor bike and set off for Weston Patrick, the village about twenty miles from Farnborough where she and Chris had bought a cottage. It wasn't a meeting I was looking forward to.

Chris had shown me so many photographs of Dragonfly Cottage that I recognised it at once. It was small and rather nondescript looking; but the house had a cared-for appearance and the garden was chock-full of vegetables and flowers. Claire Scott – at least I assumed the voice was hers – was in the kitchen singing The Mountains of Mourne, which I must say rather surprised me. She evidently heard the crunch of my shoes on the gravel path, for her face appeared at the window, and about half a second later she came fairly flying out of the door. I don't think I've ever seen a girl so alive and tingling. When she saw me her animation seemed to evaporate, and she became just another rather pretty rather puzzled girl. She gave me an uncertain smile, and held up her hand to stop me from saying anything: 'Don't tell me . . . I know. You're Jack Cunningham!'

I nodded, at the back of my mind the most terrible suspicion.

'Come on in. Johnny's always talkin' about you. . . . Would you like tea? Coffee? Or something stronger?' She put on an exaggerated brogue: 'You know we Oirish. Always a drop o' potheen beneath the sink!'

'Tea'll be fine.'

She led the way to the kitchen, and started filling a kettle. 'How's Johnny?'

It was as though I'd been poleaxed. So she hadn't got the telegram – perhaps, I remember thinking, because yesterday had been a Sunday. I couldn't think, let alone speak.

She had her back to me, and when I didn't answer I saw her go suddenly rigid. She spun round, knocking the kettle flying. 'Where's Johnny?'

As our eyes met, she knew.

The colour drained from her cheeks and the sap from her body. It was as though in an instant she shrivelled up. 'Oh Johnny,' she whispered, 'where are you?'

'I thought you knew, Claire. It happened two or three days ago.'

'Is it quite certain', she whispered, 'he's dead?'

'I'm sorry. I was with him.'

She clutched at the table, and I wondered if she was going to faint. Then something inside her seemed to snap. She grabbed the crucifix she was wearing round her neck. She tugged at it once, twice, three times; and the third time the chain parted. 'God,' she said quietly, 'you bastard. That was a bloody dirty trick.' She flung the crucifix out of the window.

I stood there like a stuffed dummy. Ladylike tears I'd been prepared for; but not this.

She let out a terrible wailing moan, and started to pound the table with her fists. She smashed her fists so hard into the table that the wood splintered, one of the legs collapsed, and cups

87

plates and a jar of marmalade slid with a crash to the floor. She ripped off the tablecloth, sending the silver and the rest of the crockery flying. Then she flung herself into a chair, curled up into a foetal ball and started to cry. I'd never have thought a human being could have so many tears in them; they poured out of her in a seemingly never-ending flood. It was, I told myself, the best thing that could happen. My hand rested a moment on her shoulder. I'd thought to comfort her, but she shied away as though I had struck her. 'I'll be in the garden,' I said. 'If you want me.'

As I shut the door she was rocking to and fro, the tears still pouring out of her. 'Oh Johnny,' I heard her whisper. 'Oh Johnny, Johnny, Johnny. Johnny I hardly knew you.'

I walked to the end of the garden, and stood staring at the neat rows of lettuces and peas. I was shaken. The intensity of her grief had brought home to me something that was obvious really, only I'd never given it much thought: that the war extended beyond the trenches, that the body limp in the wire was not the end of suffering but the beginning. It was as well, I told myself, that there wasn't anybody who'd grieve so deeply if *I* were killed. And that was the way it was jolly well going to stay. Love in wartime was better left in cold storage.

It was more than an hour before Claire Scott emerged from the kitchen and started crawling about on her hands and knees outside the window. She must, I told myself, be looking for her crucifix.

We found it hooked up in a rose bush. She ran her fingers over the cross. 'I shouldn't have done that.' Her voice was devoid of emotion.

'When he was killed,' I said, 'I felt the same way.'

She looked at me blankly.

'I was his friend, Claire.'

'Oh yes, of course. . . . Would you tell me something, please?'

I nodded.

'Was he' – her mouth was trembling – 'burned?'

'No,' I said quickly. 'I promise you. He was killed at once. He can't have known a thing.'

'How – did it happen?'

I suggested we went back to the kitchen, and I made her a cup of tea while we talked.

She nodded. She was utterly numb, utterly passive; if I'd suggested we chucked ourselves off the roof I think she'd have done it. I made her a cup of tea, and made up at the same time a story about Chris's death, which may have been based on truth but had little relationship to it. 'I suppose', she said when I'd finished, 'instead of throwing my crucifix away I ought to have thanked God he wasn't burned.'

And that, I think, was the most terrible moment of all.

I stayed with her for the rest of the morning: till a neighbour came to take her out to lunch and I knew that she wouldn't be on her own. And before leaving Weston Patrick I called on the local doctor, who promised during the next few weeks to keep an eye on her.

There didn't seem to be anything else I could do.

As I rode back to Farnborough I was depressed and at odds with the world. I couldn't forget how Claire Scott had shrivelled up in front of my eyes, how she had changed in an instant from an attractive-girl-who-has-everything to a lifeless automaton. I wondered what the future would hold for her? When I was next on leave, I told myself, I'd make a point of seeing her again.

In the meanwhile I still had twenty-four hours of *this* leave.

In my present mood I could think of only three alternatives: I could get drunk, I could pick up a girl, or I could try to get in touch with Jessica. . . . Well, I could get drunk any day at Saint Genis; picking up a girl at Farnborough mightn't be easy for someone as inexperienced in the art as I was; and the thought of Jessica made me realise how much I wanted a friend to talk to.

I thought I was never going to contact her. But after about five hours – most of which I seemed to spend on the telephone we at last got together in a somewhat dubious little restaurant in Whitechapel.

She had, she explained, come to London to work in a hospital near the docks; apparently they had a lot of shell-shock cases straight from the Front and a lot of patients minus some vital part of their anatomy. She had to be back on night duty in a couple of hours; but in those two hours we got to know more about one another than in the previous two years – I suppose because we'd both matured and both wanted someone to confide in. . . . Anyhow, she told me about the bedpans and the aching feet and the sudden smile that made them worthwhile; about the screams in the night, and the joy of helping a man to do something he had thought he'd never do again. While I told her about the stench of Archie and the beauty of the world above the clouds; the fear of being burnt slow-spinning to death, and the thrill of flying with friends in close-formation swaying together ten feet apart a mile above the earth. And eventually I told her something which I knew would mean more to her than all the other things put together. 'By the way,' I kept my voice deliberately casual, 'I saw Otto the other day!'

The coffee cup fell from her fingers.

'Jess!. . . . He's all right!'

She was trembling. Her eyes were afraid. 'You didn't' – she hesitated – 'fight?'

I shook my head; and her fear gave way to excitement. She clasped her hands, like a little girl unexpectedly offered a present: 'Oh, Jack! Tell me!'

I gave her a more or less truthful account of our meeting – its sequel I kept exceedingly quiet about. By the time I'd finished she was fairly scintillating with excitement. Love, I thought wryly, became her. Again she clasped her hands together: 'Oh, Jack! How wonderful!' She asked all manner of foolish questions. Did Otto look well: what was he wearing: had he got thinner? – she'd read somewhere the Germans were all half-starving! And when she had wrung from me the last possible drop of information, she leaned back with a sigh of content. 'Oh, I can't believe it!. . . . You men are lucky, aren't you? I mean you can fight, and still like one another?'

I nodded.

'Women', she said slowly, 'could never have that sort of relationship.'

'I can think of sorts they're better at!'

She smiled – a couple of months ago she'd have blushed. 'Why don't you get yourself a girl, Jack?'

'Didn't you know. I'm wedded to my mechanical cow. . . . Besides, the only girl I fancy isn't in the market.'

Her eyes dropped.

I decided, on the spur of the moment, to ask her something: or rather ask her *for* something: something I'd wanted for quite a while. 'Jess.'

'Hmmm?'

'I know I can't have *you*. But be a sport and let me have a photo of you.'

She withdrew. Suddenly. As though taking shelter behind a barrier she was determined would never be breached. 'Please. Don't spoil a lovely evening.'

'All I asked for was a photo!'

'But why?'

I tried to explain. 'It may not sound very flattering, Jess: but you're a sort of anchor. A sort of symbol, if you like, of all the *good* things. You know – England, beauty, goodness, innocence – all the things I value most. All the things we're fighting for. And sometimes, oh God, do I need an anchor to hang onto.'

She was twisting and untwisting her handkerchief: 'I don't know what to say.'

'Don't say anything. Just give me a photo.'

'But it's cheating! Oh Jack, I don't want to hurt you. But I'm *not* your girl. I'm Otto's.'

Well, she *had* hurt me. And I'd every intention of hurting her. 'Don't you ever get tired', I said nastily, 'of disappointing people? Doesn't your heart ever get lonely: up there in your ivory tower?'

Her eyes filled with tears. She didn't try to hide them, but looked at me very straight. 'Yes, Jack, *some* people I hate disappointing. And yes, quite often, I'm very very lonely. But I made a promise: to the man I love. And I don't break promises, especially to him. It's as simple as that. I'm going to wait for Otto, no matter how long this terrible war goes on for. So *please*

91

don't make things more difficult than they have to be. . . .'

'All I asked for', I muttered, 'was a photograph. Not to sleep with you!'

She closed her eyes. 'Oh, damn and blast the photograph! If it means so much I'll send you one.' She looked at her watch. 'Gosh! I'm late!'

I walked back with her to the hospital.

A few yards short of the entrance she came to a halt. 'I hate quarrelling with you, Jack.' She gave a forced little laugh. 'It's like having a lovers' tiff. Without the fun of making it up!'

It was exactly what I had been thinking. 'I'll be good.'

She hesitated. 'Do you think you'll see Otto again?'

'Maybe.'

'You two', she said slowly, 'mean more to me than anything in the world. You won't' – her voice faltered – 'hurt one another?'

'Good lord, no!' I spoke with some vehemence; for hadn't our friendship come within an ace of getting me courtmartialled.

She gave me a shy little kiss. 'God bless you both.' A door opened and shut. For a moment I could hear the click-click-click of her heels on the flagstones, then I was alone in the dark, my fingers touching the spot where her lips had brushed my cheek.

Oh, if only she hadn't gone to that damned dance with Otto. If only I hadn't been so preoccupied that summer with my cricket and flying. If only I'd been the one to catch her as she emerged, wings spread, from the chrysalis of childhood. If only, if only, if only.

92

7

For my return flight to Saint Genis I was given the DH2. 'We've allocated it to Eight Squadron,' Tabor told me. 'For combat testing. It'll be the only one at the Front. So don't lose it!'

'Right, sir.'

'How do you like it, by the way?'

I hesitated.

'Come on lad!'

'Well, it's got a fine view! And a forward-firing gun. That'll help with the Fokkers. But it won't be a permanent answer. It hasn't got the performance.'

'You people want to make up your minds,' he grunted. 'Do you want a plane to fly? Or to fight?'

I didn't hesitate this time. 'We want it to fly, sir. If a plane has a good performance we can adapt it for fighting. If it's a mechanical cow it's useless – no matter how many guns we cram into it.'

'Hmmm! And of the planes you've flown, which would *you* like to see at the Front?'

'The Bristol Scout, sir. She's an absolute peach!'

He was making a note on his pad when a sudden gust of wind rattled the window, and the sky darkened. 'You happy about the weather? For flying back?'

'Oh yes,' I said casually. 'I know the way.'

Half-an-hour later, as I taxied to the end of the runway, I wished that I hadn't been quite so casual.

It was one of those mornings when you can see *too* far: when the clouds one moment are distant smudges and next moment fill the sky. Right now they were filling the sky, the wind was slamming this way and that, and the first big heavy drops of

93

rain were splashing onto the tarmac. But I'd been told to be back at Saint Genis by mid-day; and I feared Uncle more than I feared the elements.

I was soon made to pay for my stupidity. No sooner had I taken-off than I ran into a belt of low continuous cloud. I couldn't very well climb through it, for fear it extended above the DH2's ceiling; so I had to fly under it – a most unpleasant experience in driving rain and poor visibility. Water came pouring into the cockpit; the turbulence made us bob up and down like a cork; and to cap it all moisture must have got into the intake-pipes, because the engine started to cough uneasily. It occurred to me – rather belatedly – that I wouldn't be popular if the experimental DH2 and I ended upside down in a field. I decided to have a look at the North Downs, and if I couldn't see a way through to turn back. Well, there was a gap of sorts at Dorking. So I squeezed through. And this was the crossing of the Rubicon; because the cloud closed in behind me, and looking over my tail I saw that I couldn't now get back if I wanted to. I flew east along the railway line, telling myself that the weather was bound to improve. Instead it worsened. The rain grew heavier, visibility shrank to a claustrophobic circle, and I was forced to fly lower and lower – in one particular valley so low that I could read the name, PADDOCK WOOD, on a railway station.

Long before we hit the coast at Folkestone I was shivering with cold, drenched to the skin and frightened. Frightened, yet at the same time curiously excited. For the weather was a challenge: as much an adversary as a Fokker or Taube; if I was skilfull I'd get the better of it, if I wasn't it would get the better of me. I worked out a compass course for Calais and headed into the Channel.

In normal conditions it is safer to fly low over the sea than over the uneven contours of the land. But in bad visibility the meeting point of sea and sky is often ill-defined, and it is all too easy to misjudge one's height and fly slap into the water. And this is what I might well have done if it hadn't been for the fantastic view from the cockpit. Certainly as we neared the French

94

coast, it was the DH2's magnificent field of vision which saved my life. For my compass course was a bad one. We hit the coast not at the beaches of Calais, but at the cliffs of Boulogne.

I was skimming the waves, expecting any moment to see a nice reassuring line of sand-dunes, when a great wall of rock came rushing at me out of the murk. I flung the DH2 aside, and our wingtip scraped past an ugly-looking headland which disappeared *upwards* into cloud. It came to me, again rather belatedly, that I was in trouble. I waited for the compass to settle, then headed north, back to the safety of the open sea. I flew north for ten minutes, trying several times to gain height, but being always forced back to sea-level by the cloud. Then I turned east, reduced speed, and headed cautiously for the lower and more friendly beaches which ran up to the Belgian border. We seemed to take an unconscionable time to get there; but eventually we hit the coast, as luck would have it at a place I recognised: Dunkirk. I zig-zagged in through the sand-dunes and picked up the main road to Saint Omer. The rain was easing off now and the sky lightening. By the time I came to the valley of the Lys sunlight was glinting from puddles and roofs, and a rainbow was climbing out of the marshes, right next to the church at Saint Genis. I landed in a shower of spray, with nothing tangible to show for my adventures: only the wisdom that comes from having made a fool of myself, and survived.

Quite a few of the squadron came running out to have a look at the DH2. Among them were faces I didn't recognise – chaps straight from Flying School who looked even younger than I was. 'What's going on?' I asked the senior pilot.

He told me that in the three days I'd been away we had lost two planes. He gestured to the DH2: 'Is she any good?'

'We'll have to make the best we can of her,' I said. 'She's all we're getting.'

It was lucky for us that autumn that the Germans didn't have many Fokkers with synchronised guns; and especially lucky for us in Eight Squadron that we had our secret weapon, the DH2.

Uncle took it up within an hour of its arrival, and when he had put it through its paces he called a meeting of senior aircrew. To my surprise I was told to attend – I suppose because of my knowledge of our new plane.

We talked tactics late into the night. We would have liked to cut down on patrolling until we had a plane that could cope with the Fokkers. But Uncle was adamant: 'My orders', he said, 'are that "full patrolling will be maintained at all times. *No matter what the cost*". So as I see it there are only three possibilities. Heavier escorts. Formation flying. And the DH2.'

We hit on no panacea, though heaven knows we talked long enough! We did, however, work out a number of ideas which, in the weeks ahead, we did our best to put into practice. And our efforts were at least partially rewarded. For in September the squadrons north and south of us lost five and six planes respectively. We only one.

So day after day that autumn our reconnaissance patrols set out not individually but in strength: usually a trio of BE2s in close formation, with a couple of Nieuports above them in the sun to take care of marauding Fokkers, and as often as not the DH2 flying behind the main formation as bait. To start with there were a fair number of skirmishes; but after a while the Fokkers tended to leave us alone and take the easier pickings which were offered to them to the north and south. I think, however, we all knew in our hearts, that we'd won not a victory but a reprieve. A trial of strength was inevitable. And one November evening as we were on our way back from long reconnaissance, the Germans staged an ambush. Our escort were lured away, and the moment our BE2s were without protection they were jumped by a trio of Fokkers. The luckless reconnaissance planes were harried out of formation; a patrolling Morane from another squadron was drawn into the fight; our escort, realising they had been tricked, came rushing back; another trio of Fokkers appeared out of the sun; Archie started loosing off at friend and foe alike, and the sky which a moment before had been an empty playground became suddenly full of wheeling planes, stuttering guns and the acrid stench of cordite.

It was my first dogfight, and I didn't like it. I took a snap shot with my rifle at a passing Fokker, and hoped he didn't have a machine-gun to reply with. Since it seemed to be every man for himself, and I started to gain height. A blue-nosed Fokker (each of our adversaries from Ronchin, I noticed, had his cowling painted a different colour) rose out of the *mêlée*, apparently with the same idea. For perhaps half a minute we clawed skyward on near-parallel courses, and I found to my delight that I was out-climbing him. When I reckoned I was in a commanding position I levelled-off and grabbed my rifle. He rose obligingly into my sights. But in my excitement I fired too soon. And missed. I saw him flinch as my bullet ricocheted off the side of his cockpit. I was taking more careful aim, when there was a violent explosion and a hole appeared in the windshield about six inches from my head. I flung the Nieuport aside. And another Fokker, its cowling bright orange, went whistling past my tail. I was considerably put out! I wasn't in a good position for a shot at him. But I was going to try. Until something – was it the way the pilot sat, or the shape of his head, or the colour of his engine cowling? – made me at the last second jerk up my rifle so that the bullet passed harmlessly above him. Otto's carpet in his study at Charterhouse had been orange. He had sported an orange scarf. Orange was his favourite colour.

I didn't know if it was *really* him. Nor for the moment did I care. I was too busy trying to stay alive.

I'll never forget that first dogfight. The guns; the smoke; the way the earth looked, falling; wind in the wires; clouds seen upside-down at the top of a loop; the exhilaration; and the fear. Nor will I ever forget its aftermath, as that evening in the Mess those of us who had survived licked our wounds and counted our losses – one BE2 and one Nieuport shot down in flames; another BE2 crashlanding on the airfield, the pilots' feet shredded to pulp; four out of six planes damaged. It made us wonder what the future held for us: whether by the time the better planes we had been promised got through to the Front any of us would be alive to fly them.

That dogfight was the prelude to a long cold winter: a purgatory punctuated by rare and all too transitory moments of satisfaction.

One such moment was when I got Jessica's photograph. I opened it at breakfast, with a great rustling of paper, and it was passed round the Mess to the accompaniment of admiring whistles. I'd hardly dared hope she would write on it; but on the back she had scrawled: 'Jack – "for the sake of auld lang syne"' – which gave me the quite unmerited reputation of being a dark horse! It also gave me something to stare at in the nights when I needed a friend.

Another if very different moment of satisfaction came a couple of weeks later, when I was on the long patrol to Ostend.

It was a miserable day, with low cloud and intermittent drizzle. For most of the patrol I flew just under the nimbostratus, disappearing into it discreetly at the first hint of trouble. Then, on my way back, as I was crossing the Ypres salient, I spotted a solitary Fokker. I don't know what got into me! Perhaps I was bored. Perhaps in a DH2 I fancied my chances. Anyhow, this time I didn't dodge into cloud. I held course. Till the Fokker spotted me.

Like a flash he went into an Immelmann turn and came at me head on.

Now that told me quite a bit about both plane and pilot. The plane had a forward-firing gun; why else would it be coming at me head-on? And the pilot was experienced – for the turn had been smoothly executed – but over-confident; there had been no hesitation, no sizing me up, no identifying the type of aircraft I was flying; simply "there's an Allied plane let's get at it and shoot it down". So what was I going to do?

This was a facet of the war in the air that enthralled me: the ritual of single combat: sizing one's opponent up, neutralising his strength, cashing in on his weakness. Often in the months to come I was to find myself alone above the clouds with an enemy scout, locked in the sort of battle which only one of us could come out of alive. I'd circle him cautiously, watching how he flew, assessing the performance of his plane seeing him eyeing me and knowing that he too was calculating: two combatants keyed-up to the ultimate pitch of skill and endeavour, each wondering who in a few moments would be plunging to destruction, and who that night would be lying awake in bed, not wanting to remember, not able to forget? Sometimes before a shot was fired I'd have the feeling I was going to survive. I had that feeling now.

I played the novice. I pretended I hadn't seen him. I kept flying straight and level, and the two planes hurtled towards one another at something like 150 miles an hour. He must have thought me a sitting duck. But a split second before I reckoned he was going to fire I opened up with the Lewis.

With a clear field of vision and a forward-firing gun that he clearly wasn't expecting, I could hardly miss. My opening burst was a fraction high and to the right. My second hit him flush in the engine.

I thought he'd pass beneath me, falling. But as my bullets tore into him he must have hauled back on the stick; for the Fokker reared up in front of me, its gun blazing wild into the clouds, its belly exposed, It was no time to be squeamish. I kept firing. Splinters of metal and fabric were ripped off the dying plane like leaves from a tree. Then I had to ram the stick forward, as he passed, disintegrating, not a dozen feet over my head.

I hauled the DH2 round, ready to fire again. But there was no need.

For a second the Fokker hung near-motionless on its prop. Then it flicked over into a vertical dive. Above the roar of my engine and the clatter of the Fokker's gun, rose another and more terrible sound: the agonised high-pitched scream of a plane in its death-dive. It was all over in less time than it takes to describe. Down, down, down the Fokker plummeted. Faster, faster, faster. A wing was ripped from its body. Its tail disintegrated. And with a thud I could hear from three thousand feet, it buried itself in a field. There was a brief pyramid of flame, a thin column of smoke, and the German pilot was dead.

He was dead. But I was alive. Alive and filled with a fierce primordial elation. So the caveman must have felt as he beat his rival's brains out on the Paleolithic rocks, or the knight as he drove his lance into his opponent's heart. And yet mixed up with my elation was another and very different feeling. Sadness. Sadness at the death of a fellow airman: sadness, and the knowledge that there but for the grace of God went I.

As I headed back for Saint Genis, I told myself that I ought to be feeling jolly pleased with myself. But it didn't work that way. By the time I landed I was bathed in sweat, feeling slightly sick, and in no mood for the welcome awaiting me – news of my victory had apparently been telephoned through from the trenches. I made my report then shut myself in my cabin, like an animal wanting to hide.

I sat on my bed and tried to sort things out. I asked myself whether what I had done was good or bad? I stared at the photograph of Jessica and asked myself what *she* would have thought? I looked out of my porthole, saw the cloud had lifted and the evening sky was quietly beautiful, and asked myself could it be right to turn God's heaven into a battleground where men burnt one another to death?

I asked myself a lot of questions that evening. But to some of them I just couldn't find an answer. So I went back to the mess and got drunk.

A lot of us got drunk a lot of the time that winter. There didn't seem to be much else to do – unless you visited the Mademoiselles in Armentières; and as far as I was concerned the thought of having to pay for it took the gilt off the gingerbread. So in the evenings we'd give one another 'shampoos' of champagne-and-whisky, squirt one another with soda syphons, play leap-frog over the dining-room tables, and sing:

"Another little drink, another little drink
Another little drink won't do us any harm."

And if you ask why we did it, the answer of course is to forget.

To forget that after the boozing would come the dreams and after the dreams would come another day when once again we'd be flying 'the mechanical cow' or 'the spinning incinerator' across the trenches to where the Fokkers with their synchronised guns would be waiting. To forget that every week new faces appeared in the Mess, and old faces vanished.

One way of ending our purgatory occurred to us after a particularly hellish patrol, when a pair of Fokkers had harried us almost back to Saint Genis. Sergeant Johnson and I were ruefully examining the bullet holes in our fuselage, when he said almost apologetically: 'Do you know, sir, how we used to deal with wasps? In mother's shop?'

'How?'

'Burn out the nest.'

I thought about it: 'You mean we ought to try and set fire to the Fokkers? At Ronchin?'

'That's the ticket, sir. With bombs.'

It may sound elementary today; but in 1915 the idea was something of an innovation. We went to see Uncle.

He wasn't exactly full of enthusiasm, but at least he gave us permission to experiment; and early one morning about a week later three of us mounted a 'surprise' raid on Saint Genis, fairly plastering the hangars with toilet rolls. Uncle was impressed. He got the go-ahead from Trenchard. And we were in business.

So in the short winter evenings, with the trenches knee-deep in mist and the western sky ablaze with the most spectacular sunsets, we experimented with different planes, different bombs, different ways of dropping them and different methods of attack; until we hit at last on what seemed an effective combination. All we needed now was clear sky and luck.

It was bitterly cold on the afternoon of November 18th, and the sky was clear. We took off at 4 p.m. Half a dozen BE2s, with our luckless observers in the front cockpits surrounded by phosphorous bombs which they intended to defuse and toss out by hand, a trio of Nieuports to take care of any Fokkers that got airborne, and myself in the DH2 to take care of machine-gun positions round the airfield. Archie, we hoped, wouldn't bother

101

us; for we hoped to come in out of a setting sun at ground level.

With Uncle leading we went winging east like an echelon of low-flying duck. . . . The Lys, I remember, looked especially beautiful as we passed over it, its banks aglow in the sunset, and the reflections of its poplars bending and breaking as plane after plane flew low over the quiet water. . . . Our first hurdle was the trenches. Those in the front of the formation managed to get across without a shot being fired; but those in the rear weren't so lucky, and the last plane but one took a burst of rifle-fire in its engine. The pilot would have been well advised to turn back; but with more valour than discretion he came limping after us, coughing gouts of jet-black smoke.

As we neared Lille conditions became difficult. It was a still evening; drifts of mist and smoke clung like dirty snow to the approaches of the city, visibility dropped to a couple of hundred yards, and among the maze of roads and railway lines we lost our way. Uncle admitted afterwards that he was about to give up and head for home, when the airfield loomed suddenly out of the murk: not where we'd been expecting it, ahead, but at right angles to the course we were flying. So much for our hope of coming in out of the sun! But at least we'd be able to drop our bombs.

What happened next has all the vividness and incoherence of a nightmare. Uncle turned away, with the idea of circling and coming in with the sun behind us. But the pilot next to him, thinking he must have been hit and was making for home, continued to head straight for the airfield. Some of us followed one plane, some the other. Our attack was piecemeal and unco-ordinated.

I saw a BE2 diving low over the hangars; I saw its bombs tossed out one after another, twisting and turning in the air, to explode along the edge of the hard-standing. Another BE2 made for a line of aircraft parked in the open. They looked to me more like Taubes than Fokkers; but at least they were German. Bombs burst among them. I saw an undercarriage collapse; but there were no direct hits and no sign of the hoped-for fires. Then I spotted a machine-gun on the edge of the airfield, the flash from its muzzle bright orange against the darkening sky. I dived on it. The gunner didn't see me till I was almost on top of him. He was a brave man. He didn't run. He tried desperately to swivel his gun toward me. But before he could fire, I gave him a burst with the Lewis. He flung up his arms and fell backwards, blood pouring from what had once been his face like water out of a tap. I hauled the DH2 round, trying desperately to tell myself that he hadn't been a man like me, only the anonymous Enemy. I can recall exactly how the airfield looked at that moment: one BE2 directly over the hangars in the act of dropping its bombs, two more coming in low over the perimeter, the Nieuports hovering overhead, and the Germans rushing this way and that, some seeking shelter, but most making purposefully for gun-emplacement or plane. Then, in an instant, the picture changed. The BE2 over the hangars vanished, and in its place there appeared as if by magic a monstrous yellow flower. One moment the plane was whole: next moment, as the phosphorous bombs in its cockpit exploded, it was metamorphosed to a myriad incandescent particles of fabric and wood, flesh and metal, bone and blood. For a second it hung like some exotic firework in the sky. Then it crashed blazing into a building behind the hangars. I know that everyone didn't *really* stand rooted to the spot in horror, that the planes didn't *really* hang motionless in the sky, that the guns didn't *really* seize up at the moment of firing. But that's what it seemed like. Just for a second. Then, as though violence itself was an opiate, the guns redoubled their clatter, more BE2s came swooping down on the hangars, and I found myself blazing away in mindless fury at a line of trenches, where men in grey-green uniforms were firing with parade ground precision at the planes. I raked the trenches from end to end. First from left to right, then from right to left. Until I suddenly realised there were no more BE2s coming in, the Nieuports were wheeling away, the attack was over.

I was the last to leave. As I scuttled hastily after the others, collecting more flak round my tail than I cared for, I passed almost directly over the building behind the hangars which had been set on fire by the burning aircraft. It looked like a farm-house; and at the back of it were a row of pens, like open stables, surrounded by high wooden walls. The pens were ablaze, and I remember thinking it lucky that the Germans hadn't kept horses in them. Then I saw something I didn't care for. In one of the pens there *was* an animal – it looked like a large dog – ringed by fire: trapped. Even as I stared at it, it leapt despairingly at one of the walls, fell back, and rolled over and over, its coat ablaze. I was so shaken that I didn't see the machine-gun em-placement. I flew slap over it.

Bullets ripped through the floor of the cockpit about nine inches from my feet, sliced through the instrument panel and knocked the Lewis-gun off its mounting. Then I was snaking away through a line of poplars. More by luck than judgment, I was alive. But I wouldn't, I told myself, stay alive much longer if I didn't concentrate. What if some luckless animal *had* been burnt to death? There was nothing *I* could do about it. It would, I decided, be suicide to go limping after the others, run-ning into every machine-gun position they had alerted. I throt-tled back, to reduce noise and the strain on the engine, and headed south. And once again luck was with me. After a long but uneventful detour I recrossed the lines not far from Loos, and crept back to Saint Genis long after the sun had set and the others had given me up for lost.

We were a glum little gathering that night in the Mess. Ten planes had taken-off. Only seven had returned; and one of these had crash-landed on the airfield with the pilot so badly wounded that he had died before we could lift him out of the cockpit. And it was pretty obvious that the raid hadn't been the success we had hoped for.

This was confirmed next morning, when our reconnaissance plane came back with photographs. Ronchin, apart from one charred building, looked very much as it had looked before. The hangars had been patched up, the craters had been filled in, the Fokkers had been wheeled out undamaged from wher-ever they had been hidden. It seemed hardly worth the loss of four good planes and six good men.

Uncle warned us to be on the *qui vive* for reprisals. And sure enough about a week later the Germans mounted a return raid on Saint Genis. They attacked at sunrise rather than sunset, and they used fighters rather than bombers. Apart from this, their raid was much the same as ours: they suffered comparatively heavy losses, we suffered comparatively little damage.

There was, however, an aftermath which, in a way, caused rather a lot of damage.

After the German planes had vanished and our guns had fallen silent, we discovered that one of the Fokkers had left a visiting card. The wreath and the cross must, I think, have been joined together when they were flung out of the plane; but the cross had broken as it hit the ground and lay in fragments in the long wet grass at the edge of the river. When we pieced it together we saw that it had an inscription: 'Jessie. RIP.' We were wondering what to make of this when a mechanic spotted the envelope, half-buried in the yew and holly of the wreath. The envelope was marked 'J. A. Cunningham'. The writing was Otto's.

I opened it in the privacy of my cabin.

Otto's letter was short and to the point.

'*Jack,*

Much benefit has your cowardly attack brought to you and your colleagues.

No military installations suffered damage. But I wish you to know that your fire bombs caused the death of four elderly women, none of them German, who worked in our kitchens. Also the death by burning of my Alsatian bitch Jessie, who was in pup.

Is this what you so-called English gentlemen call "playing the game"?

May God forgive you. I can not.

Otto.'

That evening I went for a walk by the river.

The leaves had fallen from the poplars, the reeds on the riverbank had withered and died, the ground was hard with frost. It

105

was winter. The year was dying. And with it were dying many of the ideals and loyalties which in the early days of the war we had brought with us to the Front: ideals and loyalties which, in our innocence, we had worn like armour believing it could never be pierced. But the armour was wearing thin. I was sorry – very, very sorry – about Otto's dog. But there were worse tragedies in wartime, I told myself, than losing an animal. There was no need for him to make such a fuss.

8

The ebb and flow of aerial warfare over the Western Front was like the pattern of the sea, a succession of crests and troughs. When our planes were better than the Germans' we were on a crest; when theirs were better than ours we were in a trough. That winter we were in a trough: a slough of despond, which two out of three of our squadron failed to live through.

We were Fokker fodder.

Now the Fokker wasn't all that spectacular as a plane – its performance was no better than that of a Nieuport, DH2 or Morane. It was its forward-firing machine-gun that made it so formidable. Give one man a machine-gun and another a rifle, it's obvious who'll walk away. So our opposite numbers from Ronchin had the whip-hand that winter. Their tactics were simple. They divided the Front into segments which they took it in turn to patrol; and woe betide the BE2 or formation of BE2s which ventured into their territory. After a while we got to know the German pilots as individuals. Most to be feared was their CO, Max Immelmann ('Blue Max' we called him, partly because we knew he'd been awarded the coveted medal, and partly because blue was the colour of his cowling). Another pilot nobody wanted to meet was 'The Old Red Fox', Carl Bungert, who had an unpleasant habit of materialising out of cloud, shooting his opponent down and disappearing as mysteriously as he had arrived. Nor did anyone fancy tangling with Otto who flung his orange-nosed Fokker about the sky with a panache that bordered on bravura.

What, I wondered, would I do if we met a second time somewhere above the trenches? A few months ago we had laughed and waved. Laughing and waving wouldn't be so easy now. But the alternative was unthinkable.

Towards the end of January we got another DH2, the first of the replacements we had been promised.

Uncle decided that from now on as new aircraft arrived they would be allocated to individual pilots. Since I was given the latest DH2 this suited me very well! And as soon as I'd got her stripped, trimmed and rigged to my satisfaction, I decided to try an experiment. I set my alarm for 6.30. . . . Morning after morning the bell would wake me, I'd peer out of my porthole and see the canopy of mist-cum-cloud and climb back, half-disappointed, half-relieved, to bed. Until one morning conditions were perfect: no mist, no rain, no more than a mare's tail of cloud.

I took off half-an-hour before dawn. It was nearly the last take-off I ever made. For the poplars lining the Lys came rushing at me out of the murk like a line of indignant giants – I can have cleared them by only a few inches. Nor when I was airborne were my troubles over; for I couldn't find a horizon to fly by. Gradually, however, as my eyes grew accustomed to the gloom, I got the DH2 under control and settled her into a more or less steady climb. Soon I was at 8,000 feet, flying half-in and half-out of a skein of strato-cumulus which was drifting obligingly eastward over the Front. By eight o'clock I was in position, deep in enemy-occupied territory, half-hidden by cloud, waiting for the Fokkers as they, I hoped, would soon be waiting for the BE2s.

I had hoped that I might be able to spot them as they took-off from Ronchin; but either my eyesight wasn't as good as I reckoned or cloud got in the way. For the first I saw of them was a solitary Fokker, climbing, only a couple of thousand feet below me. I altered course to get behind him, and dodged into cloud.

All I had time to notice was the colour of his cowling. It was green. So it wasn't, thank heavens, Otto. Nor was it one of the *élite*. Just an ordinary pilot. Like me.

Just an ordinary man – probably not much more than a boy –

and I was going to kill him. Deliberately. In cold blood. I adjusted the Lewis, and told myself that those who live in the jungle must dance to the beat of its drum. All the same I couldn't help wondering what sort of a person he was. Did he have a wife perhaps, or, like my sergeant-observer, a mother who depended on him, or a girl, someone like Jessica, who asked God every night to watch over him? . . . As I edged out of cloud I saw he had levelled off, not five hundred feet below me. He was shading his eyes: looking west to where our BE2s would soon be rising, like duck to the fowler's gun, out of the marshes.

He should have looked east! Back over his shoulder to where death was stalking him out of the strato-cumulus.

I stole down on him quietly out of the canopy of cloud, engine cut, the DH2 rock-steady, his back growing larger and larger till it seemed to fill the whole circle of my sights. When I was no more than a dozen yards from his tail, I took a deep breath to stop myself trembling.

Suddenly, as though at the last second he heard the scythe of death hissing down on him, he looked round.

He was no older than me. I had a glimpse of a dark good-looking face, brown eyes, a green scarf to match the colour of his cowling, and before my finger had tightened on the trigger, he had flung the Fokker onto its side. He was desperately quick. But not quick enough. The bullets which should have torn into his body missed him by inches and ripped into his engine. There was a violent explosion. A gout of smoke. And the Fokker flicked into a spin.

It wasn't a vertical spin. It was a slow flat spin: the sort of spin certain aircraft can never get out of (for no matter how violently the controls are slammed this way and that there isn't sufficient airflow over the surfaces to induce control). So the Fokker spun slowly down. Dying foot by foot. Round and round, down and down: from something like 7,000 feet to something like 5,000 feet. Then a tongue of flame licked out of the shattered engine.

'Please, God.' I whispered. 'No.'

But God probably thought it wasn't very logical of me to try one moment to shoot the German pilot in the back, and next moment to pray for him. The flames spread. They spread slowly, charring first a little of one wing, then a little of the other. Then a little of the fuselage. Then a little of the cockpit.

I shut my eyes.

But no matter how tight I shut them I could still in my mind see the handsome young pilot, wreathed in smoke, licked in flame, being burnt slowly and with terrible certainty to death. Since he couldn't get out of the spin, and since neither British nor German pilots were allowed to wear parachutes, there wasn't a thing he could do about it.

It took about three and a half minutes for him to spin burning from 5,000 feet to the ground. I don't know if he lived that long. I hope not. But he might, I suppose, have still been clinging in agony to life as his Fokker crashed blazing into a field.

As he hit the ground, sweat burst out from every pore of my body. I started shaking and couldn't stop.

I've no recollection of hauling the DH2 round and heading for cloud; but I must, I suppose, have sought its shelter like a child who knows it has done something terrible and wants to hide. . . . And it was a funny thing. It was as though I was back in the Longhorn, and Sergeant Parker was shouting at me, fiercely, over and over again: 'If you want to stay alive, *don't* go into a daydream. *Don't* go into a daydream. *Don't* go into a daydream.' I was played-out, emotionally and physically, and I'd have liked nothing better than for Sergeant Parker to take over the plane. But his voice grew louder, sharper, more and more urgent.

Frightened, I came-to with a start, and began to scan the sky as he had taught me, section by section. And saw, not five hundred feet below me, another Fokker, sunlight refracted like a parhelion from the orange of its cowling.

Otto von Searle was climbing fast, trying to cut me off before I escaped into cloud. I know it sounds fanciful, but his Fokker, with the parhelion slung round it like a halo, reminded me of an avenging angel: an angel with sword: an angel of death. Every quiver of its fuselage, every thrust of its wings, every revolution

110

of its propeller seemed to be crying out for retribution. And it came to me in a moment of clairvoyance that the pilot I'd killed had been Otto's friend.

I fled.

It was lucky for me I was above him, and close to cloud. As the first coils of white came swirling like smoke past the cockpit, Otto was still more than three hundred feet below me. He must have known I was out of range; but he opened up in fury, his bullets whistling harmlessly far beneath me. Then I was lost in the miasma of the strato-cumulus: a womb of darkness in which he had little hope of finding me.

But I was taking no chances. I turned by compass towards what I reckoned was the heart of the cloud, making like an animal in danger for the centre of a thicket. When I reckoned I was there, I throttled back – so as to fly as slowly as possible – and turned east – the direction in which the cloud was drifting – and held the DH2 steady, as close to stalling as I dared. And waited. And waited. And waited.

I nearly waited too long.

When I emerged from the strato-cumulus three-quarters of an hour later there was no sign of Otto. But I was lost. Deep over enemy-occupied territory. And I'd used up the better part of my fuel.

The gods, however, must have been watching over me that morning. Almost at once I spotted the long straight stretch of the railway line that runs from Ath to Lille, and as soon as I knew where I was it was relatively simple to find my way back to Saint Genis.

As I was taxying up to the hangars my engine coughed briefly and died. When the mechanics looked in the fuel tank there wasn't enough petrol to cover a sixpence.

I wasn't looking forward that night to going to sleep.

I sat in my cabin until well after midnight, writing letters and listening to the same old fox-trots and waltzes over and over again on the gramophone. I kept the gramophone low in the hope that it wouldn't disturb the chaps next door; but at 1 a.m. one of them started banging on the wall; so I turned the

111

gramophone off and started playing patience. As the hours passed the cards seemed to get more difficult to shuffle, the games harder to complete.

When my batman came in at eight in the morning he found me dead to the world, fully dressed, slumped over the patience cards.

I may not have slept very much that night. But I didn't dream.

In spite of its sterling qualities I never got really fond of the DH2, and I'd sometimes let one of the less experienced pilots take it up while I did a turn at artillery spotting. My observer on these latter occasions was the self-effacing Johnson; and it seemed like a routine job the two of us embarked on that February afternoon – reporting the fall of shot for our local battery. It was a fine day, which meant that the Fokkers would probably be waiting; but as the canny Johnson pointed out we ought to be able to observe the fall of shot from our side of the trenches – 'No need is there, sir,' he muttered as we walked out together to the "mechanical cow", 'to stick our necks out!' (A lot of people thought Johnson a coward, but in my opinion he simply had a well-developed sense of self-preservation, and to give him his due I don't think he was afraid so much of dying, as of what would happen if he *did* die to his invalid mother and her shop in the Mile End Road.) We took off a little after mid-day, and soon located our target: a derelict farmhouse about three miles inside the German lines which Intelligence apparently reckoned was being used as an ammunition dump. There was no sign of the Fokkers. But Archie was unpleasantly accurate; no matter how often and how violently I altered course, the shells seemed to follow us like filings to a magnet.

When we were more or less in position, Johnson unwound his aerial, a long piece of copper wire with a weight at the end of it, and started hammering away in Morse to the battery – telling them, I sincerely hoped, to get a move on. And they certainly obliged. Our key had barely stopped clicking, when a fountain of earth spurted up in front of the farm. Johnson sucked his teeth in disapproval, and tapped out the code for 400 left, 300 short. There followed a pause that seemed interminable while the battery adjusted its sights, and I weaved this way and that to stop Archie getting our range. (Our *Manual of Instruction* required us to 'observe the fall of shot by flying slowly straight and level immediately above the target'. But aircrew who followed these instructions too precisely usually found that their first stint of artillery spotting was also their last!) The battery's second shot was closer, but still to the left and short: exactly how short it was difficult to see. Johnson started peering at the sky, section by section. We were both pretty experienced at this sort of thing, and I could read his mind like a book. If we stayed on the British side of the trenches we couldn't observe the fall of shot accurately, it might take quite a while for the battery to obtain a direct hit, and all the time we were spotting we'd be Archied. If on the other hand we crossed to the German side of the trenches we could observe the fall of shot with precision, the battery would quickly achieve a hit and we could be heading for home – always provided of course we hadn't been spotted by a Fokker. I hammered on the fuselage, and pointed to the German trenches. Johnson took another careful look at the sky and nodded.

As we approached the farm, the ack-ack grew even heavier, as though the shells were massing to protect a strongpoint. German shells, in those days, contained a high proportion of black cordite; when they burst they left in their wake a residue of evil-smelling vapour, and this was now coalescing into a layer thick enough to obscure the target. So keeping an extremely sharp lookout for Fokkers, I headed for the clearer sky in the east: even farther behind the lines.

We never saw the battery's third shot; but their fourth was a beauty: spot on for direction and no more than thirty yards short.

Johnson was tapping out what we hoped would be a final correction, when there was the most appalling crash. Engine, cowling and windshield disappeared in a kaleidoscope of smoke and stars. And the BE2 reared up like a terrified horse, pawed for a second at the sky, then flopped over, controls slack, into an incipient spin. The shell must have burst within a few feet of the propeller.

I'd never thought it would happen to me. Not like this. Death in combat with a Fokker I was prepared for. But not to be blasted out of the sky by some anonymous gunner I couldn't see.

I rammed the stick forward. I kicked the rudder as hard as I could in the direction we were turning. And the BE2 trembled; hung for a moment like a ship in irons; then plunged not, thank God, into a spin but a dive. So we were under some sort of control. The engine, however, was dead: dead beyond hope of resurrection. The prop had been blown clean away, the cowling was blackened and buckled, and the engine itself was giving off the most terrifying clatter and great gouts of jet black smoke. It would never fire again. But it could easily *catch* fire. I flicked off the magneto switch.

I was quick. But not quick enough. My hand was still on the switch, when a tongue of flame came snaking out of the cowling.

I remembered the Fokker pilot. And screamed. Then something seemed to go click in my brain, and I found myself analysing the situation with clinical detachment. There must be *something* I could do . . . I kept the BE2 in a dive. The airspeed built up. The flames lengthened. They burst through the shattered windshield. They came licking like white hot whips at my eyes. I flung up a hand to guard my face. And crossed the controls.

The BE2 quivered like a struck salmon, hung for a moment as though suspended in mid-air, then keeled over into a violent sideslip. And the flames, caught by a torrent of air from an unexpected direction, were whipped away from the cockpit, were fragmented and then, as if by a miracle, buffeted out.

It was almost too good to be true. But if the worst danger had been averted a dozen remained. For we were still deep in enemy territory, falling crippled out of the sky, in our wake an ever-lengthening ribbon of smoke. The ack-ack had died away; and I

114

could picture the German gunners staring at us, shading their eyes, part-elated, part-pitying, wholly-fascinated, wondering how we were going to die – would the flames restart, would our wings be ripped off, or would we plunge meteor-like into the earth? So long as they thought we were crashing out of control, I reckoned they wouldn't fire. Which gave us one small and all too slender chance. I didn't dare pull out of the dive, because with no engine we'd have been a sitting target; but fractionally and I hoped imperceptibly I altered the angle and direction of our dive: towards the trenches, till we were plummeting like an injured skua straight for the German front line.

I didn't pull out till we were a hundred feet from the ground. For a moment I thought I'd left it too late, for the plane was travelling so fast the controls were stiff and slow to react. The ground came hurtling up at us. Figures in grey flung themselves into the mud. I could have sworn our wheels actually grazed the sandbags on the frontline parapet. Then, still travelling at over a hundred miles an hour, but losing speed every second we went scuttling at zero feet over the lunar landscape between the lines.

The Germans had been so convinced we were crashing, we were halfway across before a burst of fire from rifles and machine-guns came whistling round our tail – I could hear bullets clinking and thudding into the fuselage unpleasantly close to my back. I tried to weave. But with no engine we hadn't the speed. With every second the ground beneath us was moving more and more slowly. The plane began to shudder like a man with ague. And we were still a hundred yards from the British lines. A crater loomed up ahead: a great pit blasted out of the earth by an accumulation of explosions. I hauled back the stick. And we stalled, and slid tail-first into the crater.

There was a splintering crash, a shower of evil-smelling water, and the most horrible squelching-cum-sucking, as we settled broken-backed into the mud.

I sat in what was left of the cokpit, numb with shock, not daring to believe I was still alive. It was several seconds before I focused on Johnson's face peering at me anxiously as he tugged at my harness. 'Hop out, sir. Quick. In case she goes up.'

115

Knowing his obsession with survival I was touched that he'd stayed to help me. My back was stiff and curiously numb. Johnson had to half-haul half-lift me out of the cockpit; and when I tried to stand my knees buckled and I collapsed facedown in the mud.

The mud clutched at me like a ravenous animal. It dragged me down. It sealed up my mouth, my nostrils, my eyes. For a moment too terrifying to describe I felt I was being suffocated to death. Then, choking and retching, with Johnson's arms round my waist, I tore myself free.

'You been hit, sir?' The Sergeant's voice seemed to come from curiously far away.

I spat out a mouthful of water and mud, and said I was all right. Then, Johnson supporting me, we floundered away from the BE2. But we needn't have worried. There was no explosion – I suppose the poor old Cow was so sodden that nothing short of a flame-thrower would have touched her off. Panting for breath and dripping mud like a couple of prehistoric animals, we took stock of our surroundings.

The crater was like a medieval woodcut of hell. A pit. No colour. No movement. No life. At the bottom of it the evil-smelling water, stained by chemicals, fouled by gas; on the side of it the BE2 impaled like some dying monster, one wing folded beneath it, one raised in supplication to the sky; and overhead the Furies, the whine of bullets and the crump of shells. 'Christ!' Johnson muttered. 'It's worse than Mile End on a Saturday night!'

We were wondering what on earth to do next, when a great booming voice echoed and re-echoed round the crater. 'You airmen! You all right?' Someone with a megaphone was hailing us from the British lines.

'Yes,' I shouted back. 'We're OK.'

'Stay where you are. And keep your heads down. We'll send a patrol to bring you in.'

'Thanks awfully! Jolly good of you!'

'And bring a stretcher,' Johnson shouted unexpectedly. 'The pilot's been hit.'

116

I was rounding on him in exasperation, when my legs gave way, and he had for the second time to haul me out of the mud. It was funny. All I was conscious of was a dull ache at the base of my spine, but when I put my hand there, it came away red and wet. I immediately felt a great deal worse!

Johnson was grinning all over his face: 'Lucky it wasn't a couple of inches lower, sir!'

'Perhaps,' I said hopefully, 'I've got a Blighty one' – I had a fleeting but enjoyable vision of Jessica tending the wounded hero.

Johnson shook his head. 'Reckon all they'll give you for that is a cushion. And we'll be back on bloody dawn patrol . . . Shall I destroy the plane, sir?'

I shook my head. 'We'd better wait for the patrol. If Jerry sees smoke it'll give him something to range on.'

Johnson nodded, and we settled down to a nerve-racking wait.

It wasn't easy to sit and do nothing. We were in an alien world; the crater was claustrophobic; the silence was eerie, long spells of absolute quiet broken by the crack of a rifle or machine-gun so sudden it made us jump. It wasn't long before Johnson had a thought he didn't care for: 'Sir. . . .'

'Hmmm?'

'Suppose Jerry's sending a patrol too.'

'We're closer to the British lines,' I said. 'Our chaps'll get here first.'

'All the same, I think I'll do a recce.'

'For Christ's sake,' I said, 'be careful. The chap said keep our heads down.'

Johnson climbed cautiously to the lip of the crater. He raised his head: for no more than a fraction of a second, then jerked it down like a jack-in-the-box. Then he crawled a little way round the perimeter and did the same again. Only this time instead of jerking his head down he sort of jerked it back: jerked it back and flung up his arms and fell stiff as a board into the water at the bottom of the crater.

I tried to jump up; but my legs folded beneath me for the

third time, and I had to scramble on hands and knees to where he lay.

I felt certain he was dead. But when I got to him I found his eyes were open and he was trying to speak. I cradled his head in my lap. The bullet had smashed open the upper part of his skull, and I could see there was nothing I or anyone else could do for him.

'Mother,' he whispered. 'Mother.'

'It's all right, Johnson,' I said. 'I'll look after your mother.'

He was trying, I think, to say 'thank you'. But all that came out of his mouth was a trickle of blood, and his eyes grew wider and wider until they went sightless.

I was still sitting half-in-and half-out of the water, utterly numb, his head in my lap, when the patrol came slithering into the crater.

The sergeant in charge didn't take long to size things up. 'Leave 'im be, sir. And let's be 'aving you in the stretcher.'

'I can manage,' I muttered. 'Put *him* in the stretcher.'

'Afraid he's past 'elp, sir.'

'I'll not leave him,' I said. 'Take us both. Or clear off.'

The sergeant's eyes were sympathetic. 'You was buddies, sir?'

'Best bloody observer I ever had. His mother's got a shop. In the Mile End Road.'

'If he was a good bloke, sir, 'e'd *want* you to leave him. Soon as we start back, mark my words, Fritz'll be shelling, and we'll be runnin'. A dead man on a stretcher, and you 'obbling, sir, that would hold us up. Get the lot of us killed.'

It made sense, and I knew it. Yet the thought of leaving poor Johnson unburied, his body slowly putrefying as it sank into the mud, filled me with revulsion. 'God,' I muttered. 'This is a bloody war.'

'Right, sir. Stretcher!'

The patrol consisted of three privates and a couple of stretcher-bearers: nondescript figures in khaki who seemed to have no volition of their own, but did the sergeant's bidding like sheep under the eye of a dog. As they loaded me onto a

118

stretcher, the sergeant outlined our plan of campaign. He would, he explained, lob a grenade onto the BE2, and the moment it exploded we were to make a dash, crater by crater, for the British lines. 'And them that wants to stay alive,' he added, '*move*! And if Fritz starts shellin' don't run straight; 'ead left for them abandoned trenches. Right?'

'Right, sarge.'

He took a grenade from his belt, pulled out the pin, and lobbed it with mathematical precision into the cockpit of the BE2. As it exploded, we scrambled out of the crater.

And all hell descended on us.

If I'd been more *au fait* with the tactics of trench warfare I'd have realised that the Germans were bound to be expecting us, that they'd been playing cat and mouse in the hope of nailing both rescuers and rescued. The moment we emerged, machine-guns and rifles opened up from the German lines. Our guns replied. Then came the whine and crump of mortars, and the ground ahead seemed to well up in an effervescence of rising and falling mud. A shell burst less than a dozen yards in front of us. 'Left!' the sergeant bellowed. 'To the left!' The stretcher-bearers, like puppets jerked by a string, changed direction, very nearly tipping me out. I can't say I was enjoying myself. My back ached; my legs were numb; the whole world seemed to be disintegrating in a maelstrom of noise and pain. Then, we were half-falling half-slithering into a trench.

Or rather what had once been a trench and was now little more than an abandoned ditch knee-deep in slime. There was a sudden avalanche of earth, a bellow of alarm, and the sergeant came sliding down on top of us. Arms flailing, he lost his balance, and with a smack like an exploding grenade, fell flat on his face in the mud. His men were quick to laugh, but quicker, I noticed, to help him to his feet. The stretcher-bearer's voice was dead pan. 'Make you more beautiful than ever, sarge. My missus swears by a mud pack!'

His expletives were lost in a crescendo of shelling.

Now I can't remember how long we stayed in that ditch, while overhead the bullets whined, the shells moaned, and the grenades exploded with a crash that almost perforated our ear-drums. Nor can I remember much about our journey back through the maze of abandoned trenches, and our final hair-raising sprint for the British lines. For one of the stretcher-bearers had given me morphia.

What I *can* remember, very clearly, is everyone's mixture of concern and hilarity over my 'wound'. I had been almost mir-aculously lucky. It must have been a spent bullet that hit me: either a ricochet or a bullet whose velocity had been exhausted as it ploughed the length of the BE2's fuselage. It had come out through the pilot's seat, sliced a shallow groove across my left buttock and come to rest against the base of my spine. So you'll appreciate why, in years to come, if I was asked where I was wounded, I gave an evasive answer!

By the time I'd been carried into a dugout and a doctor had extracted the bullet, it was too late for me to return that evening to Saint Genis. So I spent the night in the front line.

It was a night I shall never forget. I wasn't in pain – except when I lay in certain positions – but the morphia had made me sick and dopy, and half the time I wasn't sure if I was dreaming or awake. I remember taking stock of my surroundings: the sand-bags, the shored-up walls, the flickering candles, the eter-nally brewing pot of tea, and these were real. Then the walls seemed to waver and be metamorphosed to those of a tumble-down cottage, the timbers over my head turned into the branches of an apple tree, and Will Willcock was peering down at me, his eyes reproachful: 'I told 'ee, zurr,' he was saying, 'no good would come o' taking the king's shilling!'

I remember other things too: the smell of sweat-damp-clothes-and-paraffin, the claustrophobia, the rat running over my face, and faintly from somewhere beyond the dugout the man sobbing away a night which must have seemed to him as endless as to me.

But nothing *really* goes on for ever. And light at last came seeping in through the half-open door, and the men in the dugout yawned and rolled out of their bunks, asked how I felt, made yet another pot of tea and started looking at their watches

120

and talking about the dawn barrage. At dawn, I gathered, the Germans invariably put down a two-minute deluge of shellfire. I looked at the roof of the dugout, and wondered if I wouldn't prefer to take my chances in the open. But the barrage, when it came, turned out to be an anti-climax. For the Germans, that morning, didn't shell the trenches but the ammunition dumps and artillery positions behind the lines. For exactly two minutes the guns roared, the shells whined, the ground shook. Then, as abruptly as it had started, the barrage lifted. And the men in the dugout relaxed and began to talk of everyday things – like getting me back to Saint Genis.

They offered me a stretcher for which I was grateful, but I said I was well able to walk – at least to a spot where transport from the airfield could pick me up; so they gave me a guide, and the two of us made our way through the secondline trenches, the support trenches and the communication trenches, until we came to a field bordered by a shell-pitted road. Here my guide and I parted company. We wished one another 'Good luck!', and he headed back for the trenches. I took my hat off to him! One night had been more than enough for me!

As we had come into the field I'd noticed three men in uniform, resting on a grass bank by the side of the road. Since I didn't fancy sitting down, I walked across to them, hoping for a chat. As I got nearer, however, I saw they were asleep, dead to the world in the pale winter sunshine. The one in the middle had a startling resemblance to Otto.

I stared at him. And the more I stared, the more startling the likeness became. It was uncanny. He had the same wiry physique, the same straight blond hair, the same classical features. For a moment I had the ridiculous idea that maybe Otto had turned spy and crossed the lines disguised as a private soldier! Then I began to realise that there was something not quite right about the sleeping figures; they were too still, too stiff, and surely it was too cold for them to be sleeping in the open? I looked more closely, and saw the bluebottles crawling across their mouths and their unblinking eyes.

I turned away, shivering.

121

For a moment I was numb with shock. Then, as the shock began to wear off, I wondered. Perhaps I ought to have another look, to make sure the man in the middle wasn't *really* Otto? I steeled myself to go back, to kneel by his side, to peer closely into his face. The bluebottles, disturbed, rose in a reluctant swarm; and I was able to satisfy myself that though the likeness was remarkable the dead man wasn't Otto von Searle.

My first reaction was relief. But as I walked to the other side of the field, feeling decidedly queasy, I found myself thinking something which really shocked me: thinking that it would have solved a great many problems if it *had* been Otto.

God forgive me, I thought. What sort of man am I turning into that I can wish my best friend dead?

9

Next morning Uncle called me to his office. He must have read my medical report, because he tactfully refrained from offering me a chair. 'How', he asked, 'would you fancy a bit of leave?'

'I wouldn't say no!'

'All you deserve', he grunted, 'is a cushion! But I've told Farnborough you'll be bringing 'em combat reports: on the DH2. Now my friend Tabor is a busy man. It may be some time before he can see you – say anything up to a week. You understand?'

'Yes, sir. And thanks.'

He went off on another tack. 'Bad luck about Johnson.'

'Yes.'

'You flew with him a lot. I suppose you'll be seeing his mother?'

It always surprised me how much Uncle knew about his aircrew. And how much he cared. 'I did promise him, sir. . . .'

'Hmmm!' He gave me a look that I wasn't sure how to interpret, and went off on yet another tack. 'Got yourself a girl yet?'

I shook my head.

'Get one!'

'Is that an order, sir?'

'No. Just advice. Might be less harrowing, don't you think, than getting to like people in the squadron?'

I knew what he meant. And I knew he was right. But I couldn't very well tell him, could I, that the only girl I fancied was in love with one of our opposite numbers from Ronchin? So I said I'd see what I could do.

I spent the rest of the day thinking about Major Bertram's

advice, first in the transport that took me to Saint Omer, then on the train to Calais and finally on the leave boat to Dover. But all I'd decided by the time I landed in England was that I'd pay a quick visit to Johnson's mother and a quick visit to Claire Scott; and that would be the end of my involvement in other people's lives: that after duty would come a bit of overdue pleasure.

Johnson's mother turned out to be a tough old lady of rising sixty. She had been confined for years to a wheelchair – suffering, I gathered, from some kind of acute arthritis – and so far as I could make out she had only two interests in life: her son and her shop. To say that his death had hit her hard would be putting it mildly. But she was a fighter. There were none of the tears I'd been afraid of, and none of the self-pity; and I think I was able to bring her some sort of comfort by describing her son's life at Saint Genis in glowing (if not entirely accurate) terms. She was certainly grateful, and kept plying me with cups of tea and home-made scones, until, as I was about to leave, she asked the question I had been dreading. She asked if I'd come and see her again.

I hardened my heart. I gave her an equivocal answer. And felt an absolute cad.

I spent the night in London, then hired a motor car and drove down to Weston Patrick.

I had tried to ring Claire Scott a couple of times; but first her number was engaged and then there was no reply. I had unhappy memories of what had happened last time I'd arrived unheralded, so I tried her a third time from the village.

It was a man who answered, and I asked if I could speak to Claire.

'Who's that?'

'Jack Cunningham. . . . I was a friend of Johnny's.'

'Johnny?'

'You know. Her husband.'

A pause. Then, in a voice that sounded decidedly put out: 'Hang on, will you?'

I began to wonder if I'd telephoned at an inopportune

moment.

'Is that Jack Cunningham?' – Claire sounded pleased but curiously breathless.

'Yes. I've got a couple of days' leave. I say, I hope you don't mind my calling you?'

'Of course not, silly! Where are you?'

'In the village.'

This time I was certain: the pause *was* an awkward one. 'Gosh! What a lovely surprise!'

For all her friendliness, I had the feeling I was *de trop*. Perhaps, I told myself, she had a boyfriend with her. And why not? Her husband was dead. 'Look Claire,' I said. 'I was only passing through: on my way to Farnborough. Can I give you a call later?'

'But you're here *now*. And I'd love to see you! Give me ten minutes. And come on over.'

'You sure?'

I *thought* I heard a man mutter something as if in protest, and a whispered 'Shut up!' . . . 'Sorry, Jack. What d'you say?'

'You sure?'

'Of course. Be lovely to see you.' She put down the phone.

There was no reason, I told myself, to jump to conclusions on the strength of a man's voice and an awkward pause. All the same, it was a good half-hour before I knocked on the door of Dragonfly Cottage.

I had forgotten how beautiful – no, that's not *le mot juste*, how desirable – she was. The first time Chris had shown me her photo I'd said 'lucky man!' The first time I'd seen her, when she had come flying out of the cottage thinking for a moment I was her husband, I'd thought what a wonderful homecoming it might have been. And now, now that my friend her husband was dead, was there any reason, I asked myself, why I should hide the admiration in my eyes as I stared at her?

'Good to see you, Jack!' She kissed me on the cheek.

From a range of about six inches our eyes met; then she drew away. I must, I suppose, have been holding myself a bit awkwardly, because she looked at me in sudden concern. 'You're not wounded?'

I laughed. 'All I need is sympathy. A cushion. And sticking-plaster once a day!'

'Oh, golly! I *am* sympathetic. Catch' – she tossed me a cushion – 'And I hope I can help with the plaster!'

She was fun.

Driving down to Weston Patrick I had imagined her as sadly beautiful in widow's weeds, a tragic Aphrodite stranded by the tide of war on barren sands. But there seemed to be nothing tragic about this beautiful young woman with her beads her laughter and her *savoir faire*, who was obviously pleased to see me, and who I found easier to talk to than any girl I'd met in all my eighteen years. We curled up in chairs on either side of the big log fire in her sitting-room, and talked and talked and talked. And it didn't take me long to discover that there was a great deal more to Claire Scott than a pretty face and the sort of figure men turned to stare at. She was the most honest person I'd ever met. She didn't – thank heavens – gush confidences uninvited; but if you asked her a question you got an answer that was at times disconcertingly straight. We were talking of Chris, and I watched her carefully to see if it distressed her to speak of him; but she didn't seem to have any sort of hang-up; so after a while, intending it as a compliment, I said that theirs had always struck me as the perfect marriage.

To my surprise the sparkle ebbed out of her. 'It was perfect', she said, 'in every way but one.'

'What was that?' – the words were out of my mouth before I realised how very personal they were. 'As your legal adviser,' I said quickly. 'I should tell you you don't have to answer that!'

She didn't smile. She sat very still, staring out of the window. Suddenly and when I least expected it, the mask of her gaiety had slipped, giving me a glimpse of what lay beneath. She turned to me impulsively: 'Have *you* a girl, Jack?'

I shook my head, and wished people would stop asking me that.

'Well, if you find one. And you *really* love one another. And she wants your child. For God's sake let her have it.'

126

I remembered my talk with Chris a couple of weeks before he was killed. I'd thought at the time he might be making a mistake; now I was sure of it. Well, it was too late for second chances, too late for regrets; but not too late, it seemed to me, to pour oil on troubled waters. 'I know', I said gently, 'Chris would have liked a child. I expect he was thinking of you.'

'But he was *wrong*.' Her hands were twisting and untwisting. 'I begged him, and begged him. A child would have been part of him. Something left. Something to live for. Now' – she shivered – 'There's nothing. Absolutely nothing. It's as though he had never been. Do you wonder I've gone off the rails?'

I didn't know what to say.

The sudden ring of the telephone made both of us start; and I for one wasn't sorry for the diversion. She picked it up automatically: 'Yes?'

I *thought* the voice on the other end of the line was a man's. I couldn't hear what he was saying, but it was obviously something that didn't please Claire; her voice was curt: 'I left a message to say sorry, it had to be cancelled.'

The telephone let out a crackle of interference and what sounded like abuse.

'I *did* say I was sorry.'

The words became angrier.

'Your thoughts, Major Armitage, are your problem. Not mine.'

This time I caught the word 'tart'.

Her head jerked up as though she had been struck: 'Just because you pay me, it doesn't mean you own me.' She slammed down the phone. Her eyes were angry: 'Sorry. That sort of thing's an occupational hazard.'

For the first telephone conversation there could have been several explanation; for the second only one. I began to put two and two together, and was priggish enough to be shocked at what they added up to.

Claire was watching me. 'I think,' she said, 'we could both do with a drink.' She collected glasses and whisky, and poured out enough to float a battleship. 'Cheers!'

As our eyes met over the rim of the glasses I found myself staring at her in a way I hadn't liked to stare before. And enjoying it. And wondering how much I'd have to pay.

She must have read my mind like a book; because she shook her head: 'Sorry, there'd be too many ghosts. And besides, it's a rule of the house. No pilots.'

I looked at her curiously.

She did her best to sound hard and uncaring; but she couldn't stop her voice trembling: 'It's just that I can't stand the sight of wings on a jacket. On a chair by the bed. In the morning. . . . Sorry to shock you!'

'I think,' I said mendaciously, 'I'm more surprised than shocked. I mean why?'

'You mean "what's a nice girl like me doing in a job like this"?'

I nodded.

'I suppose,' she said matter-of-factly, 'it's because I don't care whether I live or die. What's done to me. Or who does it.'

'Oh Claire,' I said, 'what a waste.'

'No. All that's left of me is the shell. I'm empty. I've nothing to offer anyone – except a body.'

'And isn't *that* important?'

She shook her head. 'I'll never love again. I'll never marry again. So what does it matter? Why shouldn't I do what I'm told I'm good at!'

'Because you may regret it one day.'

She sighed. 'The trouble with you men is you don't listen. Johnny wouldn't listen when I told him I wanted a child. And you're not listening now. You're thinking Time's a Great Healer and one day Prince Charming will come and make her Forget and they'll Marry and have Lots of Kids and Live Happily Ever After. But I told you I'll *never* love again. Never. Never. Never. I didn't give Johnny just a bit of my love. I gave him *all* of it. I've none left for anyone else. The thought of loving another man' – she shivered – 'it's obscene. Like blasphemy.' She took the sort of gulp of whisky that would have made me choke.

I stared at her, half-expecting her to turn in front of my eyes

128

into a raddled harlot, half-expecting to notice that she had too much lipstick, that there were flaws in her complexion, hardness in her eyes; but all I saw was a young beautiful and desperately unhappy girl, and the pity of it made me angry, and I heard the words pouring out in a great unpremeditated flood. '*Please* listen, Claire. You may think I'm a prig, and you may be right. But you can't go on punishing Johnny for the rest of your life. So he *did* make a mistake. So he *should* have let you have a child. But no matter how wrong – how terribly wrong – he was, he did it out of *love* for you. To give you another chance. To leave you free – one day – to make another go out of life. Is it fair on *him* to chuck what he's given you away?'

She stared at me, her eyes getting bigger and bigger, her hands clenching tighter and tighter, till her glass snapped and the blood came welling up through her fingers and her whisky splashed to the floor: 'I don't think you're right,' she whispered. 'But thanks for caring.'

I spent the rest of the day with her.

What she wanted most was someone to talk to: someone to share the little everyday things with: someone who demanded no special and above all no physical relationship. 'You've no idea', she said that evening as I was getting ready to leave, 'how wonderful it's been to have someone to talk to. Men don't come here to *talk*. Some'll go through the motions. But I can tell all the time what they're thinking – "Yak! Yak! Yak! When all I want is to get her upstairs and take off her clothes and find out if she's as good as she looks!"'

'I must admit,' I said smiling. 'If it wasn't for the house rule, that's just what *I'd* be thinking!'

She gave me a sisterly kiss on the cheek. 'You're very good for a girl's ego. I hope you'll come again. On one condition.'

'Which is?'

'Come because you want to. Not because you feel you ought to.'

She was more subtle than Johnson's mother; but she was after the same thing: a touch of kindness, a helping hand.

The decent thing of course would have been to give her a

helping hand. And I knew it. But for the second time in forty-eight hours I hardened my heart. I reminded myself of my resolution not to get involved in other people's affairs. I told myself I had my own problems, my own life to get on with. I said it might be some time before I was due for leave again.

'So', her lips were smiling but her eyes were lost, 'Hail and farewell!' She gave me another kiss, this time on the mouth. 'I'll remember you, Jack. And thanks for trying to turn me into an Honest Woman!'

As I drove out of the village I looked back in my mirror and saw her still standing beside the gate. We waved. Then she turned and walked back into the cottage.

What did she do, I wondered, when the door swung-to behind her and she was alone? Did she telephone Major Armitage and tell him the coast was clear? I hoped not; I hadn't liked the sound of him. But if she *did* phone Armitage (or anyone else) wouldn't the fault be mine: my fault because in my meanness I'd seen fit to give her only a limited ration of kindness, because when she'd asked for help I had prevaricated, because out of my busy life I'd felt able to spare her only a few short hours? The good Samaritan, I reminded myself, hadn't only bound up his neighbour's wound; he had carried him to an inn, stayed with him and comforted him. Why had I done less? Partly, of course, because I wasn't such a good man as the Samaritan. But (in fairness to myself) there was more to it than that. . . The first time I met Claire the depth of her grief had made me wonder if love in wartime might not have too high a price tag; our second meeting had made me sure of it. What in God's name, I asked myself, was the use of people falling in love if one of them had virtually no hope of survival? Take my case. What was the use of my having *any* friends? If I had a friend in the squadron he'd only be killed – like the Good Shepherd and Chris Scott and poor old Johnson. And if I had a girlfriend and *I* was killed, I couldn't bear the thought of her suffering as Claire was suffering. . . . So I fought shy of the friendship that Johnny's widow was hesitantly offering. Better, I reckoned, to play a lone hand, to insulate myself from caring, to be as self-sufficient and if

130

need-be as prickly as the desert cactus.

Yet even cactus, I told myself need *some* rain. And wasn't there one person who, like me, might welcome a friendship that was purely platonic?

By one of those coincidences that seem almost too wonderful to be true, I found that Jessica was due for a break from night duty and had been thinking of going down for the weekend to her parent's farm. I picked her up that evening; and she seemed, in a restrained sort of way, very nearly as pleased to see me as I her. We drove through the night, and next morning watched the sun climb out of a sea that was metamorphosed from grey to pink, and then from pink to a copper as shot through with dancing light as her hair.

It was the start of a wonderfully happy three days: beautiful surroundings, perfect weather, and the sort of easy undemanding companionship that we had enjoyed as children. This probably was the crux of it. We both wanted to put back the clock, to get away from the present, to forget men moaning away the night in darkened wards or burning slowly to death in spinning planes. So we went back to the well-loved and well-remembered paths of our childhood: by day long rambles over meadows hard with frost, the seabirds wheeling, white waves pounding; and by night semi-clandestine visits to the local pub, or searching for badger sets with a fading torch and a handful of half-frozen matches. Once or twice, it was brought home to us that we weren't *really* children – like the time I dared her to ford the Helford and without thinking, as she waded into the water, she hitched her skirt very nearly up to her waist, or when our eyes met unexpectedly in the flare of a match. But these moments we pretended weren't important. It suited both of us to play the same game.

Three days of happiness. Then it was back to reality. . . . Once again we drove by night, arrived in London as dawn was breaking over the river, and said our goodbyes outside the dingy nurses' quarters just off the Whitechapel Road. It was funny: we looked at one another, reached for one another's hands and said in unison. 'Thanks! That was fun!'

131

We burst out laughing. 'Perhaps,' I said, 'we can do it again?'

'I'd like that.'

I found myself reluctant to let go of her hand.

'Jack!'

'All right,' I said. 'I'll be good. But remember. If things don't work out, I'll be around to pick up the pieces.'

'You'd do much better,' she said, 'to get yourself another girl.'

'Do you *want* me to get another girl?'

She wouldn't look at me.

'Jess?'

'Oh, please!' She covered her face with her hands. 'Can't you *see*. It's like being torn physically in two.'

It was the nearest she ever came to saying she loved me: to letting me know that she cared. Not enough, you may think, for a sensible man to pin extravagant hopes on. But since when have love and sense walked hand in hand?

10

The moment I drove past the guardroom I could sense that something was wrong. An air of melancholy hung like a pall over the airfield; the groundcrew were going about their jobs with long faces; I almost expected the flags to be at half-mast. When I got to the Mess I discovered why. In the week I had been away we had lost two more planes: one of them Uncle's.

He and his observer had crashed on the British side of the lines. The observer had been trapped in the wreckage and burned to death. But Uncle, by a near miracle, had been flung clear and had escaped with second degree burns, a broken collar bone and a broken leg. 'The old devil's cooked his medical report,' the doctor told me. 'Says he'll run the squadron from his bed. . . . And by the way, he's been asking for you.'

Major Bertram had had his desk, his files and his telephone transferred to the sick bay, and I found him propped up in bed in his red flannel nightshirt. His leg was in plaster, and he was swathed from head to foot in bandages. I gave him a ceremonial bow: 'Hail, Pharaoh!'

'At least', he grunted, 'people can *see* I've been wounded. . . . You have a talk with Tabor?'

I nodded.

'So? When's he sending us some decent planes?'

I told him the gist of what I had learned at Farnborough: that from now on we could expect a plentiful supply of DH2s and the latest Nieuports, but nothing more.

'Christ almighty! *Still* nothing that fires through its prop? Like a Fokker?'

'Not yet. Something called an SE5 in the pipeline. And a triplane that's going to the Navy. But I wouldn't write off the

Nieuports, sir. The new ones *have* a machine-gun. On the upper wing. It fires *above* the prop.'

'How the hell do you re-load it?'

We talked technicalities: the sort of technicalities on which our lives and the lives of everyone in the squadron depended. And by the time we had sifted through the latest combat reports, the information I'd gleaned from Farnborough, and the replacement schedule for our outdated BE2s, we came to the conclusion that the tide might well be on the turn: that with the new planes we had been promised we would soon be more than a match for the Fokkers.

So we drank to ending the winter of our discontent and to the promise of spring.

The first of the improved Nieuports arrived a week later, and on Uncle's instructions I organised familiarisation flights for the less experienced pilots and maintenance courses for the less experienced groundcrew. From then on replacement aircraft were ferried into Saint Genis if not in a flood at least in a steady trickle. By mid-March our squadron could boast six DH2s, six Nieuports (with machine-guns and the improved 130 h.p. *Clergêt* engines) and six BE2s. Our outdated reconnaissance planes were no longer obliged to venture into the air unescorted. And the Fokkers from Ronchin suddenly discovered we were no longer a tasty morsel to be gobbled at leisure, but a lump of indigestible gristle on which they blunted their teeth. Indeed it wasn't long before we began to inflict on them the sort of losses which they throughout the winter had been inflicting on us.

Our skirmishing with the Fokkers that spring was, you might say, a harbinger of the wrath to come, a foretaste of the killing-time when massed armadas and circuses were to claw one another to death out of a crowded sky. But multiple battles were still in 1916 the exception rather than the rule; it was still possible to fly a two-hour patrol and not see another plane; still possible for pilots to indulge in the ritual of single combat watched only by the shifting bastions of cloud.

I had more than one such combat.

Once I was almost jumped by the Old Red Fox, only escaping because I spotted the silhouette of his Fokker reflected on a wall of cumulus as he lay in wait for me in a rift-valley of the sky. For almost an hour we played hide-and-seek-cum-blind-man's-buff in a world whose beauty was given an added poignancy by the use to which we were putting it.

Once, after a twenty minute dual of alternating exhilaration and terror, I forced a Fokker down to ground level (where my Nieuport was at its best) only for the wretched machine-gun to seize up as I was about to give him the *coup de grâce*. That German pilot was a gentleman; he realised what had happened, gave me a wave and broke off the engagement.

And that quixotic gesture, rather than the bitterness to come, is how I like to remember the war.

Twice I saw Otto.

The first time I was coming back from an uneventful patrol when I spotted him letting down towards Ronchin, the sun reflected like a gigantic catherine wheel from the rim of his cowling. I might, I suppose, have headed him off: have brought him to combat somewhere above the ancient walls of Lille. But I didn't, I turned away, and crept back by a circuitous route to Saint Genis, not knowing whether to feel thankful or ashamed.

The second time wasn't so easy. I was involved in a mini-dogfight: one 'mechanical cow', three Nieuports and three Fokkers. And the cowling of one of the Fokkers was orange. I did my best to avoid the orange Fokker, but with planes wheeling and guns clattering it was hard enough to tell friend from foe let alone one foe from another. And after a while something happened that made me literally blind with anger.

Otto shot down the poor old 'mechanical cow'.

I'd no idea who was flying it; but suddenly the dead pilot was one of *Us*, Otto one of *Them*. I dropped onto his tail. I reached for the Lewis.

He must have seen me at the last second. For as I opened fire, he flicked into a spin. A spinning plane is difficult to draw a bead on, and my bullets passed now this side of him, now the other. Then, as the range lengthened, he straightened into a dive, inviting me to follow. I didn't fall for it. I'd seen it all before: the dive that turned into a loop, and the loop that turned into an Immelmann roll which would bring him round onto *my* tail. I hauled back on the stick till the Nieuport was near-stalling. And waited, waited, waited. The Fokker went hurtling down faster and faster, then as I'd expected it started to loop. It looped gracefully, coming back towards me quickly at first, then as it lost momentum moving more and more slowly. I watched Otto, as at the last second he rolled smoothly and skil-fully out of the loop. I watched him peer downwards, first one side then the other, wondering where the devil I'd got to. I watched him shake his head in disbelief. Then the truth hit him. Suddenly. And he jerked round, to see me not below and in front of him but above and behind him, my Nieuport steady, my sights on his heart.

He must have thought he was as good as dead.

But at the moment I fired, I eased back on the stick. And my bullets went skimming over the top of his mainplane, about eighteen inches from his head.

I'll never know if he recognised me; I'll never know if he real-ised I'd spared his life, or if he simply thought me a rotten shot. Because one moment his Fokker was there, next it had toppled out of my sights and into a spin: a spin that went on and on, round and round, down and down, making me think for a moment I must have hit him, but at the last second he pulled out and went scurrying at tree top level for home. And my fury left me, and I found myself bathed in sweat and trembling. In my mind's eye I could see my bullets licking either side of Otto's body. I'd been within a hairsbreadth of killing him. And the ter-rible thing was, I *knew* that if by some miracle we were brought together, alone, we'd clap one another on the back and talk and laugh as though the years that divided us had never been. And the folly of it and the pity of it so overwhelmed me that I broke away from the dogfight and headed back for Saint Genis. When I landed, I said my engine had been playing me up. I made my report and shut myself in my cabin and got out the whisky.

After I'd had several glasses of whisky it seemed to me that Jessica was looking at me reproachfully. So I buried her photo under the pillow, and finished one bottle and started another.

But the whisky didn't do any good. There may be a saying *'in vino veritas'*. But the only truth that hit me was a hangover!

The two cars, the Delaunay and the Mercedes, drove slowly across the airfield as though in procession. In the driving seat of each was a liveried chauffeur, in the back an extremely attractive young lady. 'I think,' one of the newly-joined observers murmured, 'I'll see what they want!'

'Down, Rover!' I said unkindly. 'I'm the officer on duty!'

As I walked up to the Delaunay the young lady obligingly lowered her window. From close range she was not merely attractive but positively dazzling. I gave her what I hoped was a friendly salute: *'Bonjour, Ma'moiselle!'*

She favoured me with a smile: 'I speak a little English. Not very good.'

'I'm glad. My French is terrible! I'm very sorry, cars are not permitted on the airfield.'

'But I am waiting for Charles!'

I wondered who the lucky Charles was; I couldn't think of one in the squadron. 'Charles who, Ma'moiselle?'

'Charles Nungesser.'

'Don't think I know him.'

'Soon you will. He come from there.' She pointed to the sky. And after a moment of bewilderment, I put two and two together. . . . Earlier that morning we had received a message from headquarters at Saint Omer to say that the last of our replacement Nieuports were being flown in that evening by members of the *Cigognes Escadrilles* – the famous French squadron whose conquests, it was rumoured, were by no means confined to the air. Charles Nungesser, I told myself, must be one of the *Cigognes,* and the girl one of his conquests. I suggested we parked the cars in a safe place, and that she and her friend came back with me to the Mess.

137

It seemed to be a routine with which she was familiar; and soon the two girls were sipping champagne and bringing to our flagstoned kitchen an unaccustomed jollity and *je ne sais pas quoi*. Things were going swimmingly until — far too soon to our way of thinking — the roar of aircraft heralded the arrival of the *Cigognes*.

And what an arrival it was! The first of the Nieuports came hurtling very low and very fast over the airfield, then soared up into a victory roll. As the second Nieuport appeared we could see it had been damaged; it came in like a crab, one wing lower than the other and streaming great ribbons of ripped-off fabric. It made a hair-raising landing, and came to rest no more than a couple of feet from the hangars. The pilot, however, made no move to get out. 'It is necessary', one of the girls said, 'to assist him. He has need of the sticks for his legs.' But even as she spoke, the crash-tender and ambulance were pulling up at the side of the shattered plane.

It's hard to say which was the more bizarre: the jet-black Nieuport, adorned with every conceivable symbol of ill omen — a coffin, two lighted candles, a raven, a skull and crossbones — or the handsome but disfigured pilot, his legs broken, his jaw dislocated, his lips slashed by an explosive bullet, gesticulating excitedly as he was levered out of the cockpit and carried shoulder-high into the Mess.

One of the girls ran up to him: *'Comment, Charles! Encore blessé!'*

'Non, ma petite. C'est l'heure des réjouissances et non pas des pleurs. Mon quinzième Boche . . . et quelle bataille!'

Charles Nungesser was one of those gifted men who soar through life with the transitory brilliance of a comet. And how vividly he illuminated the scene that evening! How vividly, in between the popping of corks, the toasts, and the laughter of the girls, he described what had happened on the way to Saint Genis. 'We are over Izel-les-Hameaux, Claude and I: minding, as you say it, the business. When we see this Boche. He is taking the photographs. "Ah," I say to myself, "now shall we have the bit of sport". I signal to Claude "keep back". The two against

138

the one is not the game of cricket! Man against man is the way. Like boxers: in the ring of the clouds. So I dive on this Boche. Zoooommmmmg! I expect him to run. But, *mon dieu*, he is a wild one. Wild like me. He do the loop, the Immelmann turn, and Holy Father he is, how do you say it, behind my arse! He is firing at me! . . . I pretend the injured bird. He follow me down. I turn on him. And *olé, olé*, I am behind his arse! And that is good. . . . He twist and turn. *Il est coulant comme une anguille et d'autant plus dangereux.* We fight. *Mon dieu* how we fight. The clouds they scatter. The fields they spin like tops. Always he try the climb. But always I press him down. *Merci, ma chérie. Ce long bavardage m'a bien donné soif!* Many times he nearly have me. But in the end I have *him*. It is not his fault. It is the aeroplane, you understand. The Nieuport is more agile than the Fokker. . . . My bullets they enter his engine. There is smoke. There is flames. Ah, Holy Father in heaven there but for Your mercy it is I. . . . But he is a brave fellow, that Boche. He maintain the head. He make the stomach landing. Crrr-rummmmmp! In a field. He and his fat observer they climb out. They see me diving on them. They run. They think perhaps I give them the rat-tat-tat with my machine-gun. But I do not fire. Why should I harm them? They have fought well. They are my brothers. *Allons-nous en, Adélie. La nuit est courte.*'

Before the French pilots left they paid a visit to Uncle in the sick bay. And I reckon what happened next was a plot they concocted between them.

I had gone back to my cabin, and was re-reading a letter from Jessica – a letter incidentally that contained the surprising bit of information that Gavin, whom I still thought of as no more than a kid, was hoping any day to be going to Flying School. Anyhow, there I was lost in another world, when one of the pilots stuck his head round the door and said that Uncle wanted me to report right away to the guard room.

When I got there I found the Mercedes and the Delaunay about to leave. Adélie gave me a wave: 'Come, Jack. Sit next to me.'

I thought she was joking. But Nungesser held open the door

of the Delaunay: 'Lieutenant Cunningham. Sir!'

'I can't come with you.' I said with some alarm. 'I'm on duty.'

'Your Uncle, he give this other officer the duty.' He gestured to a disconsolate looking observer.

'Well, I don't know. . . .'

Adélie pouted. 'You are not very gallant, Jack. Don't you wish to sit next to me?'

'Oh yes, of course. But. . . .'

Nungesser and his fellow pilot seized me under the armpits, bundled me into the Delaunay, and with a honking of horns and crashing of gears we shot out of the airfield. I'd a pretty good idea of where we'd end up, and wasn't sure if I was more excited or apprehensive!

An hour later we were in Armentières, installed in what you might euphemistically describe as a high-class café. We sat in a room with a painted ceiling, rococo mirrors and marble-topped tables scattered like exotic mushrooms about a sawdust floor. Waiters with white aprons and slicked-back hair were bustling about with trays of drinks, which they looked always about to upset but never did.

'*Garçon!*'

'*M'sieu?*'

'*Six fines.*'

'*Bien, m'sieu.*'

The room was full of French and English officers. The atmosphere was heavy with smoke and heady with wine. Someone, incongruously, was playing a Chopin sonata. 'Adélie!' Nungesser ran a proprietary hand through her hair. 'We must find two of your friends for these handsome English pilots!'

'If they wish.'

My companion raised his glass: '*Vive la France!*'

Adélie laid a hand on my arm, smiling. 'And for Jack?'

Well, everyone had been telling me for the last nine months that I ought to get myself a girl, and I wouldn't have said no to Adélie herself. But I'd no intention of being palmed off with any old girl. I'd always imagined the first time would be something special, not a casual pick-up in the local whore house. And this Adélie seemed to understand: 'I will find someone for you extra nice!'

'I'd rather', I said evasively, 'find someone myself.'

Nungesser made an impatient gesture: *'Dites-lui que peu importent les apparences si elle se donne à lui.'*

Her eyes were angry: *'Charles! Etes-vous devenu un tel roué que vous avez oublié ce que c'est que d'avoir dix-huit ans?'*

Again his hand ran casually through her hair; he whispered something; and she gave him an outraged slap: *'Vous êtes un pédant!'* She turned to me: 'I understand how you feel. Follow me.'

She led the way up a short flight of stairs, put her finger to her lips and half-opened a door. Peering through, I saw another and more luxurious room, with a smaller and more intimate bar; three or four French officers and perhaps twice as many girls were grouped round the tables, drinking and playing cards. Adélie beckoned to one of the girls. She was pretty all right; and I don't know why, as she came towards us, my heart sank – perhaps because the smile she gave me never quite got as far as to her eyes. Adélie said something to her in French; and she nodded and went to join our party in the lower room.

Adélie had been watching me: 'Now, Jack. Do you see a girl that you wish for?'

She had her back to us, but I could see her face in one of the mirrors. She looked little more than a child: slim and pale, with a heart-shaped face, great violet eyes and a cloud of light brown hair; she was talking to two of the other girls; and as I stared at her she raised her head, and our eyes, in the mirror, met. I could read her reactions as though she had spelt them out. First bewilderment: then anger (which surprised me!): then a sort of wry amusement. I expected her eyes to drop. But it was I who looked away first. 'Yes.' I pointed her out to Adélie.

She shook her head. 'Oh, Jacques, I am sorry. She is the one girl – how do you say it? – she is not a girl of the house. She is a visitor. From Paris.'

I felt cheated. And obstinate. 'It's her. Or no-one.'

Adélie looked at me in exasperation: 'Go back to the others. I will talk to her.'

She must have had to do a lot of talking; because we had finished another round of drinks and were about to move into one of the upper rooms for supper, before she re-joined us. 'You are lucky,' she whispered. 'The girl's name is Nicole. She is the mistress of an officer who has been ordered far away – to the Front in Italy. She can not join him and she is bored, so she would be happy to entertain you after dinner. But you must be discreet. You must not be seen to speak with her. After we have eaten, if you go to this address, she will be waiting.' She handed me a slip of paper, on which was written in big childish handwriting: 19, *rue de la République*.

After these pleasantly clandestine arrangements, we sat down to a meal which was punctuated at frequent intervals by cries of *'Vive la France!'*, *'Vive l'Angleterre!'*, and *'Encore de vin.'* When the last of the food and the last of the wine had been disposed of, three couples went arm-in-arm up the stairs, and I in search of the *rue de la République*.

The streets were deserted, except for the occasional lorry feeling its way to the Front by the glimmer of oil lamps. The night was quiet, except for a distant grumbling of gunfire which provided a somewhat sinister accompaniment to my assignation. I found *rue de la République* all right; but where was Number Nineteen? I was striking matches and peering furtively at the number plates when a door opened on the opposite side of the street, and a figure beckoned. As I walked towards her I had an intimation that it was not so much a street I was crossing as the threshold of adolescence.

She didn't speak, but put a finger to her lips and turned the key in the lock behind us. The house was warm, the stairs dark and narrow, her bedroom small – most of it taken up by a huge double bed. She lit two candles on the mantelpiece and poked up the fire. The candlelight and the firelight were allies. The candlelight left pools of darkness round the room's periphery, half-hiding the pile of dirty clothes, the unwashed coffee-cup, the drooping fern. The firelight danced on the crochet coverlet on the bed and in her eyes. She took off her coat, shook loose the cascade of her hair and smiled an uncertain smile.

My throat was dry with an excitement that may have been old as time, but was new to me.

Like many of my generation I thought that all French girls were touched with magic. Paris wasn't, for me, the city of fountains, palaces, wide streets and pleasant boulevards, it was a gigantic brothel where women wore nothing but sheer underwear and long black stockings. In the Mess and cabins at Saint Genis we had Kirchner drawings of these delectable creatures, in varying degrees of nudity. And Nicole was like one of the better – no, the very best – of the Kirchner drawings. She had the same disobedient hair, the same impudent nose, the same generous mouth and melting eyes. I wondered, somewhat prosaically, if she spoke English: *'Quel âge avez-vous?'* I ventured.

'Dix-huit. Haighteen! I do not', she giggled, 'speak English very good.' She touched the wings on my tunic: *'Tu es pilote?'*

I nodded.

'J'adore les pilotes. Ils sont si courageux.'

Since her lips were rather less than six inches from mine I didn't have to be all that courageous to kiss her.

She smiled again, this time more warmly: *'Veux tu rester?'*

My French was so terrible I was thinking to myself that 'rest' wasn't at all what I had in mind, when it suddenly occurred to me that she was asking – as though there might be some doubt about it! – if I wanted to stay. 'Oh, yes. Rather!'

She laughed, and took a playful tug at my hair: 'Oh rathar! Rathar!' It was as though a knot inside me had been loosened; as though some instinct told me we were going to be not only lovers but friends.

I remember the firelight making patterns on her body. I remember the sweetness of her breath and the stillness of her eyes. I remember that I was nervous to start with, and then suddenly not nervous at all because she was clearly enjoying herself as much as I was. I remember that I had reckoned on staying no more than a couple of hours at the most, but ended up in her room for the night. And I remember that the morning sun, as it slanted in through the half-open window, came for both of us too soon. We lay side by side on the big double bed; and as I studied the whiteness of her skin and the beauty of her body I couldn't help but marvel that my own coarse-textured flesh should have seemed to bring her so much pleasure. Perhaps, I thought, it had all been a dream. Then her mouth and her body were pressed to mine, and the dream was made flesh and ran again its consuming course.

Later, as she made coffee, she would have slipped on a dressing-gown; but I wouldn't let her. I couldn't see enough of her. And when we had drunk the coffee, I said simply: 'When can I see you again, Nicole?'

'Oh no, Jacques! *Mon ami* – if he find out, he will kill us.'

'Then we'll have to be careful he *doesn't* find out!'

'But . . . alas, it is not possible. . . .'

I took her chin, very gently, between my forefinger and thumb. 'Don't you *want* to see me again?'

'But *mon ami*. . . . And my parents: after the war they expect us to marry.'

'That needn't worry us,' I said. 'There's no "after the war" for a pilot.'

Her eyes, unexpectedly, filled with tears. 'Do not think it, Jacques. You will live. And marry the good English girl. And make her happy.'

'I'd much rather make the naughty French girl happy. Now.'

For a moment she sat very still, then she got up and started to pace the room as though it were a cage: *'Qui peut dire: "ceci est bien" et "cela est mal"?'*

'What are you saying, Nicole?'

'That we'll have to be *very* careful.'

I was lucky enough to get a lift back to Saint Genis. The driver would have been happy to take me all the way, but I preferred to be dropped at the spot where our cart-track branched off from the main road; the last couple of miles I walked.

It was a lovely morning. The grass seemed greener than

usual, the air fresher, the sun warmer. I found myself half-singing half-humming Mademoiselle from Armenteers. I was happy. I had discovered what life was all about. It did occur to me, fleetingly, that I was in danger of breaking my resolution not to let myself get fond of anyone; but I told myself that a French girl I'd picked up in the local brothel wasn't the sort of person I was likely to Love and be Loved by with a capital L. . . . I was eighteen. And, as I think I've said, a bit of a prig.

As soon as I caught sight of the airfield I realised something was the matter. There were sentries with rifles at the gate, a guard on the planes, and groundcrew milling about like ants whose nest has been broken into. Before I was half-way to the Mess the senior pilot came rushing up to me: 'Jack! Thank God you're back!'

'What's up?'

'Your friend Gavin Pendower! The bloody fool's pinched a plane. And gone buzzing off into Hunland!'

'Gavin! But he's only a kid. He can't *fly*!'

'He can fly all right. Well enough to desert to the Huns. *And* in the latest Nieuport!'

I couldn't believe it. For a moment I stared at him, my mouth hanging open like a gaffed trout. Then my brain started ticking over. 'What', I said slowly, 'did this Gavin Pendower look like?'

'*You* ought to know! A bit older than you. A bit shorter. Good-looking chap. Fair hair. Blue eyes.'

The description didn't fit the gangling ginger-haired Gavin. It didn't fit Gavin at all. But it *did* fit another of my erstwhile friends. . . . For a moment I couldn't think how Otto von Searle could possibly have turned up at Saint Genis. Then I remembered the Fokker shot down – was it really only yesterday afternoon – by the *Cigognes Escadrille*. 'When did this chap turn up?'

'Yesterday evening, I think. Why?'

'He didn't stay the night here?'

'Why, as a matter of fact he did. In your cabin.'

I could feel fear welling up in me, like blood from a cut. I ran to my cabin. As I flung open the door I think I knew in my heart what I was going to find. That which I valued most in all the world – my photograph of Jessica – was no longer on the shelf by my bed. In its place was a letter. The handwriting was Otto's.

11

So Otto made monkeys out of us, pinched a plane from under our very noses, and went flying back in triumph to the Fatherland. That was fact. But how he managed to pull off such a coup is partly supposition, a story that has to be fitted together piece by uncertain piece. And even when one has all the pieces, there are difficulties. For through whose eyes am I to tell what happened? And whose version am I to believe? Perhaps the best way to start is by quoting from the Interrogation File on Lieutnant Kurt Fassbender, *Feldfliegerabteilung 17.*

The morning after Nungesser's visit to Saint Genis Lieutnant Fassbender was found hiding in a wood about five miles from the airfield. He was brought here for interrogation. He wasn't injured, but he was cold exhausted and frightened; facts which his interrogators, with scant regard for the Geneva Conventions, made the most of.

Interrogating Officer (in German): 'Lieutnant Kurt Fassbender: that is your name and your rank?'

Fassbender (as translated by an interpreter): 'Yes, sir.'

Interrogating Officer: 'In normal circumstances, Lieutnant, that is all we would require you to tell us. But circumstances are *not* normal. When captured, you were wearing some of the clothes of an officer of the Royal Flying Corps: an officer whose body was found close to the spot where you were hiding. Do you understand the implications that we must reluctantly draw from this?'

Fassbender: 'I can explain everything. . . .'

Interrogating Officer: 'Please answer the question. I put it to you that there are two implications. First that you killed this British Officer. Secondly that you are a spy. The penalty for either offence is the death penalty. Now do you understand this?'

Fassbender: 'Yes. But I can explain.'

Interrogating Officer: 'You will be given every opportunity to explain. But the explaining will be done *our* way. . . . Now will you please describe the events that led to your capture?'

Fassbender: 'We were shot down. Yesterday evening. . . .'

Interrogating Officer (raising his hand): 'Lieutnant! Please! If we are to believe your story you must make it convincing. What sort of plane were you flying? What was your mission? *How* were you shot down?'

Fassbender (with his first sign of spirit): 'I am not obliged to tell you these things.'

Interrogating Officer: 'That is true. But if your story lacks detail it won't be convincing, and we are hardly likely to believe it!'

Fassbender (after some hesitation): 'We were flying a Fokker monoplane. We were on reconnaissance. And that is all I shall tell you.'

Interrogating Officer: 'What sort of plane shot you down?'

Fassbender: 'I think a Nieuport.'

Interrogating Officer: 'And did you notice anything peculiar about this Nieuport? Anything unusual?'

Fassbender: 'It was painted black. Black all over. Like a coffin.'

Interrogating Officer: 'That is the sort of detail that makes us believe you – so far! Please continue.'

Fassbender: 'We were hit in the engine. It was a lucky shot, you understand. The engine caught fire. We crash-landed in a field. My pilot and I jumped out. Quickly. In case the plane exploded. And hid in a wood.'

Interrogating Officer: 'And then?'

Fassbender: 'We discussed what to do next.'

Interrogating Officer: 'And what did you decide?'

Fassbender (after a longish pause): 'My pilot speaks perfect English. He decided to walk to one of your airfields. And attempt to take a plane. . . . There is nothing wrong in this. It is the *duty* of every officer to avoid capture.'

Interrogating Officer: 'And you?'

Fassbender: 'I speak no English. I would have been more hindrance than help. I was to stay in the wood.'

Interrogating Officer: 'Go on.'

Fassbender: 'What happened next was a mistake, you understand. A tragedy. And no doing of mine.'

Interrogating Officer: 'Just give us the facts. *We* will interpret them.'

Fassbender: 'Well. . . . We were looking for a place where I could hide: near the centre of the wood. When we saw this man, fishing. He was pre-occupied with his sport, and didn't hear us. We approached him cautiously. When we got close we saw that he was in flying kit. Otto whispered that we ought to overpower him. And take his clothes. So as to make it easy for him, you understand, to enter your airfield and take a plane. . . .'

Interrogating Officer: 'Go on.'

Fassbender (in a state of nervous excitement not far removed from hysteria): 'It was a mistake, you understand. And so terrible a mistake. When I try to remember my mind goes blank. I can not think.'

The report states that at this juncture Fassbender was offered a cigarette.

Fassbender: 'Thank you. I will try to make you understand. We decide to rush this officer. We hope to give him the quick knock-out. Nothing more. But he sees us coming. He fights. He fights like the devil. We fall, all three of us, into the river. Otto – my pilot – grabs a stone from the bed of the river. He hits the officer. The officer falls. His head strikes the rocks. He lies still. When we pick him up we find – *mein Gott* – he is dead!'

The report is annotated here by both British officers: the essence of their notes being that they feel Fassbender is not, at this juncture, telling the truth – or at least not the whole truth.

Interrogating Officer: 'What did you do then?'

Fassbender: 'I say this is a terrible thing we have done, and we must give ourselves up. But Otto, my pilot, says that what is done can not be undone, and we must keep to our plan. He is senior to me. How can I over-rule him? So he sets off to search

149

for an airfield, while I stay hidden in the wood. Soon it is night. The temperature falls. I am cold: so cold that I fear I shall die of exposure. The British officer, I tell myself, is dead. He has no need of clothes. I take his shirt, his pullover and his socks. At last I sleep. Next thing I know it is morning. I am discovered. I am brought here. And now' – with dignity – 'I have told you all. And I demand that I be accorded my rights as a prisoner-of-war. As an officer and gentleman.'

Fassbender, however, was not to escape so easily. The proceedings dragged on for a further hour, a further eight pages of typescript: the Interrogating Officer searching, probing, always hinting (but never actually saying) that the more information Fassbender disclosed the more likely it was that his story would be believed. But of this – the story behind the interrogation – we in Eight Squadron knew nothing. All *we* saw was the official summary: 'That in his effort to avoid capture, the German pilot Lieutenant Otto Lothar von Searle caused the death of Captain James Cridland of the Royal Flying Corps by striking him violently on the head with a stone.'

I would never have believed it of him. But there it was. In black and white. Endorsed by the signature of an officer from British Intelligence.

And my fellow pilots and observers were very nearly as surprised as I was. As one of them put it: 'We had a splendid time with him! He seemed such a decent chap.' Then another added. 'But it just goes to prove, doesn't it: never trust a Hun!'

It was a remark which few people would have made in 1914; which not many would have agreed with in 1915; but which in 1916 met with general assent. We were learning that wars were not won by "parfit gentil knights" in shining armour, but by men who crept up behind their opponents and burnt them to death. And, it seemed, by murderers.

So we knew (or at least we thought we knew) what happened prior to Otto's arrival at Saint Genis; what happened afterwards wasn't hard to piece together. . . . Otto must have known he'd been shot down not far from our aerodrome; he must have started walking in roughly the right direction; and he must for the latter part of his journey have got a lift, because at round about six o'clock that evening a Crossley transport on its way to the Front dropped him outside the guardroom. He didn't hesitate. He walked straight in through the main gate.

The sentry on duty saw the pips on his flying jacket and gave him a hasty salute. Otto walked up to him – you have to give him ten out of ten for nerve. 'Eight Squadron *are* still here, aren't they?'

'Yes, sir.'

'Is one of their pilots Jack Cunningham?'

'Why yes, sir. I think there is a Lieutenant Cunningham.'

'Any idea where I can find him?'

'I expect in the Mess, sir. Other side of the 'angars.' He pointed.

'Thanks.' Otto started walking towards the Mess.

Afterwards, of course, there were enquiries. But when the sentry was asked 'Didn't you notice anything odd about the way this officer was dressed?', he replied 'No, sir' – for didn't all aircrew dress like a cross between Robin Hood and Scott of the Antarctic! And when he was asked 'Didn't you notice anything odd about the way he spoke?' he said no to that also – for didn't all bloody officers speak as though they'd a plum in their mouths!

So Otto cleared his first hurdle.

He didn't go to the Mess. Only as far as the hangars. And the planes.

He had arrived at a fortunate moment. It was still light; but the groundcrew – except for a small group working late on one of the DH2s – had knocked off for the day, and both hangars and parking bays were deserted. Otto studied the aircraft. The Nieuports, he decided, looked the easiest to fly. If only he could get one started. He was wondering if he dare take a surreptitious look in one of the cockpits, when he realised someone was shouting at him: 'Hey! Larry!'

He froze: mentally and physically. He thought of making a

151

dash for the nearest plane, then remembered the odds were that it wouldn't be fuelled. He thought of silencing the man who was shouting at him, then remembered what had happened in the wood. So he did the one thing which wouldn't arouse immediate suspicion. He walked towards the man who had hailed him – the man who, as they neared one another, realised he'd made a mistake. 'Oh, sorry! I thought you were my driver!' – his glance took-in the three pips on Otto's flying jacket: 'Sorry about that, sir.'

'That's all right. Who *is* your driver?'

'Larry Ingram.'

'Don't know him. But I'm only a visitor.'

An awkward pause, during which Otto realised that the man (a young observer, only a few weeks out of Flying Scool) was looking at him curiously. He couldn't think what to say, or what to do.

'Where are you from, sir?'

That seemed to confirm it; the man *was* suspicious. Otto said he was from Merville – the one allied aerodrome whose name on the spur of the moment he could remember. His only hope, he realised, was to stop the man asking questions: to throw up a smoke screen. 'By the way,' his voice was casual. 'Do you know a Jack Cunningham?'

'Why, yes. He's my flight commander.'

'I was hoping for a chat with him. We were at school together. At Charterhouse.'

The observer's suspicions – which hadn't in fact been much more than curiosity – evaporated. 'Oh, I say! What rotten luck. Jack went off to Armenteers. Less than an hour ago.'

Otto didn't know whether to be disappointed or relieved. He'd been thinking that he might as well give himself up: to me. Now, it seemed, I wasn't on the airfield. 'Do you think he'll be back this evening?'

'Not if he's any sense. Lucky blighter! I say, sir. Let me introduce you to the Mess. If you've come all the way from Merville I expect you could do with a drink.'

He was trapped. And he couldn't think how to get out of

152

it. . . . If he said he'd go back to Merville, he'd be obliged to leave the airfield. If he said he wanted to have a look at the planes, the observer would surely be suspicious. . . . And suddenly the enormity of the challenge set his adrenalin flowing. Why *shouldn't* he go to the Mess? He spoke near-perfect English, he was wearing English clothes, he was *au fait* with the English way of life. And what a coup if by some miracle he managed to pull the deception off! 'Right,' he said slowly. 'Thanks.'

Afterwards, there were enquiries about this too. But as the young observer said: 'I *did* wonder who he was to start with. But damn it, he knew Jack: even knew what school he'd been to. Besides, he seemed such a decent chap.'

Otto had any number of close shaves that evening. None closer than the first. There were only a couple of people in the flagstoned kitchen when he and the observer entered, and they, after Nungesser's visit, probably weren't as much on the *qui vive* as they might have been! The observer introduced Otto. 'This is Lieutenant Strong, sir. And Second Lieutenant Provis' – he looked enquiringly at Otto, not knowing his name. He very nearly clicked his heels and said automatically "Lieutnant Otto von Searle"! Only just in time did he remember the subterfuge he had decided on: 'Oh, sorry . . . Pendower, Gavin Pendower.'

They shook hands. And Strong said the Mess wasn't usually in such chaos, but they'd been celebrating the shooting down of a Hun. It must, to say the least, have been strange for Otto to hear his battle with Nungesser's Nieuport described at second-hand. But no stranger than a lot of things that happened that evening.

To start with he was too much on edge to relax, let alone to enjoy himself. But gradually the warmth, the drink and the *camaraderie* encompassed him in a sort of roseate glow. Unbelievable as it seemed, he was getting away with it!

When questioned afterwards one or two of the squadron admitted they had thought their visitor from Merville seemed a bit vague and non-committal and almost obsessively reluctant to talk about the war; but not one of them suspected he was anything other than a captain in the Flying Corps. As one put it: 'He knew Jack. He knew England. He knew about flying. Why *should* we suspect him?'

Otto chatted easily enough to Strong and Provis. He was introduced to two or three other people, and allowed himself to be persuaded to stay for dinner. The informality of the meal surprised him; but he was glad of the food, remembered his etiquette and was abstemious with the port. After dinner someone suggested he spent the night at Saint Genis, in his friend's cabin – 'I'm sure Jack won't be back till the morning, sir. If you stay, you could see him then.' He thought about it, and allowed himself to be persuaded again – which pleased everyone, because he seemed such a decent chap – and the duty officer showed him the way to my cabin.

I don't suppose, as he opened the door, he had the slightest premonition of what awaited him.

I don't know what his thoughts were as he stood in my cabin and stared at the photograph: the photograph of Jessica: his girl by my bed. I don't know what his feelings were as he picked it up and read the inscription.

I don't know. But I can guess.

And my guess is that this was the moment for him (my moment came later) when friendship was finally metamorphosed to hate. A hate all the more terrible because of the love that it took the place of: a love which had burned brightly once, should have burned brightly always, but was never so much as to flicker again.

What does a man do when the bottom is knocked out of his world? An introvert (like me) would probably have stayed in the solitude of his cabin. But Otto was an extrovert. He went back to the Mess. *His* refuge was talk and laughter, booze and song, and all the tinsel gaiety of a drunk.

The drunk started almost sedately: an arch little song on the gramophone:

154

Hello, hello, who's your lady friend?
Who's the little girlie by your side?

Then someone emptied a mug of beer down its horn: 'Pete! Give us a decent song! A Froggy song!' The piano was opened up. 'Orderly! Whisky for the piano!' The air, *Sous les Ponts de Paris*, was haunting and innocent; the words were neither:

> *Après la guerre finie,*
> *Soldat anglais parti;*
> Mam'selle Fransay boko pleuray
> *Après la guerre finie.*

> *Après la guerre finie,*
> *Soldat anglais parti;*
> Mademoiselle in the family way.
> *Après le guerre finie.*

> *Après la guerre finie,*
> *Soldat anglais parti;*
> Mademoiselle can go to hell,
> *Après la guerre finie.*

Applause. Another round of drinks. And cries of 'Leap-frog!'. This time the tune was John Brown's Body, and half the mess, suiting their action to the words, went bounding and crashing over the trestle-tables.

> They were only playing leap-frog,
> They were only playing leap-frog,
> They were only playing leap-frog,
> When one staff-officer jumped right over the other staff-officer's back!

It wasn't the sort of thing that would have gone on in a German Mess; but Otto, by now on his third whisky, was in just the reckless mood to join in.

155

The senior pilot brought his beer mug down with a crash. 'A soak! A soak! 'A' Flight v 'B' Flight. . . . Orderly! Siphons!' Siphons appeared as if by magic. The faint-hearted took cover. Over went the table. The offensive was launched. . . . Squirt: scream! Scream: squirt! 'Got him! Right where it hurts!' 'You bastard!' Squirt: squirt! Scream: scream! 'Orderly! More siphons!' 'Bastard am I, eh!' Squirting and screaming, till shirts were soaked, breeches were soaked, faces and hair were soaked, the walls were dripping, the floor puddling. . . . Then came a sudden tarantella from the piano, and a voice which may have been slurred and off-key, but lacked nothing in volume:

> Here's to good ole whisky,
> Mop it down, mop it down!

And after the good old whisky came the good old porter, and after the good old porter the good old brandy, and then the stout, the rum, the port and the gin. The voices grew tipsier, the words bawdier.

'I say, sir!' It was the young observer who had hailed him beside the hangars. 'Give us a song!'

He knew the Mess didn't in fact become suddenly quiet; that the British pilots and observers didn't in fact all stop what they were doing and stare at him. But that's the way it felt.

He could have refused, but that would have lost him their respect; he could have pretended he was too drunk, but that was a coward's way. Besides, wasn't this the crisis he'd been expecting, the moment of truth he'd been preparing for? He would have to improvise. He leapt onto the table. '*Achtung! Achtung!* I'll give you the Hun version of Mademoiselle from Armenteers!' His voice was guttural: a parody of an Englishman's mispronunciation of German:

> This German officer crossed the Rhine,
> > *Achtung! Achtung!*
> This German officer crossed the Rhine,

He was on the look-out for women and wine!
   Achtung! Achtung!
Look out, here he comes! *Achtung.*
Oh landlord, have you a daughter fair,
   Achtung! Achtung!
Oh landlord, have you a daughter fair,
With snow white breasts and long gold hair?
   Achtung! Achtung!
Look out, here he comes! *Achtung!*
Oh yes, but my daughter is far too young,
   Achtung! Achtung!
Oh yes, but my daughter is far too young
To be mucked about by a great big Hun!
   Achtung! Achtung!
Look out, here he comes! *Achtung!*

Otto's voice rose to a falsetto squeak:

Oh father, dear father, I'm not too young,
   Achtung! Achtung!
Oh father, dear father, I'm not too young,
I've been to bed with the parson's son!
   Achtung! Achtung!
Look out, here he comes! *Achtung!*

Laughter and cheers. Applause and shouts of 'encore'. More whisky was poured into Otto's glass. Then somebody started 'She was poor, but she was honest'; and when no-one was looking Otto tipped out the whisky.

For him the climax of the evening had come and gone, leaving him played-out, both physically and emotionally. The bravado which had brought him back to the Mess began to evaporate; and he reminded himself that he had to survive not only the evening but the next morning – and *that* would call for a clear head. So he pretended to be a little drunker than he was, said he needed fresh air and sleep, said 'see you in the morning' (when he hoped to do nothing of the sort), and set off for my

157

cabin.

No-one paid much attention to his leaving; but if one of his fellow officers had happened to follow him he'd have been puzzled. For Otto went first to the crewroom where he made a note of who was flying the dawn patrol: 'Lt. Westerman: Nieuport B103: 0730'. Then, instead of going to the barge directly across the airfield, made a detour *via* the hangars. Here he located Nieuport B103.

He was tempted to have a look in the cockpit; but thought better of it. And this, for him, was just as well; because a sentry had been watching. Afterwards the unfortunate sentry was asked 'Why didn't you challenge him?' 'But sir,' he said, 'I saw him come out of the Officers' Mess.' 'Didn't you think he was behaving oddly?' The sentry sucked his teeth and restrained himself: 'Well, sir. I knew you'd been 'aving a party!' 'But what on earth did you think he was doing: wandering about the airfield?' Again the sentry sucked his teeth: 'Lookin' for somewhere to relieve 'imself, sir' – he thought it best not to add that this was standard practice for officers after a drink. So Otto's midnight perambulation aroused no more than passing interest. Soon he was back in my cabin.

It must have been a long night for him. Some time during the small hours he must have taken my photograph of Jessica out of its frame – because next morning the frame was blank as a glassless window. And he must have written to Jessica – because there next morning the letter was, addressed very formally to Miss Jessica Pendower, propped up on the shelf by my bed. And he must have played patience – because of the order I subsequently found the cards in. What else he did, I can't say. Perhaps he slept, though I doubt it. He'd have been too afraid of missing the dawn patrol.

As I've said, you have to give him ten out of ten for nerve. He must have watched the batman taking an early cup of tea to Westerman's cabin; that was at seven o'clock. He must have walked calmly into the crewroom and pinched somebody's goggles and helmet; that was at five past seven. He must have watched the groundcrew as they trundled Nieuport B103 out of its hangar and onto the hard-standing; that was at ten past seven. He walked across to them: 'I'm flying the dawn patrol,' he said, 'instead of Lieutenant Westerman.'

The corporal in charge looked at him doubtfully, saw the three pips on his flying jacket, and thought he'd better not argue: 'Right, sir. Shall we start her up?'

'Thanks.' It was a lucky break, but no more, if you come to think of it, than he deserved.

By twenty past seven, he was strapped-in in the cockpit.

It was a cold morning, and the groundcrew watched impatiently, stamping their feet, swinging their arms and blowing on their hands as he studied the controls. After a while he thought they were beginning to look at him suspiciously. He waved away the chocks. The corporal was a bit surprised that he hadn't tested the magnetoes and revs – but that was *his* affair, and the sooner the Nieuport took off the sooner he and his mates would be back in their hut; he kicked the wooden blocks from under the wheels.

Out of the corner of his eye Otto saw a man in flying kit emerge from one of the barges: saw him shade his eyes against the rising sun, stand for a moment stock-still, then start running across the airfield, waving his arms. But Westerman was about half a minute too late.

Otto taxied fast – far faster than Westerman could run – to the edge of the airfield. He swung into wind, rammed open the throttle, and prayed that the Nieuport didn't have any unpredictable vices. He needn't have worried. His take-off was inelegant but safe. And once airborne he found the plane every bit as easy to handle as a Fokker. He risked a look down. Apart from the little cluster of figures on the hard-standing, disbelievingly waving their arms, the airfield still seemed to be asleep. But it wouldn't, he knew, stay asleep much longer. He headed east. For home.

A quarter-of-an-hour later he put down in a field on the German side of the lines. And that, you might say, is the end of the story.

But there were repercussions. . . . First, there was the letter:

159

the letter addressed to Jessica staring at me from the shelf by my bed. What on earth was I to do with it? Should I hand it over to Uncle, read it, destroy it or post it? Duty demanded I hand it over; self-interest demanded I read it and then destroy it; but surely the only decent thing to do was to post it? I was desperately anxious to be fair to Otto. For the sake of *auld lang syne*, I told myself, I ought to lean over backwards to do the honourable thing. So after much heartsearching I stuck it in the outgoing mail-box in the Mess.

Within twenty-four hours I wished I hadn't.

Next evening, when I happened to pick up my patience cards, I noticed that they were sorted into two packs: a way I never left them. So Otto must have been using them – what other things of mine, I wondered, had the wretched fellow been nosing through? Suddenly I noticed the order in which the first few cards were arranged: ace of spades on queen of clubs, ace of clubs on queen of spades. It was the same in either pack. I knew that not once in a million would those combinations turn up by chance. So Otto must have arranged the cards deliberately. Into the gipsy's warning of death.

I could picture him sitting in my cabin, his eyes returning again and again to the photograph of Jessica. And I could feel, as though it were an almost physical metamorphosis, our friendship not only withering but dying. And hatred not only taking root but burgeoning.

It was a pity. It wasn't the way *I* wanted it. But if this was the way *he* wanted it, so be it.

12

There was no doubt about it. We were on the crest of a wave that summer. We'd got the Fokkers licked.

All through April, May and June new planes arrived in ever increasing numbers at the Front: Nieuports and DH2s with forward-firing machine-guns, and graceful Sopwith Strutter reconnaissance planes to replace our 'mechanical cows'. Otto and his colleagues, outnumbered, out-manoeuvred and outgunned, had the sense to give us a wide berth. And this suited us well. Because the Big Push – the offensive which everyone believed would end the stalemate of trench warfare – was imminent; and the Flying Corps were expected to play an important part in it.

So each day, through the midsummer haze, we flew from dawn to dusk, spotting for our artillery, reconnoitring behind the lines and photographing the German defences – we must have brought back enough information to fill a volume. And each night from our barges on the Lys we watched the Army moving into position for the attack: silhouettes half-seen in the flicker of oil lamps, bumping and lurching along the potholed lane. All through the small hours we'd hear the grinding of gears the rattling of equipment, the muffled orders and the snatches of song; yet by dawn they had always vanished as though they had never been, and looking out of our portholes we'd see only the deserted road and the derelict farms. And each weekend, whenever I could get away for long enough from the airfield, I'd see Nicole.

I saw a lot of her that summer. But never enough.

Her 'friend', as she insisted on calling him, was apparently still holed up in some mountain fastness on the Italian Front

161

where she wasn't able to join him – *I* reckoned he was playing the field and didn't want her around; but this uncharitable suspicion I kept to myself. Anyhow, there Nicole was at a loose end in Paris: eighteen, beautiful and in need of consolation. How lucky I was! . . . I soon discovered that she had a passion, almost amounting it seemed to me to an obsession, for secrecy, and the first few times I saw her we seemed to be forever arranging clandestine meetings (in case, I suppose, her neighbours got suspicious and wrote to her 'friend') and forever making love with the blinds drawn and the door locked (in case, I suppose, her 'friend' turned up unexpectedly on leave). I found it a bit off-putting to start with. But when I realised this was the way it had to be, I turned the secrecy into a sort of game, a game the two of us could play as conspirators together; and for this she was grateful. And sometimes, when I could wangle a long weekend rather than a short one, I'd hire a battered old Delaunay, and we'd drive for miles into the valley of the Loire, where no-one knew us and the war was in another world. Then she'd *really* let down her hair. And those were the best times of all. No wonder, I thought, everyone had kept telling me I ought to get a girl!

I'd just come back from a particularly blissful couple of days in Touraine, when Uncle sent for me.

Though it was nearly three months since his accident, he was still limping, and his beard only partially camouflaged the scars on his neck: 'I want you', he said, 'to go and see Tabor. And chase up some new planes.'

I wasn't pleased. The Big Push was supposed to be starting any moment.

He laid a hand on my shoulder. 'Be back in forty-eight hours, and you won't miss anything. And this is important.' He went on to explain, rather to my surprise, that he wasn't happy about the performance of our aircraft – 'At the moment, I agree, we've the whip hand. But not by much. And what'll happen when *their* new aircraft arrive?'

Four hours later I was at Farnborough, putting this point to Tabor. And getting nowhere. For a reason I couldn't account for at the time, Uncle's friend Major Tabor was less forthcoming than usual. There had, I gathered, been 'unavoidable delays' with the SE5; and the "Pup" was promised to the Navy. 'Isn't there anything else', I asked him, 'in the offing?' He indicated that there might be a Bristol fighter in production by the end of the year, and perhaps a Sopwith Triplane. He promised me a flip in the prototype of the latter tomorrow. . . . Which meant I had the evening to play with.

I had been worried for some time about Jess. Apart from a grateful but rather distant 'thank you' for passing on Otto's letter, I hadn't heard from her for more than a month. The first couple of times I rang the hospital I was told she wasn't free. But the third time I got her. 'All well with you, Jess?'

'Yes, fine.' Her voice was listless. She didn't sound 'fine' to me.

'I'm at Farnborough. Just for twenty-four hours. How about dinner? At that Ritzy haunt in the Old Kent Road?'

'Sorry, Jack. I can't make it.'

'You on night duty?'

A pause, then: 'Yes.'

'Well *that* doesn't start till 8.30. I'll pick you up at six.'

'No, really. But thanks for asking me. . . . All well with you?'

'Not as well as it was a few minutes ago. What's up?'

'Nothing.'

'I may have the wings of a bird. But not its brains!'

A longer pause this time, then: 'Please, Jack. It's no good. We'll only both be hurt.'

'I'll be at the hospital,' I said, 'in a couple of hours.'

When I got there I was told she wasn't available. So I said I'd wait.

I waited, and waited and waited. After a couple of hours an extrememly attractive girl in nurse's uniform came walking up to me; she seemed to be swinging her hips a bit more than was natural: 'Jack Cunningham?'

I nodded.

'I'm Emily. A friend of Jess's. I'm awfully sorry, she can't see you.'

163

'You mean she won't see me?'

She lowered her eyelids and looked at me sideways: 'I can't think why. She must be crazy!'

I wasn't in the mood for flirtation: 'Sorry,' I said shortly. 'I'm waiting for Jess.'

She flushed. 'I *told* her it wouldn't work. Now I suppose you think I'm some sort of tart?'

I shook my head: 'Any other time I'd have jumped at the offer. But Jess and I have something to sort out. I'm not leaving till I've talked to her.'

She stared at me, tugging at her lip: 'I'll see,' she said eventually, 'if I can get her.'

About an hour later Jessica came into the waiting room. She looked thin, pale and desperately unhappy. The sheen on her hair was lacquer, the colour in her cheeks rouge, and the sparkle in her eyes – I'd have taken a bet on it – belladonna. 'I've got to be back', she said, 'in an hour.'

It was late; and about the only place still open was a tumble-down café, by the docks. It wasn't the sort of place I'd have thought Jessica would feel safe let alone at ease in; but she told me the nurses often used it because it was cheap.

'What,' I asked her when they'd brought us our tea, 'was in Otto's letter?'

'You don't beat about the bush, do you!'

'Not if we've only an hour.'

She spent a long time not looking at me, stirring her tea. Then she handed me an envelope.

There were more than a dozen pages of Otto's letter. And no wonder the damned fellow had upset her! If you cut out the sentimental verbiage, he had three things to say. He denied killing the British officer. He felt that he was being faithful to her (in his fashion!) and was disappointed that she didn't seem to have been faithful to him. And his friendship with me was very definitely a thing of the past.

We fell into this river, Otto had written: *And Kurt seized the stone, and hit the man on the head. He went on hitting him. Again and*

164

again and again. Like a madman. And the man's skull was smashed in. And still he went on hitting him. It was terrible. . . .

For more than a year, my Jessie, I went out with no girl. But I am a pilot, nineteen and flesh and blood, and who knows for how long this terrible war will last. So I begin to give the girls my company — but nothing more. And always every time I take the girl out, I make pretend it is you. And never the same girl will I take out more than once — in case, you understand, I become fond of her. And never to any girl will I give my heart or my photograph. Because of our vow and the love that I have for you. And how I hoped, my Jessie, that you had felt the same.

Once I would have given my life for Jack Cunningham. We were as David and Jonathan. But my beautiful Alsation Jessie who was in pup he set on fire and burnt alive. And my friend who had been only five days in our squadron he set on fire and burnt alive. And the girl who I love, when my back is turned, he tries to steal from me. So do you wonder that I say to him 'if you value your life cross not my path'. Yet even now, for the sake of all that is past, if we met in the battleground of the sky I would not be the first to open fire.

I handed the letter back: 'There's no need,' I said, 'to take all this to heart. He was half-tight when he wrote it. And most of it isn't true.'

'What isn't true?'

I told her about the Interrogation File on Lieutnant Fassbender: that it was Otto who had killed the British officer in the wood.

She shook her head: 'I don't believe it.'

'That was the official finding, Jess.'

'But this other German — Kurt whatever his name is — *of course* he'd say Otto did it. To protect himself.'

I didn't say anything.

She looked at me sadly: 'You've changed.'

'How?'

'You've gained something. But you've lost something too. You're harder.'

'Snails,' I said, 'have hard shells. But they're soft underneath.'

165

'So, you don't *really* think Otto's a murderer?'

I said I didn't know what to think. And that was the truth. 'But one thing I *do* know, Jess. He's no right to take it out on you.'

She smiled a sad little smile. 'That's the trouble. He's every right' – I started to say something, but she held up her hand – 'Please! When I was sixteen I thought love was all that mattered: I thought I could fly in the face of the gods. So I made a promise. Now it's very simple: either I keep that promise or I don't. I'm not, I'm afraid, like Otto. I can't have it both ways. If I go out with a chap – silly girl that I am! – I start getting fond of him, and (she sounded as though she'd a frog in her throat) giving him my photo. And wanting to break my promise. And feeling unfaithful. And hating myself. So I've made a decision. No more dates – not even platonic ones. No more Helford River – not even for the sake of *auld lang syne*. From now on I'm giving all my heart and my time to bedpans and tournequets!'

Her eyes were enormous: her skin had an almost transluscent pallor; she didn't look well; but she did look almost unbearably beautiful, and I couldn't stop staring at her. 'God,' I said. 'What a waste!'

We talked for another half-hour. But nothing I did or said would move her. She had made her decision. She didn't want – no, that's not *le mot juste* – she didn't feel able, to see me again.

It was the end if not of the world then certainly of an era.

I arrived at Farnborough next morning with a splitting headache and the mother and father of all hangovers. And my temper wasn't improved by the sight of the Triplane being wheeled out of its hangar. I thought of saying I'd decided not to fly it. Then I thought of Uncle. I collected my goggles and the manufacturer's notes.

In the eighteen months since I had got my wings I had flown pullers and pushers, monoplanes and biplanes, parasols and sesquiplanes; but never a triplane; and I can't say I was looking forward to it. According to its manufacturers this particular

166

Triplane had a higher speed, a better rate of climb, a higher ceiling and a better all-round performance than any of its contemporaries. But the same sort of claims, I remembered, had been made for the 'mechanical cow'! 'Is it any good,' I asked the corporal who was helping me to start up.

'She's OK, sir.'

That, I told myself, remained to be seen.

I found the cockpit roomy and well designed, and the view, in spite of the plethora of wings, better than I had anticipated. I couldn't tell much about her as we taxied out, though I suspected she might be a pig in a crosswind. I took her to the very edge of the airfield, swung into wind and gave her full throttle. She seemed to have quite a bit of power, and I was telling myself I'd better concentrate on keeping her straight when I suddenly realised we were airborne! I was conscious of a stir of excitement: the sort of excitement a man feels when for the first time he catches a pretty girl's eye across a room and she doesn't look away. Could it be that I was onto a good thing? I climbed to 5,000 feet. The Triplane (or Tripehound as she was subsequently nick-named) didn't appear to climb all that steeply or quickly, but when I checked my watch I found she had averaged more than a thousand feet a minute (twice as fast as a Scout could climb; three times as fast as a Fokker). I began to get *really* interested. I tried one or two gentle climbs and dives, turns and stall-turns. There was nothing special about the way she handled; indeed she was nothing like as instantly responsive as a Morane or a Bristol Scout; but she answered her controls smoothly, accurately and (for want of a better word) gracefully. She was, I decided, a nice plane to fly; but probably too lacking in *élan* to be much good at aerobatics. I tried a loop. She looped, as she had turned, with a sort of languid ennui: not particularly fast, but with such precision that as we came out of our dive we hit the slipstream we had made as we went into it. I tried a flick roll; and that was even more languid and if possible even more accurate. I tried a spin. I couldn't believe it, but that too was controlled and graceful, and she came out at the merest touch of aileron and rudder. We flew for a couple of minutes straight and level, and I got the quite ridiculous impression that she yawned and asked 'Can't you think of something a bit more exciting?' I climbed to 12,000 feet and told myself I'd be a fool to try anything *too* exciting – but I knew I was going to. I put her into a dive: 120, 130, 140, 150, 160 and that was as fast as I'd ever been in my life: 170, and her upper wing started to tremble: 180, and I hauled her out of the dive and into a loop, with a roll off the top and the second we were the right-way-up a violent stall turn that made her wings tremble like leaves in a storm; and in the dive and in the loop and in the roll and in the turn she had responded to every touch of my hands and feet. So I took her down, and landed her carefully, and went to see Major Tabor. 'How soon,' I asked, 'can you get Triplanes to Eight Squadron?'

He looked embarrassed, and started talking about 'unavoidable delays'.

'Look, sir,' I said, 'let's not beat about the bush. This is the plane we want. How soon can we have it?'

'I'm afraid,' he said, 'the Triplane has been earmarked for the Navy.'

I took a deep breath. 'If the Navy put in their requisition first, I see they must have first pick. But with great respect, sir, our need is greater than the Navy's. We're doing the fighting. Surely we're entitled to *some*?'

'Try telling that to a Sea Lord!'

I realised I was out of my depth: that my best bet was to report the set-up to Uncle, and hope he'd be able to pull strings. 'Any chance of taking the Triplane back to the Front, sir? Like the DH2? For combat trials?'

He stared at me, his fingers drumming the top of his desk. 'We've got only the one plane,' he said slowly, 'it would have to be a real emergency to make us part with her.'

I don't know to this day if I read him right, or if I read into his words what I wanted to read. I said I understood, and that I'd better be on my way, because Uncle had told me to be sure to be back at Saint Genis by nightfall – 'because of the Big Push, you know.' On my way through the hangars I collected a spanner, and when no-one was looking I loosened the piston rings in the engine of my DH2.

A quarter-of-an-hour later I was warming her up on the tarmac. The engine- – not surprisingly – wasn't running too well. 'She's no good,' I shouted to the sergeant-in-charge: 'Look at the revs!'

He sucked his teeth: 'She was OK this morning, sir.'

'Well she's not OK now, is she!'

'No, sir. I'll have a look at her.'

'Forget it,' I said impatiently. 'It may be a long job. I'll take something else. Get the Tripehound fuelled.'

He looked at me doubtfully.

I tapped the pips on my flying jacket: 'I'm in a hurry, sergeant.'

He must have thought me a real bastard. But a quarter-of-an-hour later I was climbing into the Tripehound. I didn't bother to warm her up; I was too afraid that someone would come running out at the last second and stop me. 'Tell Major Tabor', I shouted, 'there was a real emergency!' And before anyone realized what was happening I was airborne and on my way to Saint Genis.

It was the most beautiful afternoon: bright sunshine, little wind, and a cloudless sky smudged around its periphery by summer haze. I climbed to 10,000 feet and said goodbye to England and in the same breath hello to France. The view was magnificent. Behind me I could see the unbroken line of the coast from North Foreland to the Isle of Wight, the cliffs bright white in the sunlight, the waves a diamond necklace slung casually along the shore; the light was so strong I could see the pinhead dots of people on Dover pier. Beneath me toy ships were crossing the Channel: the leave-boat flanked by a pair of destroyers, three straight white furrows ploughing the blue-grey pasture of the sea. Ahead was the patchwork tapestry of France: big carefully-cultivated fields, straight roads patrolled by ramrod poplars, and distant at first but coming closer with each revolution of the prop the laceration of the Front. I wouldn't look at it. I wouldn't think of it. For a brief hour I'd make believe there

169

were only three things in the world: myself, the Triplane and the vast uncluttered playground of the sky.

There were no clouds over Northern France, and as far as I could make out no other aircraft. Nothing moved. It was like flying through a bowl of unflawed crystal, with the light seeming to come not from a single source but to be reflected from every individual particle of air. I took the Triplane to 18,000 feet: higher than I'd ever been in my life. She had the same engine as a Nieuport – the 130 hp Clerget; but she gave the impression of being more powerful – I suppose her stacked-up wings gave her additional lift. Her makers claimed that she could climb to 22,000 feet, more than twice the ceiling of a 'mechanical cow' – which, I told myself, summed up the difference between a good plane and a bad. I didn't try anything spectacular that afternoon. I did, however, for the second time, put the Triplane through every manoeuvre I could think of – loops and half-loops, spins and flat-spins, dives and spiral-dives, rolls, flick-rolls and rolls-off-the-top. And there was no doubt about it, she was the most graceful and amenable aircraft I'd ever flown. I felt like a rider who puts a new horse through its paces, and finds he is able to establish an immediate rapport. And there was one other thing I liked about the Tripehound: she had a Vickers machine-gun synchronised to fire through her prop.

It came to me that within the space of twenty-four hours I'd lost one friend and found another.

I didn't go straight to Saint Genis – I was enjoying myself too much. Instead I went down to zero feet and made a detour towards Paris, flying low over the big flat fields and the intricate network of canals. The engine was ticking over with a reassuring purr; the Triplane was so stable that she pretty well flew herself; the sun was shining; I was happy and relaxed. I rediscovered that afternoon something I had been in danger in the last few months of losing: my love of flying.

I put off letting down at Saint Genis until the sun was setting. And what a sunset it was! The heat-haze of the afternoon had vanished, leaving the horizon clear, the shadows sharp and the countryside bathed in a radiance like liquid fire. Even the Front took on a sort of macabre grandeur: the wire glittering, the trenches a mosaic of ebony and gold. It was the sort of evening when God seemed firmly ensconced in his heaven and it was good to be alive.

The moment I landed, Uncle sent for me. His eyes were bright with excitement: 'The Big Push', he said, 'is fixed for July 1st. The barrage starts tonight.'

The guns opened up at midnight.

There were an incredible number of guns, massed along a twenty mile strip of the Front on either side of the River Somme; and they fired non-stop, day and night, for five days: million after million shells pouring down like cosmic hail onto the German defences. It was the most terrible bombardment of the war. We at Saint Genis were fifty miles north of the Somme; but even on the airfield the ground shook, doors were blown open, glass was shattered, and each night the sky was lit as by a continuous sheet of summer lightning. It seemed impossible for anything or anybody on the receiving end of such a holocaust to survive. But we had to be sure. So each day – though the weather was vile, with low cloud and driving rain – our planes took off to photograph the German positions.

Imagine our amazement when we discovered that the Germans were still very much alive. And our terror when we discovered that in order to find out what was going on we had to fly *through* the barrage of our own shells.

The Germans were alive because the soil in the valley of the Somme is basically chalk; chalk is ideal for quarrying; and the Germans had quarried trenches forty feet deep, reinforced with timber and stone, and secure against any number of direct hits. It was impossible to smother all these trenches all the time; and the moment our barrage shifted from one line to another, the Germans emerged, manned their guns and started firing. Several of our planes, in those five days, were brought down by German fire from the ground. Several more were brought down by our own shells. And this, for me, was one of the most terrify-

171

ing moments of the war: flying at fifteen hundred feet (we couldn't get higher because of the cloud) and looking back at the semi-circle of guns, their muzzles pointing at *us*, their shells passing all around us, so close that the plane quivered and jerked in their slip-stream. It was, of course, only a matter of time before one of them would register a direct hit.

On the eve of the offensive a Staff Officer arrived from Army Headquarters to thank us for our co-operation during the bombardment, and to explain what was expected of us once the attack got under way. 'Your main job', he told us, 'will be to see where the advance is going fastest. So we know where to send in the cavalry.' He spoke as if victory was already assured. And few of us doubted him.

July 1st dawned misty and still. I was flying the first patrol, from 7.15 to 9.15; and as zero hour was 7.30 I reckoned I ought to have a grand-stand view of the PBI going over the top. The bad weather by now had moved east into central Europe, and there wasn't a cloud in the sky as I took off, only a soft white ground haze which the heat of the sun would soon disperse. The barrage, of course, was still going on; but now the cloud had vanished I was able, thank goodness, to get above the trajectory of the shells, and from 8,000 feet could see the full effect of the week's bombardment. About fifty square miles of the Front had been blasted to a pock-marked desolation: there wasn't a tree, a blade of grass or one stone left standing on another. And still the shells came pouring out of the sky, covering the German trenches in what looked like a canopy of white cotton-wool. I glanced at my watch. Only a minute to go. I found myself edging closer to the lines.

It was as though the world stopped in mid-rotation – as indeed for some hundred-thousand French, German and British soldiers it was about to. One second earth and sky were trembling under a hail of shells. Next second there was silence: absolute silence: a silence the more unnerving because everyone knew what it heralded. The silence lasted for perhaps ten seconds. Then everything happened at once.

A pair of mines – the fruits of long weeks of patient tunnelling

– exploded just short of the German salient at La Boiselle, flinging a great column of smoke and debris 3,000 feet into the sky. For a moment the column hung expanding, like the silhouette of a great black tree; then it fell to earth in a widening cone of dust. The Triplane bucked like a frightened horse. Whistles blew along a ten mile stretch of the Front. And the infantry went over the top.

From my aerial perch, I could see all too clearly what happened. The infantry threaded their way through the allied wire. They seemed to be moving with painful slowness – which was hardly surprising seeing they were weighed down by a minimum sixty-six pounds of equipment and had been ordered to 'go forward deliberately, as on a parade ground'. Once through the wire they formed up into a solid line and advanced with fixed bayonettes on the German trenches. The Germans, meanwhile, had emerged from their dug-outs and manned their machine-guns. Bullets ripped into the infantry like hail into blossom. The first British line faltered and fell. Another line formed up and tried to advance; but they too were mown down. The same thing happened to a third line, and to a fourth and to a fifth, and so, throughout that long and terrible morning, *ad infinitum*. With the best will in the world troops can't advance when they are dead. And that is the story of the Battle of the Somme: total casualties one million plus, total gains a few square miles of mud.

For the Army, idealism perished on the Somme and nothing was ever quite the same again. It was summed up by the poets in the trenches. Before the battle they wrote:

If I should die, think only this of me:
    That there's some corner of a foreign field
That is for ever England. There shall be
    In that rich earth a richer dust concealed;
A dust whom England bore, shaped, made aware,
    Gave, once, her flowers to love, her ways to roam,
A body of England's, breathing English air,
    Washed by the rivers, blest by suns of home.

After the battle they wrote:

Good-morning; good morning!' the General said
When we met him last week on our way to the Line.
Now the soldiers he smiled at are most of 'em dead,
And we're cursing his staff for incompetent swine.
'He's a cheery old card,' grunted Harry to Jack
As they slogged up to Arras with rifle and pack.
But he did for them both by his plan of attack.

For Eight Squadron the Somme was not so much a disaster
as a non-event. 'For months', I wrote in my diary, 'we've been
preparing and practising, hoping to give our chaps in the
trenches a helping hand. But no luck. No flares, no signals,
none of the manoeuvres we had rehearsed. Something must
have gone *terribly* wrong'. It was, I felt, too bad. But because I
was young, and because we airmen ate, slept, moved and
thought in another environment to the men in the trenches
(almost in another world) I didn't concern myself all that much
with the Somme. A-third-of-a-million men may have died and
two-thirds-of-a-million may have been crippled, but I didn't
know one of them; I was less moved, I think, by the holocaust
than by Claire Scott throwing her crucifix out of the window.
And there is perhaps another reason why the decimation of our
Army made so little impression on me. We were about to be
decimated ourselves: about to be plunged into a valley of darkness every bit as filled with death as in the days when we were
Fokker fodder.

For the Germans, late that summer, produced a magnificent
new fighter.

The Albatri arrived at Ronchin in September. And they
arrived not in dribs and drabs but *en masse*. Two *Jastas* (or
fighter squadrons): twenty-eight planes, complete with spares,
replacements and hand-picked pilots. Now the Albatross's performance was good but not spectacular. She had a top speed of

110 (faster than a DH2 or a Nieuport, but no better than my Tripehound), and reasonable all round manoeuvrability (again nothing like as good as a Triplane). What made the Albatross so formidable, what sent us toppling flame-wrapped out of the sky, was its armament. The best *our* planes could boast was a single drum-fed machine-gun. The Albatri could boast a pair of belt-fed and synchronised machine-guns. It was like a boxer with one hand fighting a boxer with two.

And there was another reason for the Germans' instant and spectacular success: their invention of the *Jasta*. The purpose of the *Jasta*, in the words of the German High Command, was 'to establish complete air supremacy over a limited section of the Front'. This was achieved by concentrating the best planes and the best pilots into a number of crack squadrons: squadrons trained to fight not as individuals but as a unit. The unit's tactics never varied. The Albatri would climb high into the sun behind the German lines and lie in wait for the inevitable Allied reconnaissance-planes and artillery-spotters; when they saw these planes they would descend on them *en masse*, and shoot them down. Simple. Effective. And unanswerable. For the Flying Corps that autumn were still committed, no matter what the cost, to a policy of continuous patrolling. We were obliged, in other words, to head east, day after day, to where the *Jastas* were waiting: better planes, with better guns in greater numbers. The war in the air became suddenly less individual, less chivalrous, and decidedly less enjoyable. As the Somme, for the Army, marked a watershed between idealism and disillusion, so for the Flying Corps, the *Jasta* marked a watershed between flying-for-fun and flying-to-kill.

It was a change of attitude brought out very clearly by two incidents in the Mess, one at the start of that autumn one at the end.

I was playing cribbage with a young observer only a few weeks out of Flying School, when our senior pilot came into the Mess: 'We've just had a message from Merville,' he told us. 'Boelcke is dead.'

'I'm sorry,' I said.

The observer I was playing with looked at me curiously: 'He was a Hun, wasn't he?'

I nodded.

'And you're *sorry*!'

I felt suddenly and depressingly old. How could I make the youngster understand the way we had felt in the early days of the war? Was it worthwhile explaining to him that in the last twelve months Oswald Boelcke had shot down five of our squadron's planes, and that each time we had received a letter from him addressed to 'the relatives of my comrades of the air': that whenever Boelcke shot down a plane and the crew survived, he visited them in hospital, made sure they were being well-treated and brought them gifts of fresh fruit and schnapps. 'He was a good man,' I said.

The senior pilot nodded: 'Merville are sending a wreath. Uncle reckons we ought to. What do you think?'

'Good idea.'

So that night we made a cross out of holly and ivy and wrote an inscription: 'To the memory of Captain Oswald Boelcke, our brave and chivalrous foe'. And next morning I dropped the wreath on the airfield at Lagincourt – and wasn't surprised when I got back to hear that planes from six other squadrons had done the same.

That was before the *Jastas* got to work. Before the Fall.

A couple of months later I was playing another game of cribbage with another and even younger observer – the other chap had lasted only a week – when the senior pilot came into the Mess with a face like a boot. 'Lanoe,' he said, 'has been *carboneezayed*.'

Lanoe Hawker was the doyen of the RFC, a pilot whose courage and skill had earned him the VC, the DSO, and the admiration of everyone who knew and cared about flying. There was a stunned silence. If Lanoe had fallen, what hope was there for the rest of us?

'Who,' I asked, 'got him?'

'Richthofen.'

Another silence. Manfred von Richthofen, one of the new

176

generation of *Jasta* pilots, had hardly endeared himself to his opposite number by having a silver trophy made to commemo- rate each of his kills – 'like a bloody hunter, mounting his victim's head'. The senior pilot's voice was angry. 'God, I'd like to get that bastard in my sights. And watch him fry. All the way down.'

But when next week the two of them met above the woods of La Neuville, it wasn't von Richthofen who fell flaming out of the autumn sky.

That night Uncle sent for me: 'How do you fancy taking over as senior pilot?'

I shrugged: 'If you can't think of anyone else.'

'I'm asking because there *is* an alternative. I could have you posted home. To training.'

I was dog-tired. I'd flown seven hours that day, and nearly been killed three times. My God, I wanted home. But experienced pilots were needed at the Front more desperately now than ever before. And there was Nicole. 'Don't think I fancy training,' I said.

He stared at me: 'How old are you, Jack?'

'Nineteen. If you think I'm too young, it's all the same to me.' Behind me a door swung-to with a crash, and I found my head jerking round, as though I half-expected an Albatros to come zooming into the room.

'That's not what I was thinking at all. Sure you *want* to stay?'

I didn't trust myself to speak. So I nodded.

'How about some leave? Before you take over?'

I thought of the upper reaches of the Loire and the vineyards and the quiet little Huguenot silk towns and Nicole with her hair down. 'That', I said, 'would be very nice.'

And so it was. Very nice indeed.

We had four days together. Longer than we'd ever had before. I think quite simply they were the happiest days of my life.

I had no inkling, when I arrived back at Saint Genis, of the surprise in store for me.

I had a chat with Uncle about my duties as senior pilot, then made my way to the Mess. I'd been told that a couple of replacement pilots had just arrived from England; but I didn't ask their names or anything about them, because I knew I'd meet them at dinner. And sure enough, about half-an-hour before the meal, they came into the mess. I happened to have my back to them as they entered; but the moment one of them spoke I spun round, disbelieving.

And there he was: tall, gangling carroty-haired and grinning all over his face: 'Good evening, sir.'

'Good God!' I hammered on the table for silence. 'Hey, everyone! Meet the *real* Gavin Pendower!'

13

Gavin always insisted that his posting to Eight Squadron was pure coincidence; and if this was the way he wanted it, I didn't argue. Anyhow, here he was: scatterbrained and irrepressible as ever, about three inches taller than when I'd last seen him, and, as I soon discovered, a pretty competent pilot. On duty I don't think he ever once took advantage of our friendship, saluting me and calling me sir with almost embarrassing punctilliousness; but in our free time we dropped quickly into the easy-going relationship we had enjoyed as children.

One of the first things we talked about was Jessica. 'She didn't look too well,' I said, 'when I last saw her. I wish she'd forget Otto.'

'You know how it is with Jess. Once she makes up her mind there's no shifting her. And her affair with Otto was more than a schoolgirl crush, you know. And Jack. . . .'

'Hmmm?'

'I don't know if I ought to tell you this. But it worries me. I still think of Otto as a friend. If we met, I . . . I couldn't kill him.'

A DH2 took off with a sudden roar, and my head jerked round like a puppet's. I was on edge, and I knew it: 'Now listen, Gavin. And this is an order. If you meet Otto von Searle you're to kill him. Understand? Kill him dead as a dodo. I'll tell you why. . . .'

I was telling him why in some detail and with some vehemence, when I suddenly realised he wasn't listening: that he'd switched off: that he didn't want to know. I was angry. 'Gavin! For God's sake!'

'Sorry. You're right. I know you're right. But I can't help the way I feel.'

It was no use, I told myself, losing my temper. 'When I arrived at Saint Genis,' I said slowly. 'Believe me, I felt like you. In fact I was very nearly courtmartialled, for larking about with Otto. But that was eighteen months ago. I've learned a lot in eighteen months. And believe me, it's kill or be killed.'

He looked at me, and I could read his mind like a book. He was thinking about me exactly what I, eighteen months ago, had thought about Uncle: that I was uncaring, that the war had made me bitter and twisted. And suddenly – maybe because of Jess – I was desperately anxious for him *not* to think of me like that; I wanted him to think of me as someone to admire, not to pity. 'Talking,' I said, 'won't get us anywhere. Come on! Grab a Nieuport. And see how long you can stay on my tail.'

It may have been running away. But what a wonderful world it was to run to. Beneath us, dappled in sunlight and shadow, the winter fields; around us few but how splendid clouds, and above us that radiant world where the light is bright as God's bedside lamp and the silence more absolute than a cloister.

We climbed away from the Front, levelled off at 10,000 feet, and played Chase-me-Charlie among the bastions of cumulus.

Gavin turned out to be a good if somewhat reckless pilot. And as we stooped and soared, wheeled and cartwheeled about the sky, I found myself wondering how I'd assess him if he were flying an Albatross? I would, I decided, have to be *very* careful, but I'd get him in the end: if I taxed his patience for long enough, he'd try something a bit *too* reckless, and that would be that. I decided to teach him a lesson. I went into a tight turn, and he followed, trying to get on my tail. This was standard practice. I stayed turning: five, ten, fifteen, twenty complete circles, keeping always just out of his sights. By the end of the twenty-fifth circle Gavin was bored and losing patience. I could guess what he was thinking: 'this could go on for ever. I'll have to try something else'; I could see him forgetting the cardinal rule that the pilot who breaks a circle first is in jeopardy. I kept turning, watching him like a hawk, waiting for him to break. And the moment he broke, I broke too, but in the opposite direction, and hauled the Triplane into a stall-turn and dropped onto his

180

tail. He hadn't the slightest idea where I was. And now he made his second mistake. He looked below him and above him, to the right and to the left; only last of all did he look behind him, to see me sitting rock-steady on his tail.

'Two bits of advice,' I said, when we had landed and were walking back to the Mess.

'I'd be grateful.'

'You did OK – made me quite glad you weren't an Albatross! But unless the other chap is out-turning you, *never* break a circle.'

'Right, sir.'

'And if you lose sight of your opponent, look behind you first. It's common sense. If he's behind you, you're in *real* trouble. And you've got to act fast. If he's any other place, he's got a deflection shot, and that's more difficult so he'll want to get close. And that gives you time. Right?'

'Right, sir. And thanks.'

It would be nice, I told myself as we headed for our respective cabins, to have someone to take under my wing: someone to pass my knowledge on to: a friend to relive the past with. And we all needed a friend that winter. For the Albatri were too good for us.

We would send our luckless reconnaissance planes across the lines at different times and different heights and different places, we'd send them over singly or in pairs or in formations of up to a dozen, we'd send them over unescorted, lightly escorted or heavily escorted. The result was always the same. They were shot down. The life-expectancy of the air-crew who came to us that winter dropped to eleven days. . . . New aircraft were what we needed, as no-one knew better than Uncle. He sent message after message, asking for Triplanes; but the Navy wouldn't release them – though they did eventually send one of their own squadrons to the Pas de Calais. 'Maybe,' I suggested, 'we ought to settle for SE5s or Bristols?'

Uncle shook his head: 'Tripehounds I want. And Tripehounds I'll bloody well get!'

I shrugged: 'You'd better get 'em quick!'

181

He looked at me thoughtfully, stroking the great black arras of his beard: 'So you hear it too. . . .'

'Hear what?'

'"Time's winged chariot hurrying near."'

'I hear,' I said. 'But I don't listen.'

The truth was that we all heard Death hurrying after us that winter. And he sought us out, not only in our waking hours but in our sleeping. Often in the small of the night we would dream he touched us, and would wake moaning or screaming or grinding our teeth; and some of us would reach for the bottle and some would turn on the gramophone and some would pray. But it made no difference. Next morning on the dawn patrol, whether we'd been on our knees or at the bottle, he snuffed us out impartially as the fancy took him.

Sometimes I'd find it difficult to sleep, and Gavin and I would go drifting down the Lys on a home-made punt and make believe we were on the Helford. And sometimes I'd lie awake and listen to the water whispering past the barge, and make believe I was on the Loire and Nicole was in my arms and there was no more war. Then I'd hear the grumble of guns, and would roll over to face the bulkhead, hands pressed to my ears, my eyes screwed tight.

I reckon not one of us would have survived that winter if we hadn't found an ally in the weather. Winter in 1916 came early to the Western Front; and throughout the latter part of November low cloud hung pall-like over the exhausted armies. How the troops in the trenches must have cursed the bitter wind and the driving rain; but we welcomed them, for they kept us grounded. The days *we* dreaded were when the cloud lifted, and the fields lay sparkling with sunlight and frost. December 2nd was such a day, and we lost a Strutter and its escorting Nieuport; December 9th was another and we lost two Strutters. As Uncle put it, if we were going to be killed anyhow we might as well go out in a blaze of glory. We got in touch with Merville and planned an ambush.

The two squadrons built a scale model of the Front between Armentières and Ypres; and for the whole of one wet and

182

blustering weekend we rehearsed our tactics, moving aircraft about our model with a precision we only hoped we could match in practice in the sky. We didn't need to be told that if we got things wrong we'd be massacred: that knowledge was at the back of all our minds as we waited for the weather to clear. We waited, and waited. Until on the evening of December 23rd the wind veered north and the temperature dropped, and this we knew was a sign the cloud was about to lift.

December 24th dawned bitterly cold, with a green-as-applemint sky and flurries of snow. There was still a scattering of cloud, and this we welcomed because it gave us the sort of cover we needed for our ambush. Our plan was simple – as it had to be in the absence of air-to-air radio. At 0930 a single Strutter, escorted by a trio of SE5s, was to take off and head southeast for Lille; this was the diversion, its sole objective being to draw part of the *Jasta* away to the south. At 0945 another single Strutter was to take off and head northeast up the valley of the Lys in the direction of Bruges. This was the bait. Escorting the Strutter there would apparently be only a single aircraft, myself in the Triplane. What we hoped the *Jasta* wouldn't realise, until too late, was that nine fighters from Merville and nine from Saint Genis had taken-off half-an-hour earlier and were lurking in formation among the clouds, ready to dive on the Albatri the moment they dived on the Triplane and Strutter.

I can't say that I fancied being cast as bait; but as Uncle pointed out, the *Jasta* would be particularly keen to get at the Triplane, the one aircraft which had their measure and had already shot two of them down.

So there I was on Christmas Eve, heading northeast up the Lys, keeping half-an-eye on the Strutter beneath me and one-and-a-half eyes on the clouds above. As we crossed the lines there was no sign of the *Jasta*, but Archie was accurate. It would, I thought, be ironic if after all our scheming we were shot down from the ground! We followed the river, weaving this way and that to avoid the flak. Beneath us the fields were alternately dark with shadow and bright with sun. It was a lovely day.

Suddenly I saw them: a formation of eight or nine aircraft high up and to the right. They seemed to be climbing away from us, into the sun, and I was still trying to make out if they were Nieuports or Albatri when they disappeared into cloud. I waggled my wings and pointed, and the Strutter pilot and observer peered anxiously at the underbelly of the cumulus.

As we made our way up-valley, now more on the *qui vive* than ever, the cumulus thickened. This was a development I didn't care for; for I had visions of our being jumped by the *jasta* without our fighters realising what was going on. I signalled the Strutter to lose height and zig-zag.

We were keyed-up, ever moistening our lips and staring this way and that like children lost in a darkening wood. Any second we expected the worst: the sharklike Albatri streaming down on us through a gap in the clouds, guns clattering. I ought to have remembered that war brings always the unexpected. The first Albatross that we spotted emerged from the clouds not in a menacing dive but a frightened spin, streaming smoke.

I had about two seconds to make up my mind what had happened, and what to do. Somewhere above the clouds, I told myself, the *jasta* must have bumped into our fighters before the trap had been sprung. So it was every man for himself. I signalled the Strutter to run for it, and dived on the luckless Albatross. About the last thing the German pilot can have expected, as he pulled shuddering out of his spin, was to find a Triplane, waiting. He hadn't a chance. He tried desperately to turn to face me; but his engine was damaged, and he could only limp round slowly, losing height. For a second I thought of holding off, and letting him crash-land in a field. Then I realised that with the courage of despair, he was trying to bring his guns to bear on me. I banked sharply onto his tail, and gave him a burst with the Vickers. From a range of ten yards I could hardly miss. I could see the pilot's body quiver and jerk as my bullets thudded into him. He slumped over the stick. And the Albatross went into the sort of dive from which there was no pulling out: down and down: faster and faster: to shatter into a myriad fragments on the bank of the Lys.

It didn't seem much of a victory.

I'd barely got my breath back, when two more planes came, tumbling out of a gap in the cumulus: an SE5 and an Albatross, twisting turning diving climbing spitting flame locked like wild-cats in a combat that could end only in death. And the SE5 was getting the worse of it. I hauled my Triplane into a climbing turn and went to his aid. But the German pilot must have had his wits about him; he saw me coming, broke off the engage-ment and climbed back into cloud. The SE5 to my surprise, made no attempt to follow, but kept flying straight and level up the valley of the Lys. I wondered if the pilot was wounded. I lost height and edged in beside him. And the closer I got the more damage I saw; his rudder was colandered like a sieve, and a line of bullet holes ran diagonally across his fuselage. The pilot was sitting bolt upright, clutching the stick. I waved at him to turn for home, but he took no notice; and suddenly his plane, hit by a patch of turbulence, rocked uneasily and went into a shallow glide. The pilot made no effort to correct it. And as I stared at him, I saw why. Blood was oozing out of his mouth; his eyes were fixed on a horizon more infinite than any he had ever flown by.

And still his SE5 flew gracefully up the valley, like a ghost ship breasting a quiet sea. It flew on and on, gradually losing height, until I wondered if by some miracle it was going to land itself; but at the last second its undercarriage hit the branches of a tree and it toppled onto its nose and lay for a moment as though surprised it could have been so clumsy. Then it burst into flames. The flames spread. There was a violent explosion. And suddenly all I was staring at was a charred stump and a hole in the ground. I flew round and round the place where a second earlier there had been a plane and a man. It was the fin-ality I found hard to accept. I kept peering at the crater as though I expected some phoenix to rise from the ashes.

Then, when I least expected it, I realised someone was call-ing me: was shouting at me again and again, his voice getting ever louder and more urgent. It was Sergeant Parker: 'If you want to stay alive, *don't* go into a day-dream. *Don't* go into a day-

185

dream. *Don't* go into a day-dream.'

I came-to with a start, looked back, and saw the Albatross ghosting down on me out of the sun. I turned to face him.

I can remember the way the sky looked, turning: twin mountain ranges of cumulus, and between and above them the aircraft wheeling like gulls against a backdrop of sea. I can remember the way the sun looked, great shafts of light gilding the fringe of the cumulus with a hem of fire. I can remember the vapour trails, the streamer of smoke, the plane fluttering earthward like an injured bird, and the distant rattle of Vickers and Spandaus. And I can remember the Albatross, as I turned to face him, hesitating; and I knew what he was thinking – that he'd lost the element of surprise, that he'd have to be careful. But he was five hundred feet above me, and he had me in trouble. If I ran for it he'd dive on me, if I tried to engage him he'd have the priceless advantage of height. I took a quick look down, crossed the controls, and the Triplane dropped like a stone. It was the last thing the German pilot had been expecting. By the time he'd started to follow me down I was at ground level, snaking for the woods. If he'd stayed high he might have been able to pick me off; but as I'd hoped he followed me all the way down and tried to batten onto my tail. The moment he opened fire, I skidded into a near-vertical turn round the edge of a copse. As I turned, I could see his bullets scything into the branches not a dozen feet from my head. I turned tighter and tighter. A Triplane at ground level is more manoeuvrable than an Albatross, and it wasn't long before I began to out-turn him. He saw what was happening. Afraid that if he tried to turn any tighter he'd spin-in, he broke away. And the moment he broke, I broke too, climbing flat-out for cloud. Now climbing was the Triplane's forte – her stacked-up wings gave her a quite extraordinary degree of lift – and looking back I saw to my satisfaction that I was leaving the Albatross behind. It was I now who was the higher: I who had the advantage.

If he had tried to follow me, I'd have turned on him. But he realised he had been outmanoeuvred, and prudently put his nose down and headed for home.

For a moment I thought of following him. But it would have been a long chase. And looking up, I saw that high above me our SE5s and Nieuports were still dog-fighting with the *jasta*: three dozen planes, clawing one another to death among the ramparts of cloud. I was tempted to leave them to it: tempted to say to myself that I'd destroyed one plane and frightened off another, and that surely was contribution enough. But I knew very well that much as I wanted to opt out, when it came to the crunch I wouldn't. . . . Yet there was no need, I told myself, to rush blind into trouble. I headed for the cumulus, intending to climb through it, to emerge above the *mêlée*, and give myself the advantage of both height and surprise.

The moment we entered cloud I knew it wasn't going to be easy. Greyness closed round the Triplane like the strands of a web; air currents clutched at her with unseen hands, jolting her this way and that and knocking her off-course; I needed all my strength to keep her under control. We climbed up and up: 5,000 feet, 8,000 feet, 10,000 feet — I'd no idea the cloud extended so high. It was bitterly cold. Ice started to form on the surface of the wings, and I was beginning to feel decidely uneasy when we broke through into another world.

One second I was peering into Stygian darkness, next second the sky was blue as gentian, the upper-surface of the clouds was white as snow, and the light so bright that I had to screw up my eyes. For a moment there didn't seem to be another aircraft in sight. Then I spotted them: a couple of miles to the south and a couple of thousand feet below me, in a great blue valley between the clouds. They were still at it, hammer and tongs. About ten of them and perhaps twice as many of us. Wheeling, circling, diving, climbing. Slugging it out. Evenly matched. Neither willing to be the first to cry 'enough'.

I reckon it was my arrival that tipped the scales. And if this sounds conceited, let me hasten to add it wasn't me the *jasta* pilots feared, it was the Triplane.

I took my time. I manoeuvred into the sun. And waited until an Albatross, more canny than his fellows, disengaged himself from the *mêlée* and came climbing towards me. He must have reckoned that the sky above him was a refuge; he can have had no premonition that death was waiting for him in the halo of the sun. I watched every move he made: watched him level off, check his guns and peer down at the planes beneath him, selecting a victim, little thinking that he himself had been already selected. I saw him, like the careful pilot he was, look behind him, look above him, and last of all look into the sun. I saw him stiffen. I saw him shade his eyes, for a moment disbelieving, then believing all too well. I saw him slam over the stick. But he was too late. Even as he started to turn my bullets scythed through the rear of his fuselage. His rudder disintegrated. His elevator flew spinning into the air. And the Albatross keeled over into a horrible corkscrew dive: out of control: falling turning, turning falling: round and round, down and down: faster and faster. And there wasn't a thing the pilot could do. His skill was of no more use to him than his courage. He could only sit there, slamming his useless control-column this way and that, as first one wing and then the other was ripped away from the fuselage to leave him spinning earthward, pressed by centrifugal force into the coffin of his cockpit as he plunged like a meteor to destruction.

I ought, I told myself, to have got used to this sort of thing by now. If it hadn't been him, it would have been me. . . . All the same I couldn't help wondering what sort of person he had been, what eyes would weep for him.

Then, for the second time that morning, I heard the voice of Sergeant Parker: '*Don't* go into a day-dream! *Don't* go into a day-dream!' I stared this way and that. And saw the planes not a thousand feet beneath me. Climbing.

There were three of them. Two Nieuports and an Albatross.

And the nose of the Albatross was orange.

In an instant my sickness vanished, my shaking stopped, and I found myself sizing the situation up with the detachment of a surgeon about to operate. . . . One of the Nieuports was climbing parallel to Otto von Searle: was climbing steeply, but not steeply enough; and I could see that before long Otto would turn on him, from above, and that would very likely be that. But the second Nieuport was in a better position, slightly above Otto and behind him, and I could guess what this second pilot was thinking: that the moment the German levelled off he'd drop on his tail.

Sometimes, even now, I lie awake at nights and think how different my life might have been if that morning I had been a little less careful, a little less selfish. Some pilots would have dived straight in, guns blazing. But before I killed Otto von Searle I wanted to be very very certain that no-one was going to kill me. I looked above me; I looked behind me; I looked into the sun. I spent about ten seconds making sure that the sky, in all the places that mattered, was clear. And in those ten seconds Otto levelled off.

I saw what happened next as though it were some drama I was watching from the wings of a stage.

Otto turned on the Nieuport. But the Nieuport pilot was no fool; it was what he'd been expecting, and before Otto could open fire he went into a spin. Otto hesitated, then followed him down, not noticing the second Nieuport which had levelled off above him and was about to drop onto *his* tail. The pilot of this second Nieuport was fast and skilful; but something about the way he flew – a sort of slap-happy recklessness – made me stare at him, suddenly afraid, in my mind the first suspicion of the tragedy about to be acted out. A second later, as I saw his registration number, my fears were confirmed. It was Gavin.

From this moment everything that happened had the inevitability of a Greek tragedy, the end of which is writ plain in its beginning.

Otto followed the first Nieuport down, firing: firing but missing because a spinning plane is a difficult target. Gavin followed Otto down. And I waited, half-horrified half-elated, for him too to open fire. He closed-in to point-blank range, to the sort of range he couldn't miss from. But he didn't fire. He simply sat there, his sights on Otto's back, his finger a thousand miles from the trigger. My first thought was that his gun must have jammed. Then, in a moment of truth, his voice came to me above the pulse of the Triplane's engine – 'If we met, I . . . I

189

couldn't kill him'. And I suddenly knew – knew with as much certainty as if he had told me on oath – that Gavin had recognised our erstwhile friend.

'Kill him!' I whispered. 'Kill him!'

But I'd got it the wrong way round. Otto, warned by the sixth sense that pilots live by, looked back. He saw the Nieuport on his tail. Quick as a flash, he toppled into a spiral dive. I'll never know why Gavin followed him. Perhaps he'd decided belatedly to fire; more likely it was a reflex action born of his months of training. Anyhow, down the two of them went.

I was too far above them to be anything but a spectator. I could only watch, sick with horror, knowing what I was going to see, yet when I saw it unable to believe what my eyes were recording. . . . Otto's dive steepened. His speed built up. Suddenly he looped. At the top of the loop he rolled into an Immelmann turn. And Gavin, uncertain where the Albatross had got to, pulled out of his dive, peering this way and that.

'Gavin!' I screamed. 'Look out! He's in the sun!'

But even as my words were whipped away in the slipstream, Otto dropped on his tail, firing.

His bullets thudded into the Nieuport's engine. The engine caught fire. And the Nieuport reared up like a terrified horse, hung for a moment on its prop, then toppled almost lazily into a slow flat spin. Round and down, down and round: the smoke thickening: the flames spreading: the heat intensifying, melting wood and metal, fabric and cloth, flesh and bone.

A veil of red dropped like a curtain of blood across my eyes. The self-control which up to now had always come to my aid in a crisis deserted me. I heard myself screaming again and again: 'Bastard! Bastard! Bastard!' I flung the Triplane into a dive. I'd kill him. If I had to follow him to the very vaults of hell, I'd kill him. If it was the last thing I did on earth, I'd kill him.

Otto von Searle didn't follow Gavin down. He was too experienced for that. He pulled out of his dive: took a look round: and saw me falling on him, like the apocryphal angel of death. He dived for cloud.

I think I'd have got him: in fact I'm certain I'd have got him. I was lining him up, when there was a sudden crack, a violent explosion and my windshield disintegrated. I flung the Triplane aside. And another Albatross, guns yammering, flashed past my tail. By the time I'd shaken him off and got back into my dive, Otto was disappearing into the cumulus.

I was literally mad with rage. If I couldn't kill Otto I'd kill the other bloody German. He was coming at me again. And I hauled the Triplane into a stall turn, hung for a moment above him, then as he passed underneath me flung the stick forward and tried to ram him. Luckily for both of us the Albatross pilot had his wits about him. He cartwheeled away, our aircraft passing so close that I could see the individual strokes of paint on the big black cross on his tail.

The shock sobered me up. I was shaking with fear now as well as with rage; torque from the prop was pouring in through the shattered windshield; the engine was vibrating and misfiring; and neither the Triplane nor I was in any state to be airborne. We were lucky. For at that moment the dog-fight broke up.

The Albatri must have had an agreed signal to disengage, because one second the sky was full of cartwheeling planes, next second the *jasta* were forming into a close-knit V and heading for home. Battered and exhausted, we also formed-up and went limping down the valley of the Lys.

By nightfall we had managed to piece together a pretty accurate picture of what had happened. The Germans had lost four Albatri, with another four badly damaged – heavier losses than they had suffered in all the previous three months. Our losses were two Nieuports, two SE5s and a Strutter, with another couple of machines (including the Triplane) damaged badly enough to be grounded. It had, everyone seemed to think, been 'a damned good show'; and from the point of view of the War (capital W) and the Squadron (capital S) I suppose that was right. But there was nothing good about it as far as I was concerned. In fact you might take the view that after the events of that morning, life for me was never quite the same. . . .

I was pretty accustomed by this time to dreaming that I was

being burnt alive; in fact such nightmares no longer made me scream – for which I was thankful, since terror was a state in which I didn't like the chaps in the next-door cabins to see me. But on the night of Gavin's death I had a new dream: more terrifying in a way, because it was more inexplicable. Through the mists of sleep I saw a face, blurred and indistinct, distant at first but coming gradually towards me. Coming closer and closer, until it seemed that the face and I were staring at one another nose to nose, separated by no more than a sheet of glass. The face was familiar, yet at the same time curiously blurred so that I couldn't identify it. And this worried me. Whose face could it be? My own? God's? Someone I knew? The pilot I'd just killed? Or was it the pilot waiting for me in the sun, the pilot who was soon to kill me?

I woke trembling, covered in sweat.

After a while I got out of bed and peered through the porthole.

It was a beautiful night. The ground was white with frost; the sky was hung with the sort of stars that make diamonds look like paste; and faintly above the whisper of the Lys I could hear what sounded like church bells.

The bells had me puzzled for a moment. Then I remembered. Of course: it was Christmas Eve.

Christmas Eve. And it seemed only yesterday that Gavin and Otto and I were kneeling side by side at the midnight service in Helford Church. Now Gavin was dead, Otto had killed him, and I was eaten up with hate.

The bells had no message for me.

They were a mockery.

Next morning Uncle called me to his office. 'I'm giving you four days leave,' he said cheerfully. 'Recommending you for an MC. And getting you posted to England: as an instructor.'

Someone on the far side of the airfield started testing a Vickers, and the crack-crack-crack made me flinch and peer anxiously over my shoulder. 'Thanks for the leave,' I said. 'And the gong. But I don't want a posting to England.'

'Indeed! And why not?'

'Because I want to stay here.'

He looked at me curiously: 'Why?'

I was surprised at how matter-of-fact I sounded: 'Because I want to kill Otto von Searle.'

His eyes darkened, and he gave me the sort of glare that struck terror into the hearts of aircrew straight out of Flying School. 'I'll have no personal vendettas. Not in my squadron.'

'I know what you're thinking,' I said. 'But I give you my word. Nothing I do will involve the squadron. When I stop doing my job as senior pilot – *that's* the time to send me packing.'

His fingers drummed the top of his desk: a sure sign he was undecided. 'You're pushing yourself too hard, Jack,' he said eventually. 'Enjoy your leave. And when you get back we'll talk again. Maybe we'll see things differently.'

I nodded. There was no point in telling him that my mind was made up: that in the ring of the sky there was no longer room for both Otto von Searle and I.

I had kept track of Jessica through her parents, and knew that she was now nursing in a hospital on the outskirts of Boulogne.

I rang the hospital up.

It was some time before I got through to the person I wanted – the Sister in charge of the ward where Jessica was working; but when I did make contact I found myself talking not to the dragon I'd been afraid of but to someone who sounded as though she could be a friend. . . . Yes, Miss Pendower knew her brother had been killed. Yes, the hospital were aware they were twins and were keeping an eye on her. . . . I asked the Sister if she'd find out whether Jessica would like to see me. And almost immediately she came back with the reply I had hoped for: 'She says "yes", Lieutenant Cunningham. If you call tomorrow evening, she'll be off duty at six. But might I have a word with you first? Sister Jardine: Ward Dumont D'Urville.'

193

The hospital was an ugly great barracks of a place; about the only attractive thing about it was its view over the Channel. Sister Jardine, on the other hand, turned out to be every bit as attractive as she had sounded – a slip of a girl with an elfin face and great brown eyes which looked as though they'd seen just about everything but could still raise a smile. I have to admit, however, that the conversation which took place in her office wasn't quite what I had expected.

'I don't', she said, 'usually chaperone my nurses. But there've been incidents lately. And I don't want Jessica upset. She's still in shock.'

'I understand. . . . What sort of incidents?'

'Our nurses,' she said, 'are all volunteers. They're unpaid. Some of them take to the easiest way of earning money a woman has. And the word gets round.'

'Good Lord!'

'Sorry to shock you.'

I was about to tell her that a slip of a girl wasn't likely to shock a pilot who'd spent a couple of years at the Front, when something about the way she was smiling made me wonder if two years in the wards of a hospital mightn't be a more comprehensive education than two years in the cockpits of aircraft. 'Right,' I said. 'I'll remember not to pay her!'

'Forgive me for ever thinking you might! But I wanted to be sure of you. We're all very fond of Jessica.'

'Is she a good nurse?'

She nodded: 'People with broken hearts very often are.'

It occurred to me that Sister Jardine seemed to know a great deal about Jessica. 'I didn't think her heart was broken,' I said slowly. 'Only locked away.'

'If something is divided, Lieutenant Cunningham, it stands to reason it's broken. But let's not become too clinical.' She stood up. 'Would you like to wait for Jessica here, or in the ward?'

I hesitated.

'My boys,' she said, 'are always glad of someone to talk to. If you're not afraid?'

'I'm afraid of a lot of things,' I said. 'But I don't *always* run away.'

At the entrance to the ward she stopped, and looked at me very straight. 'Be gentle', she said, 'with Jess. And don't be surprised if you find her changed.'

'Right.'

'And be gentle', she added, 'with the boys. They're most of them blind.'

Ward Dumont D'Urville was reserved for the victims of mustard gas. There were about two dozen of them. All of them had difficulty in breathing, and most of them, as Sister Jardine had warned me, were blind. I can remember the screens round the beds of those who were close to dying; I can remember the aseptic smell (a mixture of Coal Tar soap and surgical spirit); I can remember Jessica turning as I came in and holding up her hand, fingers spread, and pointing to her watch to tell me she'd be five minutes; and most of all I remember the atmosphere. Incredible as it sounds, the ward had the sort of peace that one associates with a cloister; it was as though the men who lay there had passed beyond suffering and found on the other side a sanctuary. I sat by the bed of a private – a chap even younger than I was – and not knowing what to say asked him what part of England he came from. He said 'Manchester', and I wondered what on earth we'd find to talk about. But he made it easy for me. He discovered I was a pilot, and asked me what it was like to fly. . . . It seemed no time at all before Jessica was walking past the end of the bed. She gave me a smile and a nod.

'I must go now,' I said to the private.

I could see his blind eyes staring at the door as it swung-to behind her: 'You're not', he said, 'walkin' out with Angel?'

'You mean Jessica?'

'Angel's what we calls her. You her boyfriend?'

'Just her friend.'

'Be good to her, sir. Poor little kid. She's just lost her brother.'

I told him I knew; and that his Angel was in safe hands.

She was paler than usual, and, not surprisingly, more sub-
dued; she was also dog-tired; but my first impression was
that she seemed to be less affected by Gavin's death than I'd
feared. Twins, I knew, often had a special sort of relationship,
an almost physical interdependence; and quite frankly I hadn't
known what to expect. . . . However, she seemed pleased to see
me, and for awhile we talked easily enough, most of the time
about her work. It was only gradually that I began to realise
something was missing, something was wrong. . . . Now I don't
know how to explain what was missing without seeming crude
and unfeeling; but the fact is that I found I was no longer conscious, as I always had been in the past, of her physical pres-
ence. I tried to tell myself that I wasn't being fair to her: that
with her twin brother hardly cold in his grave she could hardly
be expected to sparkle. Then we had a conversation which
made me think. We were talking of Gavin's death.

'What time', she asked, 'was he killed?'

'Must have been about half-past ten. In the morning.'

She nodded – as though this confirmed something she
already knew: 'And how?'

'It was Archie. A direct hit. He can't have known a thing.'

'Please tell me the truth, Jack.'

'But I am!'

She shook her head: 'He was burned to death. Slowly. I
know.'

Well, I had my story, and I was going to stick to it. Some-
things, I told myself, it was better not to know. 'No, Jess. I was
there. I know what happened.'

She gave me an understanding smile: 'All right. Forget
it. . . . Anyhow, I'm glad he wasn't crippled. Or disfigured. For
Gavin that would have been worse.'

I wouldn't have thought myself anything could be worse than
death; but I wasn't going to argue.

'I mean,' she went on, 'he was such a *physical* person.'

I looked at her curiously. I couldn't think why she was going
on so about her brother's death. It was as though she was trying
to tell me something.

'Just the opposite', she added, 'to me. We were complementary.'

Now I hadn't thought about it before. But when she put it into words, I realised she was right. We are all part-flesh, part-spirit. In Gavin's case the flesh had been predominant – he had loved football, beer and girls; in Jessica's case the spirit – she loved lame ducks, lost causes and Chopin. Now I don't mean that Gavin was insensitive and Jessica blue stocking. Nothing could be further from the truth. But a childhood incident which I now remembered summed up the difference between them. . . . It was on their eleventh birthday; one of the Pendower's cats was expecting kittens, and the twins had been promised one each. The cat produced no fewer than five kittens, ranging from a superb and excessively greedy ginger tom, to a tiny tortoiseshell female, beautifully marked but so small as to be almost the runt of the litter and having at feeding time to fight desperately for survival. Gavin chose the magnificent tom, Jessica the diminutive female. By the time they were eighteen it probably wasn't surprising that Gavin had become a slap-happy pilot, and Jessica a dedicated nurse. Then Gavin was killed. Now if they had been merely brother and sister, I don't doubt that Jessica would have been heart-broken. But no matter how deep her grief and no matter how long it lasted, I doubt if she would have been altered basically as a person. However, they were twins: linked at birth and after birth by bonds which made them uniquely inter-dependent. And I think that when Gavin died, part of Jessica died with him: the physical part. And I think that was why I could look at her now, across the table in the bistro, and feel that something was missing.

It came to me that Otto von Searle had even more to answer for than I'd thought. And the hate that was in me was fanned to the fury of an inferno.

'Jack!'

I came to with a start: 'Hmmm?'

Jessica was looking at me with a curious intentness. 'I know', she said, 'you don't want to talk about Gavin's death. I know

197

you pilots have a sort of code: to cover things up: and that you think I'm morbid keeping on about it. But I'm worried' – her hands were twining and untwining – 'and I'm asking for help.'

'Of course,' I said unguardedly, 'I'll help.'

She gave me a trusting smile. 'I suppose it's because we were twins. But I can see Gavin's death so terribly clearly. I know *when* he was killed – I could feel it, like a physical shock. And I know *how* he was killed – in spite of what you tell me that he was burned. But I – I don't know how to explain this – but there are some things I *don't* know and *don't* understand. And I've a feeling I ought to: a feeling that something important happened. So please tell me.'

Well, what would *you* have told her? . . . 'Why yes, your brother *was* burned to death. He caught fire at about 6,000 feet and spun burning all the way to the ground. Slowly. And there's something else you ought to know: the chap who shot him down was your boyfriend, Otto von Searle'?

The first she might in time have been able to live with. But never the second.

'Honestly, Jess,' I said. 'Cross my heart and all that. There isn't anything to tell. Our squadron and some of the chaps from Merville were in a dog-fight. There were planes wheeling about all over the sky. And a lot of ack-ack. Gavin's plane got a direct hit. He must have been killed at once. I suppose he might have been burned, just for a second. Or his body might have been burned: afterwards. But nothing – well nothing unusual happened.'

'Is that the truth?'

'Of course.'

'Will you swear it? On the Bible?'

'If you want me to.'

I could see she didn't believe me. The old Jessica would have tried to wheedle the truth out of me. The new Jessica seemed to have neither the weapons nor the inclination. She gave me another understanding smile: 'All right. Forget it.' And we went back to talking about her patients in Ward Dumont D'Urville.

Though she tried not to show it I could see that she was desperately tired, and after a while I suggested she had an early night. She made a token protest, saying it wasn't fair on me, when I'd come all the way to Boulogne. But she soon allowed herself to be persuaded – which made me more conscious than ever of the change in our relationship. So I walked her back to the nurses' quarters, a row of drab little huts in the grounds of the hospital. As we said good-night she reached apologetically for my hand: 'It's only nine. What'll you do for the rest of the evening?'

'Have a drink and an early night, I expect.'

She told me the name of a café by the waterfront where there was usually a bit of life; and after I'd given her the sort of kiss that I might have given my sister, I made my way to this café and ordered a bottle of wine, and set about trying to convince myself that she was in shock and that the old magic would one day return.

The café was bright and cheerful, recovering from Christmas and getting ready for the New Year. More than 90 per cent of its clientele were French; but there was the occasional British soldier or seaman, and a couple of girls who looked as though they might have come from the hospital. I caught one of the latter eyeing me, and after a while she came across: 'Do you always drink on your own?'

She was pretty in a disorganised sort of way; and I thought 'Why not?' I pulled up a chair for her, and asked the waiter for a second glass.

'Here', she said, 'is to ships that pass in the night.' She knocked back the wine like lemonade; and I wondered if she too had things she wanted to forget.

By the time we had finished the bottle we were both thinking of the same thing. But something about me seemed to worry her. 'Didn't I see you at the hospital?' she asked eventually. 'Earlier this evening?'

'You might have.'

'Visiting a buddy?'

'No. One of the nurses.'

199

'Which one?'

'Jessica Pendower.'

'The one with auburn hair? That all the men call Angel?'

I nodded.

'Not poaching, am I?'

I thought about it. Every pilot, I told myself, was living on borrowed time. The odds were that within a week I'd be dead. So what the hell did it matter who I went to bed with? Jessica wouldn't care. Nicole would never know. I looked at her and wanted her, and knew instinctively how it would be: uncomplicated and satisfying, and in the morning I'd offer her a present and she'd refuse, but I'd leave one all the same because it had been fun. 'No,' I said. 'You're not poaching.'

My instinct turned out to be right, even down to her refusing but my leaving the present.

There was, however, what you might describe as an unexpected interlude. We were asleep in one another's arms, when I started dreaming: dreaming that I was staring up at a cloud which was curiously opaque. The cloud came nearer and nearer, taking on the semblance of a face. I moaned, rolled away from it and covered my eyes. But still the face drew nearer: expressionless, enigmatic; until we were staring at one another, nose to nose. I felt that I ought to recognise it, but couldn't. It wasn't myself. It wasn't Otto. It wasn't Gavin, or Uncle or Chris. So who on earth was it? It could only, I decided, be the pilot waiting for me in the sun. 'When?' I whispered. 'When?'

Then came the flames: little tongues of red and gold, lapping the face's periphery. The flames spread. They grew brighter and fiercer, singeing hair, melting flesh, charring bone. And still the face stared down at me, disintegrating in the heat, but never altering its expression – though I could now see that tears, big glistening drops of moisture, were rolling slowly out of its eyes.

I screamed.

I grabbed pillows, blankets, anything I could lay hands on, and tried to smother the flames.

200

I tried to stamp on them. I tried to beat them out with my hands. And as I pounded them I could hear myself screaming. And someone else screaming too. A girl.

I woke covered in sweat. To find the bed stripped of blankets and sheets, and the girl the far side of it, naked, her eyes wide with terror. And my feet stamping, my hands clawing, at flames that only I could see.

'Jack!' she was screaming. 'Wake up! Wake up!'

I stared at her. And slowly my hands unclenched. And the flames subsided.

'Oh, Jack!' she whispered. 'You're all right. It was only a dream.'

I couldn't stop shivering. And she came hesitantly round the bed, her eyes very wide, and took me gently as though I was a child in her arms. 'You're all right.' She repeated it over and over again. 'It was only a dream.'

I stared at the scattered bedclothes and naked girl, and was appalled. 'Susan! Are *you* all right?'

'I'm fine. You didn't hurt me.'

'Oh God! The flames. I could *feel* them.'

'There're no flames. Only me.'

I clung to her. Clung to her as a ship in peril clings to its last anchor, knowing that if the anchor parts, it is lost. And in the hour when I needed a friend as I'd never needed one before, she brought me back to sanity.

'Help me,' she said. 'With the bed.'

As I've said, she was naked; and the bed-making could hardly have been other than erotic. Our eyes kept meeting.

It took a long time. It took a very long time indeed. But eventually I began to think of other things than the face of the unknown airman.

By the time I got back to Saint Genis I'd had plenty of time to think over my decision to kill Otto von Searle. I hadn't changed my mind. In fact now that I'd seen the effect his bullets had had on Jessica, I was more determined than ever.

201

I knew that Uncle wouldn't approve, so I had to act fast. I went straightway to the cemetery at the edge of the airfield, took one of the wreaths from Gavin's grave, carried it back to my cabin, and wrote a note; brief and to the point.

Otto,
    The sky isn't large enough for both of us.
    I challenge you to single combat: you in your Albatros, me in my Triplane.
    I shall be waiting for you above the trenches at 10,000 feet, midway between our airfields. I shall be there tomorrow, the first day of 1917.
                        Jack.

When I read the note, it sounded theatrical and melodramatic. But it said what I wanted to say. So I put it into an envelope which I addressed to Lieutnant Otto von Searle; then I wired it into the wreath.

I had put my name down for the last patrol of the day; and at 3 p.m. I took off, with the wreath in the back of the cockpit, and headed for Ronchin.

It was a miserable afternoon, with mist and low cloud providing plenty of cover. The German gunners must have reckoned the weather too bad for flying, because the only place I ran into Archie was round the airfield. And here I was lucky; for I managed to drop the wreath and make my getaway at the cost of nothing more serious than a line of bullet holes through the lowest of the Triplane's wings. Within three-quarters of an hour I was back at Saint Genis.

You might have thought, that evening, that I'd be tortured by remorse, or at least by doubt. But I wasn't. I had made my decision: and that was that. The consequences I didn't want to think of. I spent a couple of hours in the hangar, helping my long-suffering ground-crew to patch up and check the Triplane; then I went early to bed. My greatest fear was the weather: that it might on New Year's Day be too bad for flying.

14

New Year's Day dawned bitterly cold, with a raw wind slamming this way and that in violent gusts, and flurries of sleet. But as I made my way at first light to the hangars, I saw to my satisfaction that the clouds were broken and reasonably high. With luck I'd be keeping the rendezvous.

I had a careful look at my Triplane. The mechanics had done a good job on her. Her engine was sweetly tuned, her fabric was smooth and glossy as the coat of a well-cared-for dog, and her scars had been neatly stitched and doped. I knew she wouldn't let me down: that if I was soon to fall flaming out of the winter sky the fault wouldn't be hers.

I went into the Mess for breakfast. Once or twice before as I'd sat down to breakfast it had occurred to me that I might be eating my last meal on earth. On previous occasions I'd dismissed the idea as melodramatic: told myself that no matter how great the danger the odds were with me. But they weren't with me now. And I knew it. The Albatross was as good a plane as the Tripehound. Otto was as good a pilot as I was. I had, at best, no more than a fifty-fifty chance of ever sitting down to breakfast again.

At 9.30 I gave the Triplane a twenty-minute test flight, and checked that her Vickers was firing freely. And when I had landed, I supervised her re-arming and re-fuelling myself.

The mechanics were patient and understanding. Unlike some of our pilots I'd always got on well with the men who serviced my planes. We understood and I think respected one another – at least I certainly respected them. I never asked them to 'rig' imaginary defects to get me out of a dangerous patrol; and in return they never did the sort of botched repair that

203

could have landed me in trouble in the air. Yet because of the rigid barrier that existed between officers and other ranks, we never really got to know one another. Which made what happened next the more unexpected. . . . All my mechanics realised something was up. They were used by this time to pilots who slept beside their machines, who insisted on starting them up in the middle of the night, who checked their rigging and tuning with morbid obsessiveness. They were used to it. They understood. And some of them cared. . . . At 11.30 they wheeled my Triplane onto the hard-standing and started her up. As I changed places with the sergeant, he said, almost apologetically: 'Take good care of her, sir. We want her back in one piece.'

'I'll try.'

'And yourself, sir.'

All I could think of saying was 'Thanks, sergeant. Thanks very much.' Then I was taxying to the edge of the airfield.

The sergeant, I told myself, was a jolly decent chap. He had been servicing the Tripehound every day for the last six months, and it struck me as a pity that the only thing I knew about him was that he had a seven-year-old daughter who was the apple of his eye. It seemed silly that we should have been dependent on one another for so long and yet be strangers, and I told myself that when I got back I'd make a point of getting to know him better.

When I got back.

If I got back.

And suddenly all the things I had ever wanted out of life but had never had, came crowding in on me: people I had liked but had never properly got to know, places I had wanted to visit but had never set eyes on, things I had wanted to do with Nicole but hadn't been sure if she would be flattered or shocked, and Jessica, and all the dreams I had ever dreamed of she and I together on some deserted Cornish shore, and all the tomorrows I had taken for granted would be mine . . . and here I was, throwing them all away. I cursed myself for a fool, and wished I had never thrown down the challenge. But thrown it down I had. I couldn't with honour back out.

I took off in a flurry of sleet.

I reckoned I could be at 10,000 feet by a-quarter-to-twelve, and at the rendezvous a few minutes later. I didn't, however, want to get there early – because this might have given me an unfair advantage over Otto, might have smacked of lying-in-wait for him. I would, I told myself, approach the rendezvous-point at exactly 10,000 feet at exactly mid-day.

This, however, turned out to be easier said than done. Because of cloud. Thunderheads of cumulus were rolling out of the north like gargantuan snowballs: great fluffy masses, with their base at three-to-four-thousand feet and their summits at thirteen-to-fourteen-thousand. In between them the sky was gentian blue, and the sun was shining with the brilliance of a light that knows it's liable any moment to be snuffed out. It was a day to savour the beauty of the earth and the splendour of the sky. But all I could think of was that Otto had two machine-guns to my one: that, and the fact that it was coming up to mid-day and the rendezvous was in cloud.

I climbed through a rift in the cumulus, and broke into clear sky above the thunderheads. This, it seemed to me, was as near to the rendezvous as I could get.

I looked carefully this way and that.

There was no sign of Otto.

I flew up and down above the thunderheads, waiting.

To say I was keyed-up would be a considerable under-statement. My mouth was dry, and I found myself having fre-quently to moisten my lips; while my eyes were continually darting this way and that, now scanning the ever-shifting folds of cloud, now peering at the shafts of sunlight. The last thing I wanted was to be 'jumped'; one burst from Otto's Spandaus, and the fight would be over before it had begun. I scanned the sky section by section, with many an anxious glance behind me and into the sun.

But mid-day came and went, and there was no sign of Otto von Searle. ˙

I told myself it must be the cloud that was making things

difficult; that he must be waiting (probably as puzzled as I was) in some valley between the banks of cumulus. With a good deal of difficulty I pinpointed my position, and let down into open sky as close to the rendezvous as I was able.

If I had been keyed-up above the clouds, I was positively neurotic among them. I wanted to look a dozen ways at once. In my imagination I could see Albatri emerging from each and every cavity in the cumulus; I could see them ghosting down on me along each and every shaft of sunlight; and every time the Tripehound trembled in an air current I suffered the vicarious thud of bullets. I wandered through the valleys between the clouds, like a deep-sea diver who explores a reef, knowing that somewhere among the shadows there lurks another and more deadly shadow, the shadow of the giant octopus, waiting.

By twelve-thirty I was cold, frustrated and bitter. Otto, it seemed, was not only a murderer. He was also a coward.

I'd never have thought it of him. But what other explanation was there? The cloud wasn't so thick that we could go on missing one another *ad infinitum*. Even now, as I looked down, I could see the battered streets of Armentières. *I* was in position. But my erstwhile friend, I told myself, was obviously afraid to face me.

And with this uncharitable thought my life would have ended – if the German pilot had been a better shot.

I heard the staccato crack-crack-crack, and saw tracer whipping past in between the Triplane's wings.

I cartwheeled frantically into a turn, and the Albatros flashed by not a dozen feet from my tail.

I was about to follow, when some instinct made me look back, over my shoulder.

And my heart seemed to shrivel up and stop pumping.

For above me, waiting, was another Albatross. And above that another. Three of them; and the uppermost a brilliant pillarbox red. There was only one German pilot, I knew, who had his aircraft painted red – von Richthofen.

So that swine Otto had had me ambushed!

I had no time for anger, nor bitterness, nor even fear. Every fibre of my being was concentrated on the one thing that mattered.

Staying alive.

The immediate danger was so enormous that there seemed to be no way out. Every road was a *cul-de-sac*, with death at the end of it. Whatever I did, the Albatros above me was going to drop on my tail. For a second I started to follow the plane that had fired on me down, pretending the danger from above was something I hadn't seen. Then, the moment the higher Albatross started battening onto my tail, I flicked into a spin. His bullets passed first one side of me then the other; then skimmed inches beneath me, smashing through the struts and wheels of the Triplane's undercarriage. I pulled out of the spin and started frantically to climb.

And as I climbed I looked this way and that for von Richthofen. He was in the one place I didn't want him. Above me. Waiting.

And I realised how it was going to be. The other pilots were inexperienced. Richthofen was the one I had to watch out for. He was, I remembered, ice-cold and a deadly shot; if he got me in his sights I was dead. So what could I do? If I fought, with the Triplane's superb manoeuvrability I might be able to prolong my life; I might even be able to shoot one of the less experienced Albatri down; but they'd get me in the end. If I wanted to live, my only hope was the cloud. And quickly. For already the planes beneath me had pulled out of their dives and were coming at me again. I swung downwind, and made for a mass of cumulus which looked agonizingly far away, but which came closer with every revolution of the prop.

I wanted to climb. But Richthofen was above me: waiting. So I had to dive. One of the other Albatri was on a converging course. I gave him a long-range burst. I doubt if my bullets went within fifty feet of him, but he shied away; and I swung back towards the cloud.

Richthofen saw what I was up to. He headed me off.

He was like a master-player at chess: always one move ahead of me. I could read him like a book. Let the others kill me if they could. If I looked like escaping, he was always there, at no great risk to himself, to pick me off. His plan had the sort of cold-blooded logic that made me think it was all too likely to work.

I looked desparingly at the cloud. In four minutes, maybe three minutes, I'd be safe. But one of the lower Albatri was coming in on my quarter. And above me von Richthofen was watching. Waiting.

A split second before I thought the German pilot was going to fire, I crossed the controls. The Tripehound shuddered: slewed sideways: seemed to hang in mid-air. And the Albatross's bullets went whistling past in front of me. So did the Albatross.

I hauled up my nose, and gave him a hopeful burst.

It was my lucky day. But not his. I saw the pilot double up: slump over his stick. And the Albatross, engine screaming, cart-wheeled into the sort of dive from which there is no pulling out.

I didn't watch. The second I realised I'd hit him, I had thoughts for only von Richthofen.

I hoped he'd dive on me – that would have given me the chance to mix it. But he stood off, between me and the cloud; and opened fire.

I sideslipped, and his bullets passed inches in front of me. I slithered frantically into a turn, and his bullets passed inches behind me. God, he could shoot! It was only a matter of seconds before he got me.

I had to take a risk.

I hauled the Tripehound into the sort of climbing turn that only she was capable of. Climbing and turning. Near-vertical. Straight at him. As though I was trying to ram him. I was quick. But so was he. Again he stood off, and gave me a deflection burst: a burst that started behind me, came closer and with a terrible finality closer, until it was slicing through the Triplane's wings; across its fuselage: straight at my head. I ducked.

Now I don't suppose for a second I *really* ducked under the tracer. But that's what it seemed like. And the gods must have been watching over me. A foot lower, and von Richthofen's bullets would have beheaded me. A foot higher and they would have ripped into the engine. As it was, they hit nothing more vital than the windshield, sending bits of cockpit-shield and cowling spinning off like leaves into space. The engine gave a protesting cough, but kept firing. And I was turning onto von Richthofen's tail.

I never had him in trouble. But I had him startled. He whipped into a vertical turn. And the pair of us went round and round, turning tighter and tighter, trying vainly to get onto one another's tail. The Triplane had the edge on the Albatross for manoeuvrability. But von Richthofen was a superb pilot. And he had an ally: his companion.

I wanted three pairs of eyes: one to watch Richthofen, one to watch the second Albatross, and one to watch *my* ally, the fast approaching cloud.

If the second Albatross had had his wits about him, he'd have dived straight in and finished me off. But he held back – I suppose through fear of getting in his flight-leader's way – and with every circle Richthofen and I completed, the cloud drew nearer. He realised what was happening: I saw him wave at his companion, beckoning him in. But his fellow pilot got the message too late.

One moment the light was brilliant, next moment a great wall of cumulus was blocking off the sun. Our circles became kaleidoscopic, as we turned now into blue, now into black. Then, mercifully, the first eddies of vapour were swirling over my wings.

But suddenly, at the last second, von Richthofen broke circle, turned, and fired. At the very moment I was thanking God I was safe, his bullets ripped into my tail-plane.

I toppled into a spin: almost in the same moment pulled out: and burrowed into the cumulus, like a terrified fox to earth.

The cloud was a sanctuary. What did it matter that aircurrents were rocking the Triplane like the waves of the sea, that vapour was pouring in through the shattered windshield, that the engine was running rough and misfiring. For the moment I was safe. I turned for what I hoped was the centre of the cumulus, knowing the longer I stayed hidden the better my chances of survival.

To start with all my attention was concentrated on the plane: on keeping it under control (never easy in cloud) and assessing its damage (extensive but mercifully, it seemed, superficial). After a while, however, I began to think of what had happened.

And the more I thought about what had happened, the more bitterness, like some insidious poison, seeped into the very core of my being. Three years ago Otto and I had been – he'd said it himself – as David and Jonathan, bound one to another by the sort of friendship we never doubted would last for life. Two years ago, we had waved and laughed and played 'chase me Charlie' among the clouds, comrades of the air. A year ago we had refused to fire at one another. My God it was different now! Gone was our friendship: snuffed out our comradeship: not only were we trying to kill one another, we were doing it with hatred, with malice and without honour. How, I asked myself, could Otto have sunk so low? How could the boy who had raised his glass to 'knights of the air' have turned into the sort of bastard who refused a challenge and had his challenger ambushed.

It struck me as a tragedy.

I was still brooding over it an hour later when I staggered back to Saint Genis.

I was so eaten up with bitterness it never occurred to me that the real tragedy lay not in Otto's conduct, but in my interpretation of it. That as, that night, I tossed and turned and dreamed and screamed, Otto von Searle was on leave in Berlin where he had been for the past week: that my challenge lay in his room at Ronchin, unopened.

I knew as soon as I shut my eyes that I was in for a bad night. And it wasn't long before my dreams were embarking on a familiar course.

As was often the way, they started innocuously, almost

210

idyllically, with Jess and I walking hand in hand along some lonely strip of shore. Only this time there was a third person with us: a dream child, a little girl of perhaps three or four who kept running laughing into my arms, while Jessica watched, smiling. Then the child vanished; and suddenly (as is often the way in dreams) Jessica and I were no longer on the beach, but riding into a clearing. It was a clearing we had been to before: a strip of level ground beside the Helford, and in it the familiar cottage and cider-apple and the mud-pilot. And in my dream I told Jessica that I wanted a word with Will Willcock, and dismounted and walked across to him and peered intently into his face, as though committing his features to memory. Then Jessica and mud-pilot vanished, and the world of my dreams became suddenly very still and very quiet.

And in my sleep I moaned and covered my eyes.

For I knew what was coming.

The face.

It was always the same: a face that was somehow familiar and yet unidentifiable. Not mine, not Otto's, not – if photographs could be trusted – the father I had never known – not – I had just checked the likeness – Will Willcock's, not – if I could trust my memory – any pilot I'd ever met. Yet if he was my executioner, the pilot who was going to kill me, why was *he* crying? Why were tears rolling endlessly out of those great sad eyes?

'Who *are* you?' I whispered.

The face dissolved in flames.

I moaned. I'd taught myself not to scream, but I couldn't help moaning. And my moaning went on and on, until the chap from the next cabin came in with a bottle of whisky.

211

15

Most of us go through a period in our lives that we would like to forget; I certainly wish I could expunge from mine that January and February of 1917.

I couldn't get over the fact that Otto had refused my challenge and had me ambushed. I nursed my hatred, and planned revenge. He couldn't, I told myself, run away for ever; one day I'd catch up with him. So as well as flying my normal quota of patrols I took to sneaking off at sunrise and sunset, ever hopeful of spotting the glint of orange on an Albatros's cowling. I met several Albatri those first few weeks of January, but never the one I wanted. I shot three of them down, and wished each time it had been Otto – especially the one who burned slowly, all the way from 14,000 feet to the ground.

Then Uncle sent for me.

He got out a bottle of whisky – which struck me as ominous, as though he had some pill he was anxious to sweeten. He raised his glass: 'Here's to your M.C. – which came through this morning. And your retirement!'

I put the whisky down: 'Say that again?'

'Your MC. It's in this week's honours. Congratulations! And I've fixed you a posting to Brooklands. As an instructor.'

'But I don't *want* to be an instructor.'

He raised a Mephistophelean eyebrow: 'Needs must when the devil drives.'

'Look,' I said desperately, 'you can't have many pilots who *want* to stay with you and be killed!'

His fingers drummed the top of his desk. 'You querying my orders, Jack Cunningham?'

'Yes, I bloody well am!'

He gave me the sort of glare that eighteen months ago would have made me quake in my shoes.

'Forget the act,' I said sourly. 'Just tell me why.'

He took his time over answering. 'The CO of a squadron', he said at last, 'has an obligation to his aircrew. He has to strike a balance. He has to push them hard, to turn them into the best possible fighting machine; but not too hard, in case they crack up. Now *I'm* not pushing you, Jack. But you're pushing yourself. And much, much too hard. I asked you to stop, but you didn't. Now I'm damned if I'll sit on my arse and watch a good man – and a good friend – kill himself. So it's *finis*. Back to Blighty.'

'But, sir! We've been together two years.'

'And you're the best senior pilot I've ever had. Don't think it's been easy.'

'Suppose,' I said carefully, 'I promise to ease up?'

'You mean you'll stop this bloody silly feud? With Otto-whatever-his-name-is?'

'I might.'

He looked at me thoughtfully: 'I don't understand you and this Otto. Eighteen months ago I very nearly had to have you courtmartialed: for refusing to fire at him. Now you're obsessed with killing him. You want to talk about it?'

Well, I certainly wouldn't have minded someone to confide in: someone to take the place of the father I'd never known, to advise me like some ancient all-wise god. But as I looked at Major Bertram, I hesitated. He looked tired and old: an Atlas worried almost beyond endurance with the burdens which had been heaped on him. For heaven's sake, I thought, hasn't the poor old bastard troubles enough of his own without being landed with mine. 'Things between Otto and me,' I said slowly, 'are so complicated I think we're the only two who can sort them out.'

'So?'

'So will you give me twenty-four hours: to make up my mind? Then I'll promise either to stay and be good. Or go quietly.'

He nodded, adding that he didn't *want* to lose me; but the

213

decision was mine.

And that's how we left it.

We both felt that we had been reasonable – as in a way I suppse we had. But we had forgotten one thing. That in war, time is something which can't be bought. It is nearly always later than you think.

Uncle and I seldom went on patrol together – it not being a good idea for CO and senior pilot to be simultaneously at risk. But next morning, due to a combination of mishaps and misunderstandings, we found oursleves at 8,000 feet over Tournai: he in a Strutter, taking photographs of the railway sidings; me in the Tripehound providing him with cover. It was Albatross country, and we were both very much on the *qui vive*. Thank goodness, however, there was a fair amount of cloud about, and this we hugged with more discretion than valour; until at the end of a nerve-racking three-quarters-of-an-hour we had the photographs and were on our way home. As we re-crossed the Front I remember telling myself that German aircraft seldom ventured onto our side of the lines : that we were as good as safe.

I should have known better.

I didn't see them till the last moment. The *Jasta*. Coming down in line astern like hornets out of the sun.

I waggled my wings. Fired a burst with the Vickers. And pointed.

Uncle saw them. Hesitated. And dived for cloud.

Sometimes I lie awake at night and ask myself if there was anything more I could have done. Perhaps if I'd kept a better lookout, or guarded Uncle's tail more closely, or positioned myself more skilfully? Perhaps, perhaps, perhaps. . . .

They were on us before we could reach the cloud.

I saw the Strutter haul up into a climbing turn as the first of the *Jasta* tried to fasten onto its tail. Then another Albatross was coming at me. I zig-zagged frantically, trying not to be driven too far from Uncle. But no sooner had I shaken the first Albatross off, than another took its place. There were too many of them.

For a couple of minutes the sky was full of diving planes, clattering guns, trails of vapour and exhaust. Then it was over. Reinforcements from Saint Genis were climbing to our aid. And the *Jasta*, not wanting to be drawn into a dogfight on the British side of the lines, reformed and headed east. But not before they had colandered the Strutter's tailplane and shot off its rudder controls.

The Strutter went into a spin.

Now Uncle was a superb pilot, and if courage, skill and ingenuity could have got the Strutter out of that spin he would have done it. He came out of cloud at about 10,000 feet, spinning not fast and vertical, but slow and flat; and I could see that he still had the aircraft under some sort of control – that is to say although he couldn't get it out of the spin, he could stop the spin getting worse. He tried everything. He tried every possible combination of elevators and ailerons; he tried every possible setting of the engine; his observer even crawled out of the cockpit and tried to haul over the rudder by hand. But it was no good. Nothing worked. No matter what they did, the Strutter went on spinning, quite slowly, round and round, down and down, all the way from 10,000 feet to the ground. It took about five minutes. And for every second of those five minutes Uncle and his observer must have known that they were going to die.

They ploughed into a field about a mile behind the lines.

They ploughed into it hard, but as luck would have it with their wings near-parallel to the ground. The Strutter did a sort of skidding bounce. Its fuselage broke in half. And both halves came to rest quite close together at the edge of the field, one half on its back, one on its side. I waited for the explosion. And the flames. But nothing happened. There was no movement. Only the sort of stillness that precludes much hope of life.

The field was small and had been recently ploughed in preparation for spring sowing; it was wet, uneven and not the sort of place an aircraft would have much hope of taking-off from. But I didn't care. If there was the slightest chance of Uncle or his observer being alive, I was going to take it. I crash-landed

215

the Triplane, as close to the wreckage as I dared. Her undercarriage collapsed, and she tipped onto her nose. I scrambled out, took a deep breath, and ran, terrified of what I was going to find, to the Strutter.

In the rear cockpit the observer was dead, his back so broken that he seemed to have jack-knifed almost in two. In the front cockpit Uncle was hanging upsidedown from his straps; one leg was at a most peculiar angle, the other embedded in the instrument panel. His eyes were open, but it was some time before they focused on me: 'Jack?'

'Keep still,' I said. 'You're all right.'

'Bugger off. She'll blow up.'

I told him to hang on. That the ambulance would be with us in a minute.

His eyes closed.

His left leg was spurting blood, and looked liable any moment to part company from the rest of his body. I was terrified to touch him. But I couldn't stand there and watch while he bled to death. I ripped off my shirt, made a makeshift tournequet, and tried to remember where the pressure point was in a thigh. 'You're making a mess', I said, 'all over your nice cockpit. So I'm going to bandage you up.'

The moment I started to apply pressure, he fainted. But at least I managed to stop the worst of the bleeding.

I was wondering if I dare try to lower him out of his harness, when I heard a shout: 'They're both ours!' And, looking up, saw a man with a rifle climbing out of the ditch at the edge of the field, and behind him, thank God, another two men with a stretcher.

He was still breathing as they lifted him out of the cockpit. Still breathing as they tied him onto their stretcher. And still breathing as a couple of hours later they carried him into the hospital in Saint Omer. He stopped breathing, for a moment, while they were operating; but the anaesthetist knew his job and turned up the oxygen, and he started again. And he was still breathing next morning as I sat by his bed in the hospital ward. Though by now he had only one leg.

216

I don't think the doctors expected him to regain consciousness. But he did. A little after mid-day his eyes opened. And he recognised me: 'Jack?'

'We were wondering when you'd wake up!'

'Where. . . . am . . . . I?'

'In hospital. In Saint Omer. Lucky blighter! Another few days and you'll be home in England!'

His eyes closed. After a while I realised he was trying to say something: something about the squadron.

It struck me as really rather sad: that on what looked like being his death-bed it was the squadron that mattered to him most: not wife, nor girl, nor family, but a collection of inanimate planes. If I were dying, I thought, I'd be asking for Jessica. Or Nicole. Then I thought again, this time with more perspicacity: Eight Squadron, I told myself, had been Uncle's creation; his child; and he thought of it not as planes but as people: 'The Squadron's all right,' I said gently.

'They need you, Jack.'

I couldn't think why they needed me more than anyone else; but I didn't want to upset him. 'Don't worry.'

'Stay and look after them, old chap. They need someone who cares.'

I felt trapped. But as I've said, you can't argue with a man who might be dying: 'I'll look after them,' I said.

'Thanks.' His hand closed on mine. His eyes focused on things I couldn't see, and he drifted off into the no-man's-land between life and death.

What, I wondered, was he seeing as he skirted that 'undiscover'd country': phantom aircraft of the future, ghost pilots of the past? I sat for a long time by his bed, not daring to disengage my hand, telling myself it would be no hardship to go back to Saint Genis, that I hadn't really wanted to be an instructor.

That night it was touch and go. But by the time I left the hospital next afternoon he was trying (albeit without much success) to sit up in bed, and to bellow (albeit mutedly) at the nurses. I knew then that he was going to be all right.

When I arrived back in Saint Genis I found the squadron in some confusion. So I telephoned Trenchard, got his authority to take over, and set about continuing Uncle's regime with the minimum of fuss.

The aircrew could have been difficult. For the Albatri were giving us a bad time, conditions on the airfield were primitive, and Uncle had been not only the best but also the best-loved CO on the Front – I couldn't so much follow him as come chronologically after him. Most pilots and observers, however, gave me the same unquestioning loyalty that they had given Uncle; and though I say it myself I believe in time I would have made quite a passable CO.

But it was not to be. For in the eyes of our headquarters at Saint Omer, it seems that I had blotted my copy-book.

A few days after telephoning Trenchard I found on my desk a memo from headquarters, asking why I had (a) 'deliberately crash-landed (my) aircraft in a field' and (b) 'absented myself from (my) place of duty for 48 hours without permission of leave'?

If I'd been older and wiser I would have written a tactful letter and gone to make my peace with headquarters in person. As it was, I wrote a hurried *not* very tactful letter and forgot them. But they certainly had the last laugh. A fortnight later a signal arrived from Saint Omer to say that a Major James Featherstone Calvert was to take command of the squadron 'forthwith'; while I was to revert to my position as senior pilot.

I think the squadron was more angry and upset than I was. As far as I was concerned, provided the CO did a good job I didn't mind who he was.

Unfortunately Calvert *didn't* do a good job. And this is certainly one reason why those early months of 1917 were such an unhappy time. It was tragic to see Uncle's creation, the work of years, whittled away until it was virtually destroyed.

James Calvert was a fine-looking officer of the old-school, with many excellent qualities. He was ambitious, efficient and a man of great personal courage; he was also an excellent pilot. The trouble was that for the past year he had been in charge of a training school in England, and he seemed to think that operations could be run on the same tight inflexible lines as training. 'He'll be OK,' I kept telling our long-suffering pilots and observers. 'Just give him time to learn.' But he never *did* learn – at least not while I was with him. Our discontent increased. Our losses mounted. Our *ésprit de corps* evaporated. By the end of the month we had degenerated from *élite* to just another squadron of Albatross fodder.

I think that in a curious way this worried me less than it worried the rest of the squadron; for I had a special reason for wanting to go on flying from Saint Genis. . . . Uncle, in his wisdom, had tried to scotch my vendetta with Otto. Under Calvert it was allowed to run riot. And it ran riot until, like a cancer, it took root in the very core of my being. Then it ran an all-consuming race with me: a race which could have no winner and only one end.

I couldn't think where Otto had got to. The bastard, I told myself, must have a guilty conscience and be lurking, somewhere, behind the lines, afraid to face me. In my saner moments I had to admit that there were other and much more likely explanations for his absence – he could be on leave, or posted to another squadron, or even dead. But for a lot of the time that winter I *wasn't* sane. I had now been flying over the Front for more than two years. On some days, it's true, I hadn't flown at all; but on other days I'd flown two or even three times. Let's say a total of a thousand sorties. A thousand sorties, on most of which I had been fired on: on any of which I might have been killed, on many of which I very nearly had been killed. I had come to the end of my tether. I had defeated the 'inner *schweinehund*' again and again; but he always returned, and each time I clambered into the cockpit he had to be defeated again. I had shot down twenty-three German planes. Twenty-three ghosts to walk my dreams: twenty-three faces to stare at me out of the night, some ringed with flame, one in particular (and he my most frequent visitor) bathed in tears.

It was this last apparition I dreaded most. How long would it be, I wondered, before somewhere above the clouds I met him?

I hoped soon. I began to go looking for him.

Now you might think that a pilot *looking* for death would find him easily enough; and of course if I had merely wanted to kill myself I could have done so a dozen times in a dozen ways. But it wasn't as simple as that. I wanted to take Otto with me.

So I became, that spring, a killer: a rogue male: an outcast from the herd: a creature condemned by its obsession to live beyond the pale. Such develop a terrible cunning. And are dangerous.

The skies from Ypres to Arras were my hunting ground, the winter clouds my cover; and as I hunted Otto von Searle the *jasta* hunted me. They hated the Triplane (which had been repaired and flown back to Saint Genis); for it was the one aircraft able to stand up to and outmanoeuvre them. I was never foolish enough to tangle with one of their large formations, but when they ventured up in twos or threes I'd try to pick one of them off, then use the Triplane's fantastic rate-of-climbing to escape. And each time I sent a German flaming through the winter sky, I wished with all my heart it was Otto. And each time I fought a German plane I wondered what the pilot looked like, wondered if his face would be familiar, wondered if he was the one who was waiting for me. So you might say that I was ever-seeking, yet ever-fearful of finding that which I sought.

If it hadn't been for my weekends with Nicole I would have gone quietly out of my mind. She knew something was wrong, and wanted to help. But I told her what would help most would be if the two of us played a game: a game called 'Let's Pretend There Isn't a War'. So if we couldn't get far enough away from the Front to avoid hearing the guns we'd pretend it was thunder; if we saw a man with only one leg we'd pretend he must have been thrown from his horse; and if, in some quiet retreat, we heard the rumble of approaching transport we'd pretend it was Some Fearful Monster, and run into café or copse and hide our eyes. And the game that we played brought us wonderfully close to one another: like lovers who together face a common danger, or delight in a common fantasy.

Nicole, of course, wasn't the only one who realised I was

cracking up. My fellow pilots and observers realised it too. They were for ever urging me to apply for a job back home as an instructor. And one of them must eventually have taken it on himself to get in touch with Jessica. Because quite out of the blue, I suddenly found her one evening sitting in the Mess, with the aircrew crowding round her like bees round a honey pot.

Beautiful young nurses didn't appear all that frequently in the Mess, and there was a general reluctance to let her go. But when she had finished her drink, she said firmly that I was taking her for a walk by the river.

As we made our way down the tow-path I was conscious of two things: of her beauty, and of the constraint which hung like an almost physical barrier between us. She looked at me reproachfully, and I knew all too well what was coming. 'I've been hearing,' she said, 'about this feud between you and Otto.'

I muttered that she shouldn't believe all she heard.

'Please, Jack. We've always been honest with one another.'

'Well, we *are* at war with Germany,' I said. 'It's my job to fight German pilots'

Her eyes closed, as though in pain. 'This is different. And you know it. This is a *private* war. And I beg you, implore you. For both your sakes. Stop it.'

I couldn't think of anything to say. There was a long and awkward silence.

'Jack!'

'Hmmm?'

'You and Otto are the two people in the world I love most. If you've any feeling for me, any feeling at all, please stop it.'

I began to feel an absolute cad.

'Would you like me to grovel? I'm not ashamed to.' Much to my embarrassment she dropped to her knees in front of me in the mud. 'I beseech you. In God's name. Stop this evil thing you are doing.'

'For heaven's sake, Jess!'

'Promise you'll stop it. I'll do anything to make you stop. *Anything, anything, anything,*'

It made me angry to see her humiliate herself. 'Don't try to

221

bargain,' I said, 'for his life.'

She flinched as though I had struck her. Her eyes, as she got to her feet, were angry: 'Oh, you blind fool. Don't you think I care about *your* life?'

Well, I didn't know what to think, and I didn't know what to do. I only knew that I didn't care for the sort of person I was turning into. And suddenly all the tension which had been mounting over the last few months built up to the point where I couldn't stand it. I'd had as much as I could take. I was quitting. Maybe it was the coward's way out; maybe I was breaking my promise to Uncle, letting the squadron down; but I didn't care. I'd come to the end of my tether. 'All right.' I said. 'I'll stop.'

For a moment she couldn't believe it. Her eyes opened wider and wider, and she clasped her hands in front of her like a little girl at a party who is offered the coveted prize. 'Promise?'

'I promise,' I said, 'to put in for a posting to England. As an instructor.'

I thought she was going to cry. Then I remembered this was something she never did. She grabbed the lapels of my coat and buried her face in my shoulder. For a long time she simply clung to me, neither moving nor speaking. Then I realised she was whispering, 'Oh, thank you! Thank you! Thank you!' over and over again.

I had learned in the past two years to keep my emotions on a pretty tight rein, and her gratitude embarrassed me almost as much as her humiliation: 'Come on, Jess,' I said gently. 'Pull yourself together.'

'Oh, Jack! Let me be happy!'

We were both of us happy that evening. It was as though from both our shoulders a burden had been lifted. And perhaps because of this, we managed to recapture something of the *rapport* which we had known as children. Perhaps one day, I thought, in some distant time or place we may even recapture it all.

Next morning she went back to Boulogne, and I put in my application for a posting home.

Calvert said he'd be sorry to see me go, but he endorsed the

222

application on the spot. He would, he promised, get me to Blighty within the week.

Thank God it was over.

It seemed too wonderful to be true.

I knew that when it came to leaving Saint Genis I'd have mixed feelings – I had, after all, spent the two most eventful years of my life here; I'd met some wonderful people, flown some wonderful planes, had some wonderful times. But my overwhelming feeling was of relief: relief that my battle with the inner *schweinehund* was ending, that the killing was over. Perhaps in time, I thought, I'll even be able to sleep and not to dream. . . .

Then everything happened at once.

The moment I saw the letter I knew it was from Nicole – who else would address me as 'Lt. Jacques Cunningham'.

It was an almost incoherent letter: a mixture of French and schoolgirl English, smudged with tears.

My darling Jacques,

Never may I see you again. Mon ami *in Italy has the most bad wound. He has lost the leg, and has what I think you say the gangrene. He is calling for me and I must go to him.*

I do not wish to go. But mon ami *needs me and my parents say I must. But oh Jacques I do not wish to leave you.* Et pendant tout le temps que je serai en Italie je m'imaginerai que je suis dans la vallée de la Loire. Et chaque fois qu'il me prendra dans ses bras, je m'imaginerai que c'est toi.

All my life will I remember you, and the wonderful times we had and the wonderful things we did and the wonderful games we played, and never in all my years will I play these games with any other man. Oh, Jacques! Jusqu'au jour de ma mort chaque fois que je verrai un aéroplane, je penserai à toi. Et à toi en moi. Je t'aime. Je t'aime. Je t'aime.

Do not think bad of me because I leave you. But as I said that first night we made love, marry the good English girl and make her happy.

May God walk with you and fly ever with you in your airplane.

Nicole.

223

The letter had no address to which I could reply.

I borrowed a friend's car and drove like a maniac to the apartment she had rented on the outskirts of Paris. It was dark by the time I got there.

Her apartment was empty. None of her neighbours had any idea where she had gone.

I stood in the street, numb with shock, staring up at the window of her bedroom. The moon came out from behind the clouds, and I thought of Heine's poem:

> *Still ist die Nacht, es ruhen die Gassen,*
> *In diesem Hause wohnte mein Schatz;*
> *Sie hat schon längst die Stadt verlassen,*
> *Doch steht noch das Haus auf demselben Platz.*
>
> *Da steht auch ein Mensch und starrt in die Höhe,*
> *Und ringt die Hände, vor Schmerzensgewalt;*
> *Mir graust es, wenn ich sein Antlitz, sehe —*
> *Der Mond zeigt mir meine eigne Gestalt.*

(The night is still, the street is quiet, this is the house where she used to live; she left the town some time ago, but the house still stands where it used to be. And there I see a man staring upwards, and he wrings his hands in anguish. I shudder when I see his face; it is myself the moon reveals to me.)

I couldn't believe that I was never going to see her again.

I reminded myself that parting had been inevitable: that now I had opted for a posting to England I wouldn't in any case have been able to see so much of her. But I hadn't wanted the parting to be like this: at her instigation, and final. What *I'd* had in mind had been not good bye but *au revoir*, with flying visits to Paris whenever I could snatch a few days' leave, and maybe in time her coming to join me in England. It came to me that I had been taking too much for granted. It came to me also, not for the first time in my life, that one never knows what one wants till it's gone.

I spent the night in Paris; and most of the next day in cajoling her parent's address out of reluctant friends.

By the time I returned to Saint Genis it was late at night. The Mess was deserted except for a couple of pilots swapping reminiscences. From what they were saying I gathered that one of them had had a narrow escape on the mid-day patrol. 'That Hun,' he was saying, 'could fly like the devil. One second he was below me, coming straight at me. Next second, for Christ's sake, he was on my tail!'

'I'll watch out for him,' the other pilot said. 'What colour was his cowling?'

'Orange.'

Time seemed to stand still.

It was as though events were building up to a predetermined climax. As though Otto and I, having dug a pit for ourselves, were fated to fall into it.

16

I lay awake into the small hours, wondering what to do.

If I went to one extreme I could spend my last few days at Saint Genis searching for Otto. If I went to the other extreme, I could say I'd finished with flying over the Front and refuse to get off the ground. I thought of my promise to Jessica, and discarded the first alternative; I told myself that refusing to fly was cowardly, and discarded the second. In the end I decided I'd fly normally, neither searching for Otto nor avoiding him. So what happened would be in the lap of the gods.

I slept badly; and was thankful next morning to be woken by the sound of rain on the deck of the barge. It rained for most of that day. Only a couple of patrols took off. And I wasn't on either.

Next morning it was raining again: great thunderheads of cumulus rolling out of the west, and water sluicing into the hangars and turning the lower reaches of the airfield into a quagmire of mud. But a little after mid-day the clouds lifted and broke, and the rain gave way to sun. Planes started taking off at 2 p.m., and I worked out that provided the weather held, I'd be flying the last patrol of the day. I checked that the Triplane was armed and serviceable, and waited.

Time dragged. I'd done everything that had to be done. My cabin was in apple-pie order; letters to my mother, Jessica and Nicole were written sealed and stamped. All I could do was wait. Wait and try not to think; and keep telling myself that the sky was vast and Otto and I weren't really likely to meet.

I took off at 5 p.m. In a couple of hours it would be dark. Surely, even on the run from Arras to Ypres, I could keep out of trouble for a couple of hours!

It was an evening of violent contrast. One moment the sun was bright and the atmosphere oppressive; next moment clouds were blotting out the sky, and it was raining cats and dogs to the accompaniment of thunder. However, after I'd been airborne about an hour the weather took a turn for the better, and the clouds began to roll away into central Europe, leaving the Front washed clean by rain and bathed in sunlight. I didn't like it. Without the protection of cloud I felt naked: bereft of sanctuary. Away to the south I spotted what looked like a solitary aircraft, high above me, on the German side of the lines. I turned away from it. But a few minutes later I spotted something I couldn't with honour turn away from: an Albatross climbing purposefully towards me out of Ronchin.

I stared at it.

And shivered.

For it was haloed by a parhelion: a great circle of light refracted from the orange of its cowling.

Otto von Searle and I kept coming towards one another, as though impelled by a magnetism over which we had no control. It was too late now for second thoughts, too late for regrets. As we eyed one another across the sky which in our folly we had transformed from playground to battleground, we both knew that before the sun dropped below the horizon one or both of us would be dead.

I was at twelve thousand feet, he at ten; and I let him climb up till he was level with me. That, I reckoned, was only fair.

As though acknowledging the gesture, he rocked his wings. Then we turned to face one another.

I was ice-cold. This, I told myself, was my forte: single combat, man to man, plane to plane. And now as never before I'd need every iota of my expertise. I watched him, knowing his skill and his fire-power, edging (I hoped imperceptibly) higher, as I waited for him to make the first move.

I might have known he'd do something brilliant! He went into a dive, and as soon as his speed built-up, hauled the Albatross into a loop. I felt certain he was going to do an Immelmann turn off the top of the loop, and come out facing in the opposite direction. Instead he kept looping. Until I suddenly realised he was plummeting down on me, upsidedown, firing.

Bullets flashed inches wide of the Triplane's wing. If I hadn't cartwheeled aside, the flight would have been over before I'd got out of my corner! I slithered from turn to sideslip, and as he hurtled past, gave him a burst. It missed by a mile. Then he was pulling out of his dive and coming at me again. God, he was fast! He must, I told myself, be flying the latest and most powerful Albatross: the DV. Again, as I flung the Triplane aside, his bullets missed me by inches.

It was his fire-power against my agility.

Time and again he came at me, firing; and time and again at the last second I flung the Triplane aside. We were both angling for a mistake. If I turned too soon, too late or in the wrong direction, he'd get me; if he came too close, so that I could use the Triplane's better manoeuvrability, I'd get him. Once I thought I had. As he tried to follow me, climbing, I spun round and gave him a deflection burst. Bullets shredded his wingtip. He toppled into a spin. For a moment I thought it was all over. Then, when I saw that he wasn't seriously damaged, I cursed. He'd be more wary than ever now of closing in. But at least I was above him.

For a moment, like combatants panting for breath we drew apart. Then once again we were wheeling, watching, seeking one another's tail. I decided to try and lure him into a circle.

I let him get *almost* onto my tail, then started turning. Tight: but not as tight as I could. Never quite letting him get into a position to fire, but always giving him hope that if he turned that little bit tighter he'd make it. Then, the moment he was committed to circling, I began to turn in earnest, tighter and tighter, coming gradually round onto *his* tail.

After five or six circles he realised what was happening. I could see him fighting desperately to turn more steeply. I could see the wings of the Albatross trembling. But with each circle, I turned that little bit inside him, got that little bit closer to his tail. Until the Albatross came drifting crablike into my sights. I reached for the Vickers.

But at the last second he flicked over into a spin.

I was after him, firing.

My bullets flashed past his tail, first one side, then the other. Then suddenly – don't ask me how he did it – he'd pulled out of the spin and, just for a second, hauled up his nose to face me. The twin-Spandaus clattered. Bullets scythed through my undercarriage. Pain knifed through my leg. And it was my turn to fall twisting and turning, like an injured bird, towards the gyrating earth.

I pulled out at a thousand feet and took a quick look at my leg. Blood was welling out from below the kneecap, but not in any great quantity; I reckoned I must have been hit by a ricochet. It was nothing, I told myself, to worry about. In any case I hadn't time to worry. For he was diving on me again.

Engines screaming, wings trembling, guns clattering, we wheeled like angry eagles across the sky.

And what a sky it was! Even as we fought, I realised that away in the west the sun was setting through a veil of cloud, and that its rays were metamorphosing the sky around us from blue to gold. It had happened, I remembered, once before: when Otto and I had met for the first time above the trenches. It had been dawn then; and in our innocence we had twisted and turned like dolphins at play. It was twilight now, and we were neither innocent nor playing. I felt suddenly very tired and a thousand years old. It came to me that my leg was injured and my plane damaged: that I was sick and faint: that my vision was blurring: and that Otto von Searle was getting the better of me. I had, I told myself, to do something desperate. And fast. I had to find an ally. But where?

My idea owed nothing to chivalry. It was born of the primordial instinct to survive.

I put my nose down, and made for ground level.

I levelled off at zero feet, in quiet rolling country about a dozen miles behind the allied lines. Otto followed me. And here among the big bare fields, rutted tracks and regimented lines of poplars, we played out the final movement of our ritual dance of death. One second he was on my tail; but I skidded round the periphery of a wood. Next second I was on his; but he cart-wheeled across the face of an escarpment, so sharply that I very nearly flew into it. We weaved in and out of ruined buildings. We jinked through the skeletal trees of what had once been a wood. We followed a river, our bullets ricocheting off the water and into the reeds. Then I was streaking flat-out down a long straight road, with Otto behind me, closing. The road went on and on: one side a line of poplars, the other a succession of big open fields. I knew that Otto was gaining on me. That there wasn't a thing I could do about it. That any second he'd fire. I heard the stacatto bark of a machine-gun. I flinched: waiting for the thud of bullets.

But it wasn't the Triplane that reared up, streaming smoke.

It was the Albatross.

My allies had come to my aid. . . . I'd known for some time that they were close at hand. Troops. Some resting behind the lines, some moving up towards the Front. Most of them had barely heard the sound of our aircraft before we had flashed past them. But somewhere along that stretch of long straight road an anonymous gunner, more alert than his companions, had seen us coming, and given Otto a burst from his Vickers: a burst from point-blank range.

The Albatross reared up, hung for a moment on its prop, then settled into a shallow glide.

I'd neither strength nor inclination to give it the *coup de grâce*. My leg was numb; my foot was wet with blood; my eyes kept playing me tricks – the fields, I told myself, couldn't *really* be undulating like the waves of the sea; Otto couldn't *really* be flying slap into them. . . .

But he was.

He made no effort to pull out of his glide. He flew on and on, gradually losing height, till his wheels were almost feathering the grass. I pushed my dizziness aside and went after him: watching, knowing what was going to happen yet when it *did* happen unable somehow to believe it.

His wheels brushed the grass quite gently. It wasn't a bad landing at all. But the Albatross didn't stop. It careered on and on, out of control, straight for a line of poplars. It scythed into the poplars at something like eighty miles an hour. Its wings were knocked off and went sailing through the air like the vanes of a disintegrating windmill; and its fuselage came to rest in the next field. I waited for the explosion; but it didn't come. I waited for Otto to crawl out of the cockpit; but he didn't move. Perhaps, I thought, he's hanging there upsidedown: like Uncle: bleeding to death.

I took a look at the field, and saw that it was flat and free from obstruction. I wondered how badly the Triplane's undercarriage was damaged, and decided to risk it. I couldn't very well fly away and leave him, could I: maybe injured, maybe dying?

I put down beside the line of poplars, and taxied to the spot where Otto von Searle had ploughed through them. There were ripped-off branches, a buckled wing, fragments of undercarriage, and in the next field, half-on-its-side, the fuselage. I levered myself with some difficulty out of the cockpit. Everything was very still, except for the stir of a sunset breeze; and very quiet, except for a solitary lark singing away in the gloaming – I must, I suppose, have landed close to its nest.

I hobbled across to what was left of the Albatross.

Otto von Searle was dead. A line of bullets had ripped open his body from shoulder to waist. At least, I told myself, it had been quick. I stared at him, unable to think; unable to feel; unable to accept what had happened. There was a leaf in his hair; one of last year's leaves, dead and shrivelled; and for a reason I can't explain it seemed wrong that the leaf should be there, so I moved it, very gently, as though afraid I was going to wake him. Then I saw the wallet, half-hanging out of his flying jacket.

I took the wallet, and opened it; and found myself staring at the photograph of Jessica. *My* photograph, which he had taken (how very long ago) from my cabin in Saint Genis. The photograph was red with blood. And as I stared at it I started to tremble. I trembled so violently that the photograph slipped out of my fingers. I tried to catch it; but the breeze took hold of it and sent it spinning away into the poplars. I tried to hobble after it, but my leg gave way. I told myself it didn't matter. We would

231

neither of us have her now.

I walked slowly back to my plane.

I ought of course to have stayed with her: to have had her patched up, and my leg attended to. But what with shock and loss of blood, I didn't really know what I was doing. I only knew that I didn't want to stay in that terrible field, with Otto's blood-soaked body and Jessica's blood-soaked photograph. So with much heaving, cursing and wincing I climbed back into the cockpit.

The last thing I saw before I revved up was the photograph of Jessica; it had fallen to earth at the foot of one of the poplars; and I remember thinking that even if it rained all day and every day for a millennium that wouldn't be rain enough to wash away the blood. Faintly above the purr of the engine, I heard the lark, still singing away in the twilight. Then I was taxying to the edge of the field, and swinging into the worst take-off of my life: crosswind, and not so much over the poplars as in between them. I remember laughing like an idiot as the branches flashed past within spitting distance of the wing.

Once airborne it was darker than I had anticipated. The sun had set, and only above the western horizon was there evidence of the disappearing day. I flew west to where the light was – it was so much easier than searching in the darkness for Saint Genis.

I was alone. In all the vastness of the sky no-one else was mad enough to be airborne. And my aloneness gave me time to think. . . . What mattered most, I tried to tell myself, was that I was alive and Otto von Searle was dead: that it was I, not he, who would know the warmth of the sun and the softness of women's lips. For a while I was conscious of a wave of primordial elation: like the animal who, after bloody combat, bays over the body of its rival. But man is not animal alone; and mixed up with my elation was sadness: sadness and a sense of irretrievable loss. And as I flew on through the darkening sky, it was these emotions which gradually superseded all others. As a great gold moon came climbing out of the Channel, I couldn't help thinking back to our friendship, to the days when we had been as David and Jonathan. I remembered my joy when Otto had been made a monitor, his joy when I'd got my First XI Colours; I remembered his anguish when he thought I had been injured, and my fury when I thought the Longhorn pilot had slighted him. Our friendship in those days had been very real: 'a joy to our friends, a consternation to our foes'. So what had happened to it? What had happened to us? Where had we gone wrong? I flew on and on, asking a lot of questions but not finding many answers. I was over the Channel now, and the waters beneath me were dappled with moonlight. With man asleep, the world had reverted to quietness and beauty. The water fascinated me: especially the path of moonlight beckoning westward into the Atlantic. Perhaps if I followed it I'd find myself in Lyonesse or Avalon or Brandon's 'Islands of the Bless'd'! It was a tempting thought. I was telling myself how wonderful it would be if I could touch-down on some undiscovered shore, where I could close my eyes and not hear the guns, sleep and not dream, wake and not have to battle with the *schweinehund* . . . when the engine spluttered, coughed and cut dead.

I reached without enthusiasm for throttle-lever and switches; I juggled with them, but the engine wouldn't restart. A glance at the petrol gauge told me why. We had run out of fuel.

So what! The sea beneath me was beautiful, mysterious, inviting: a short cut to my undiscovered shore. I shut my eyes. I let go of the stick. And the Triplane stalled, and heeled over into an apologetic spin.

It was the pain that saved me. As we started to spin I must, by instinct, have stamped automatically on the rudder to correct it. Hard. With my injured leg.

The shock was like a douche of cold water. I woke up to what was happening. Had I survived two years at the Front, I asked myself, only to let myself be snuffed out like a pricked balloon? I saw that I was still at 7,000 feet, and not impossibly far from land. I turned downwind, for France. . . . It was good to stop thinking about Otto, to know that once again I was flying, not fighting for my life. . . . I was down to 5,000 feet before I spotted

233

the coast. It was difficult by moonlight to tell what sort of coast it was – cliffs would be bad, sand-dunes OK, open beaches best of all. I headed hopefully towards it. By the time I was down to 2,000 feet I could see that it was cliffs; I could see too that we hadn't a hope of clearing them, that somewhere close to the meeting-place of rock and sea we'd run out of height.

I had almost given up hope when I saw the beach: the narrow strip of sand at the foot of a horseshoe bay. With cliffs rising sheer on three sides, it was a hellish place to get at. But I reminded myself that even without her engine the Triplane was wonderfully manoeuvrable. 'Come on!' I muttered to her. 'We can make it!'

I reckoned we had just enough height and just enough speed to get as far as the beach. And that's the way it was. As we neared it, however, I saw to my consternation that it was strewn with outcrops of rock, and was less than a hundred yards in length – though that hundred yards lay mercifully close into wind. I approached it slowly, clinging as long as I could to what little height I had, my leg aching, my eyes watering, the Tripe-hound bucking uneasily in down-draughts from the cliffs. Distances were hard to judge. One moment I thought I was a hundred feet up, the next flying slap into the sea. As the beach came rushing towards us, I waited till I could see the reflection of my wheels in the sea-wet sand. Then, at the last second, I straightened her up, hauled back on the stick, and prayed.

But by this time we had used up almost two-thirds of the beach, and I could see that even if we landed in one piece we'd never pull up before we crashed into the cliffs. I shut my eyes. And the Triplane, as she had done so often before, saved my life. As she hit the sand her undercarriage collapsed. She slewed sea-ward, and smashed not into the cliffs, but into a low-lying outcrop of rock.

Rock like a battering-ram burst through the bottom of her fuselage. There was a terrible splintering crash. And in a maelstrom of sea and spray, sand and stars, noise and pain, I passed out.

I must have been unconscious for quite a time; because when

I came-to it was pitch dark, and little waves were sucking and swirling round my feet. Since I didn't fancy being drowned, I tried to move my feet, but found that I couldn't. My prospects, I decided, weren't too good. I tried to lever myself up with my elbows; but this wasn't very successful, and hurt so much that I slid back gratefully to unconsciousness.

I'm not sure what happened next. I can remember the sound of waves, the repetitive cry of a seabird, the cold, and the sea creeping gradually higher over my body. I can remember thinking that it was no good complaining: that I'd brought it on myself: that if it hadn't been for my vendetta with Otto von Searle I'd be sleeping peacefully in England. At such moments I must have been conscious. But at other moments I was obviously either delirious or dreaming. Because, once again, I kept seeing the face.

I thought I'd seen the last of him! But there he was, staring down at me out of the starlit sky, flame-wrapped and weeping those endless tears. I was frightened, but I was also intrigued; and after a while curiosity began to get the better of fear, and I found that I could look at him and no longer tremble and moan. Who *could* he be? There had been a time when I'd felt certain he was my executioner; but this no longer seemed to make sense – unless by some miracle I was going to be rescued and drafted back to the Front. It was too much of a mystery: too puzzling to cope with.

The tide was still rising. The water was up to my armpits now. And I was mustering what little strength I had for a last effort to hoist myself clear, when I heard the voice.

At least I *thought* it was a voice. A single shout: '*Voilà!*'

I started threshing my arms about and yelling for help. And after a couple of minutes – as though in a dream too wonderful to be believed – I heard the splash of oars and the creaking of rowlocks.

They were French fishermen, setting their lobster pots. Big slow-moving men with strong hands, garlic breath and a bottle of rough red wine which they kept thrusting into my mouth as they struggled to dislodge me from what was left of the fuselage.

They were wonderfully gentle.

I owe them my life, my legs, and I should think about a bottle and a half of rough red wine.

When I came out of my stupor I was in bed.

17

As I regained consciousness, I couldn't for a moment think where I was. Then I smelt the familiar aseptic smell, and saw above my bed the familiar night light. I was in hospital.

My first reaction was relief: I was alive. I felt for my legs. They seemed to be encased in some sort of plaster; but at least they were there. I told myself I had a lot to be thankful for, and drifted back to unconsciousness.

Next time I woke it was daylight, and a man on the opposite side of the ward was screaming; I had a headache, a foul taste in my mouth, and a nagging pain in my legs. I told myself not to worry: that things would gradually get better. But in this I turned out to be wrong. The man – I learned later that he was shell-shocked and minus both his arms – went on screaming intermittently round the clock; neither my head nor my legs stopped aching; and no matter how many gallons of water I drank my mouth remained perpetually dry. I began to wonder if my relief had been premature. It was the start of the worst few weeks of my life.

The trouble was that they kept pumping me full of morphia, not realising I was allergic to it. The morphia made me sick and depressed. It was the depression which was worst. I didn't seem able to snap out of it. I lay there day after day, refusing to speak, staring vacantly at the ceiling, and cursing the Face which kept appearing, disappearing and reappearing when I least expected it. I told myself that I had killed my best friend, that I had lost the only two girls I'd ever care for, that I'd never climb into an aircraft again. I wished the fishermen hadn't found me. . . . It was lucky that my body turned out to be more resilient than my mind. The injuries to my legs were

pretty unpleasant (one broken, and one with multiple frac-
tures and a bullet wound), but they weren't the sort of injuries
that a man of twenty in hospital would normally have died
from. In time they started to heal; and as soon as they started to
heal the doctors were able to cut down on the morphia and I
began to come out of my depression. Towards the end of the
third week I was told I could have visitors. I remember thinking
that in my present mood I didn't want to see anyone, and I very
much doubted if anyone would want to see me. But here again I
turned out to be wrong. And never for as long as I live will I
forget the people – many of them quite unexpected – who came
to visit me that spring.

The first of the good Samaritans was in nurse's uniform. Now
I had realized for some time that I was in the hospital near Boulogne – the one where at the end of last year I had visited Jessica. I had been wondering if she would come to see me, and
hadn't, to be honest, been looking forward to a visit from her. I
needn't have worried. The face staring down on me wasn't
Jessica's. It was a pretty face in a disorganised sort of way, with
a generous mouth and eyes that were smiling: 'Hail, voyager!'
she said. 'Our paths cross again!'

'Susan!' I wasn't sure if I was more surprised or delighted.

I thought at first that perhaps she had been transferred to my
ward on duty; but she assured me her visit was purely social,
and of this I was glad. She stayed a long time – so long that she
had in the end to be chased away by the ward sister – and before
she left she had a look in my locker and extracted a pile of washing which she said she would cope with. She also extracted
three letters: the letters to my mother, Jessica and Nicole,
which I'd written at Saint Genis and which had been for-
warded, together with my personal belongings, to the hospital.
She asked if I wanted them posted.

I shook my head.

She looked at me curiously: 'Why write 'em then?'

'I wrote them before a special patrol,' I said. 'In case I didn't
come back.'

She bit her lip. 'Sorry. . . . But – now you *are* back, why hang

238

onto them?'

It was a good question; and when I had thought about it, I asked her to burn them. This she promised to do. And before she left she made another and very different promise. 'I hope,' she said, as she stood up, adjusting her cape, 'you won't be staying in that bed much longer.'

'Why?'

She kissed me on the mouth. 'That's all you'll get in *that* bed! I mean the very idea! In front of all the patients!'

As I watched her walk out of the ward, I told myself I couldn't any longer pretend I had no incentive to recover.

I had about a dozen visitors during the next week. All of them cheered me up and helped my recovery. Two in particular.

Sister Jardine came to see me the next day. And she started talking almost at once about Jessica. She thought I might be wondering why Jessica hadn't been to see me; the reason, she explained, was that she had been transferred to another hospital, the odds were that she didn't even know I was wounded let alone where I was. She offered to write and tell her.

I shook my head.

Her big brown eyes were full of concern: 'I don't want to interfere. But Jess is very fond of you. . . .'

She wouldn't be very fond of me, I thought, when she knew I'd killed Otto. I shut my eyes and wished I could as easily shut from my mind all that had happened between the three of us.

She reached for my hand: 'Sometimes it helps to talk.'

I was still in the aftermath of depression and was about to tell her to mind her own business, when I had second thoughts. Maybe she was right; maybe I was wrong to keep everything bottled up inside me, to spurn every offer of friendship. 'If I talked all night,' I muttered, 'you still wouldn't know the half of it.'

She smiled. She drew curtains round the bed — provoking ribald comments from my fellow patients. She kicked off her shoes: 'I'm happy,' she said, 'to stay the night!'

Well, we didn't quite talk until dawn. Only till 3 a.m.

She was a wonderfully patient and sympathetic listener; and

though I didn't start by telling her everything, that is the way it ended. And what a relief it was! Just to talk things over: just to share my experiences and emotions with someone who cared. You could, I suppose, say that at the end of it all we arrived at no solution: that we hit on no panacea by which I could Live Happily Ever After. Yet something she said brought me comfort. 'Do you know,' she said, 'what I think is the saddest thing, yet in a way the most wonderful thing, in all you've told me?'

I shook my head.

'That last time you and Otto met. That you let him climb up till he was level with you. And that he rocked his wings to say "thank you". Don't you see what it means?'

'Not really.'

'That you and Otto haven't changed: not deep down. That you were both still decent people. Oh, can't you see! What's happened hasn't been *your* fault. Or *his* fault. It's the fault of this bloody stinking war.'

Well, it wasn't quite the way I saw it; but the thought was certainly a comforting one, and at 3 a.m. I wasn't going to argue.

Before she left she kissed me good-night. It was a very different kiss to Susan's. But it meant every bit as much to me.

I heard my next visitor before I saw him.

A great booming voice echoing like a foghorn round the ward, the tap-tap-tap of crutches on the linoleum floor, and there he was, the nurses hovering round him like harem-girls a potentate. 'Good Lord,' I said. 'Long John Silver himself!'

Uncle prodded me with one of his crutches: '"Why lie ye here all the day idle?"'

'Because,' I said, 'they haven't taken me out of plaster yet.'

'Have you asked 'em to?'

'No. But. . . .'

'Ha!' Another prod from his crutch, and more giggles from the nurses. 'He always was a lie-a-bed. You'll have to watch him, my dears. Or he'll take root!'

I was about to say indignantly, 'That isn't fair'; when I suddenly realised it was; that for the past month I'd been lying in

240

bed like a cabbage, making not the slightest effort to help myself. Uncle's jibe had been shrewdly placed. He sat down; and we talked all afternoon about flying. We talked – and this surprised me – not of the past but of the future. And the more we talked the more it became apparent that Uncle certainly didn't regard his career in the Flying Corps as over. Since losing his leg he had been promoted, had been given an important job in the War Office, and had still found time to fly several of the Corp's most promising prototypes, including – lucky devil – the Camel. I began to tell myself that what he could do with one leg I surely could do with two.

My talk with him did me more good than a whole pharmacy of medicaments. And that evening, when the doctor came through the ward on his rounds, I asked him how long it was going to be before I could walk.

So my visitors set me on the road to recovery. I was still, however, very conscious of the fact that a vital spark was missing: that I was still only half-alive: that I was making an effort not because I wanted to but because I knew I ought to. All this was changed by the letter.

What memories came flooding back as I stared at the familiar hand-writing. I tore the envelope open, uncertain if I was more pleased to hear from her or fearful of what she might have to say. The letter was quite a long one.

My darling Jacques,

I am requesting a friend to translate this letter into English, because – as you know! – my English is not good, and I wish to be very certain you understand what I write.

Much has happened since last I saw you.

My friend is dead. He was a brave man, Jacques, and a good one. But he lost first the one leg with gangrene, then the other leg. He would not have been happy to remain alive. So perhaps God in His way was merciful. Before he died he wished that we should marry, and how in the circumstances could I refuse him? So the one week I am married, and the next week I am the widow.

Now I do not know the customs in England [much to my

241

amusement Nicole always thought of England as another world and the English as another species!] *and if you think it wrong because I was married that I now should write to you, I can only say I am truly sorry and I do not wish to be wicked. But my heart is ever with you. And my body ever longs for you. And if you wish again to see me I will very gladly come.*

Please do not be angry with me, Jacques, but write and say that I may once again be with you.

Nicole.

How in God's name could she ever have thought that I'd be angry! I felt as a man who has been imprisoned in a dark room, when unexpectedly a window is flung open, and the light he had given up hope of ever seeing again comes flooding in.

Next day I was taking my first tentative hops across the ward. Three weeks later I was transferred to a convalescent home on the outskirts of London.

18

I was sent to a country house in Surbiton: one of those last bastions of a way of life which was dead but refused to lie down. I remember the highly-polished silver dishes (full of poached haddock, kidneys and scrambled eggs) set out on the sideboard for breakfast; the deck chairs beneath the cedars, carefully arranged so that we needn't look into the sun; and the beautiful Waterford glasses, which each evening were filled with port. For a while it was good to relax in a world as far removed from the Front as Avalon from the innermost circle of the Inferno. I wrote a lot of letters – three in one week to Nicole; did a lot of swimming – which I'd been told was good for my leg; and had my penultimate encounter with the Face.

I don't know why he came back on that particular night; but there he was. I no longer threshed about like a gaffed salmon when I saw him. For quite a while now I had been more puzzled by him than afraid; and this time I was particularly puzzled, because his image seemed to be more indistinct than usual, as though he was fading into some limbo where I couldn't follow. Who *could* he be? Why was he weeping? Why did his expression never change? Why was his head ringed with flame? I felt certain I had seen him somewhere before. But though I stared and stared, and racked my brains, and dredged back into the farthest corners of my memory, I couldn't place him. I woke frustrated. What an anti-climax, I thought, if I never find out who he is!

A couple of days later I received an invitation to go to Charterhouse, to attend the unveiling of a memorial plaque to Gavin. I thought for a very, very long time about whether or not I should go. For I knew who else would almost certainly be at the ceremony: the one person I didn't yet feel able to face. In the end, however, I accepted. I couldn't keep running away from Jessica for ever.

It was soon after this that I was summoned to the War Office. On Uncle's advice I had applied for a job in the newly-formed recruiting department of the Flying Corps. This department was now of some importance; for pilots at the Front were being killed more quickly than they could be trained and replaced – and this at a time when the General Staff were at last beginning to understand the importance of air power. To cut a long story short I landed a plum job. I was given a Sopwith Camel, and told to embark on a series of demonstration flights and lectures all over the United Kingdom, starting at the public schools and universities. My short-term objective was to stimulate recruiting to meet the immediate needs of the war. But there was also a long-term objective; and it was to this that I gave my heart. Already in the summer of 1917 there was talk of creating an Air Force which would be a separate Service: a Service orientated to the air as the Navy is orientated to the sea and the Army to the land. The moment I heard the idea I knew that this was my dream: that this was the star I'd hitch my waggon to. The war, I told myself, won't last for ever; and when it's over we can get back to flying instead of fighting, to mastering not one another but this wonderful new element which had been added to our lives.

So I discarded my crutches, and graduated to a stick. I familiarised myself with the Camel – she was a sweet and wonderfully sensitive plane to fly, though no aircraft for me ever quite measured up to my Triplane. And I worked out a schedule of places to visit. One of the first places on my list was Charterhouse; and since I had to be there in any case on the afternoon of June 13th for Gavin's memorial service, I arranged to give my lecture that evening.

So in due course I found myself in the school chapel, taking part in one of those services in which God seems fated to play second fiddle to the Union Jack. For the Pendower family I'm sure it was a deeply moving occasion; but I have to admit that

244

more than once I found my attention wandering. Wandering to Jessica. . . . Poor kid, I thought; the service must be an ordeal for her. But she got through it without a tear: without in fact the slightest sign of emotion, looking all the while like some beautiful sleepwalker, whose body goes through the conventional movements of kneeling and standing but whose mind is in another world. Our eyes met just the once. And then for the only time in the service her expression changed. She shivered, and looked away. Perhaps, I thought, it would be best if I didn't try to speak to her.

I was still uncertain what to do when the service ended. Most of the congregation filled out through the cloisters; but Jessica said something to her parents and stayed kneeling – though whether this was because she wanted to pray, because she wanted to avoid me or because she wanted to be alone with me, I wouldn't have liked to say. I followed the others into the cloisters; and here I waited for her, pacing up and down beneath the stone arches, staring absentmindedly at the plaques and the paintings, not knowing whether or not I wanted her to come.

After about five minutes she emerged through the south door. She saw me, hesitated, then, looking more like a sleepwalker than ever, came slowly towards me.

'Hello, Jess.'

'Hello, Jack.'

'I wanted to see you,' I said. 'But now I don't know what to say.'

'There's nothing *to* say, is there?'

We walked side by side in silence through the cloisters.

And suddenly when I least expected it, when I most certainly wasn't thinking about it, I saw him.

The Face.

There on the wall of the cloisters: the painting: 'The Crucifixion' by the Master of Aacher: Christ on the cross: His head ringed by a golden halo of flame, and His eyes weeping those everlasting tears, weeping not for Himself but for all time and for all mankind, weeping for Otto, Jessica and me. 'Of course,' I whispered, '*that's* who it was!' I walked up to the painting. I ran my hand over it, wondering.

Jessica was staring at me: 'What's the matter?'

I hesitated: 'It's a long story.'

I thought she was going to let it pass. She looked at me. She looked at the painting; then, to my surprise, she sat down on the flagstones beneath it. 'Go on.'

So I told her everything. About my dreaming and screaming in the night. About the faces of the pilots I had killed; and how they had haunted me, and His face in particular, and how I'd felt certain He must be the one who was waiting for me in the sun. And when I had finished, she said simply. 'Oh Jack, isn't this a terrible war! No wonder He's weeping!'

For a while we were silent; then she started plucking at the hem of her skirt. 'Jack!'

'Hmmm?'

'This, this thing, between you and Otto' – her voice faltered, and she wouldn't look at me – 'Was it *my* fault?'

'Of course not.'

'I mean' – her voice was so low that I could hardly hear what she was saying – 'Was it because of me?'

'No, Jess. I promise you. You were caught up in it. But you weren't the cause of it.'

'What *was* the cause of it then?'

Well, I ask you! What could I tell her? I suppose it might have made her more sympathetic towards me if I'd told her that Otto von Searle had shot down her brother and that I'd hunted him down and killed him out of revenge; but it would have made things even more hellish for her. Poor kid, I thought; she's been through enough. There are things it is better she should never know. 'I talked about this,' I said, 'to your friend Sister Jardine. And she thinks that what happened wasn't his fault, or my fault, or anyone's fault. It was simply the bloody war.'

'And is that how *you* see it?'

I looked at her very straight. 'Yes.'

She thought it over; for a long time; then she said slowly. 'And you think that's how *I* ought to see it? No blame? No bitterness? No evil? Just the war?'

'If you can.'

She looked at me, shivered, and as quickly looked away. 'Not yet. But maybe one day. When I'm old.'

I couldn't think of anything to say that wouldn't sound either maudlin or trite.

Eventually she stood up. 'So this is good-bye.'

I knew she was right: that ever since Otto had taken her to that damned dance while I stayed behind with the Longhorn, our relationship had been star-crossed, that between that day and this too many terrible things had happened between us for our relationship to end any other way. But the fact that parting was inevitable, didn't make it much easier. I thought of all that might have been, and couldn't bear to look at her. I heard a voice that I didn't recognise as my own: 'God be with you, Jess.'

'And with you.'

She held herself very straight as she walked out of my life. As she passed from cloisters to courtyard, the sun caught her hair, transforming it for a moment to an avalanche of fire. I shut my eyes. And when I opened them she was gone. But I could still hear the click-click-click-click of her heels fading *diminuendo* to a silence that went on and on and on.

I sat there for a long time, thinking of all the things that we had shared once, might have shared always, but would never share again.

When, later that evening, I gave my talk to the school I didn't keep to my prepared script. I talked more about flying than fighting – fighting was something I'd had my fill of. I could tell that some of the boys were disappointed; they had expected tales of combat, tales of Huns shot flaming out of the sky, and here I was talking about what the earth looked like from 20,000 feet, the birth of clouds, moonlight on struts and the *camaraderie* of the air. But others, I think, saw what I was getting at: saw that when the war was over the sky *could* become not a battle-ground but a meeting-ground; that man's growing mastery of the air *could* be used to knit nation more closely to nation. And if all this seems of no more substance than a pipe-dream, I can only ask you what would life be worth without its dreams?

When I had finished my talk and the boys had filed out of hall and gone back to their houses it was still light, so I went and sat by myself on a seat overlooking the playing-fields: the very seat where less than three years ago Otto, Jessica and I had sat side by side in friendship. Now Otto was dead – and I had killed him. Between us we had broken Jessica's heart – and my instinct told me that she would never marry. And I – even I who had come out of it best of all, was hobbling about with a stick and had just seen the death of the most treasured of my childhood dreams. . . . And the sad thing was that as far as I could make out all three of us, according to our lights, had acted honourably and decently. . . . So was Sister Jardine right? Were we simply victims of the War? Was it no fault of ours that the things we had made one another suffer read like a chapter out of Dante's *Inferno*? It didn't quite seem to add up. . . . But it was a lovely evening, and I had grown tired of asking questions I couldn't answer. I told myself that only one thing mattered.

I was alive.

And as I sat there, watching the sun drop slowly toward the hills, I was conscious of a feeling not far removed from content. I had come out of the night: not, it is true, unscathed, but at least in one piece. With any luck, I told myself, I'd be able to spend the rest of the war in Blighty; and hadn't Nicole promised that if I wanted to see her she would come?

It was a funny thing: but as my thoughts turned to Nicole, my content seemed to become more firmly and deeply rooted. How wonderful it would be, I thought, if I could get her to England – perhaps smuggled in in the back of a Strutter or RE8!

I was walking back across the playing fields, thinking of the games that she and I had played once and might with a bit of ingenuity soon be playing again, when I heard the aircraft.

The sun was setting and throwing out great shafts of red and gold as the Triplane passed almost directly overhead, flying west into the sunset. I shaded my eyes and watched her silhouette growing smaller and smaller until she was no more than a pinhead of fire. I expect that in fact she was flying straight and level; but the sun was sinking so quickly that the aircraft appeared to be rising out of the very orb of it, climbing up and up into a sky which would soon be filled with stars.

And it came to me how lucky I was: to have been born at the very moment when man was taking his first tentative step along the road which will one day lead him to other worlds. Later pilots would fly faster, climb higher and control planes which would make our Shorthorns and Triplanes seem like primitive toys. But it was *my* generation who were first to venture into a world where no men in history had ventured before. We were the young eagles, flexing our wings in an untried element: the young salamanders, venturing for the first time into flame. And time cannot dim the joy nor diminish the wonder of our venturing.

It was almost dark by the time I got back to the house where I was staying the night. And darkness, after the heat and turmoil of the day, was welcome, a prelude to sleep: a sleep which for the first time in years held the promise not of faces ringed with flame, but of dreams of where I was going and of who was going there with me.